For Laurence G. Boldt
(November 18, 1954 – March 28, 2024)

BIG
LAKE
TROUBLES

BIG
LAKE
TROUBLES

A Novel

Jeffrey D. Boldt

atmosphere press

Published by Atmosphere Press

Cover design by Matthew Fielder

The author gratefully acknowledges that his poems (1) *Fragment of Summer* first appeared in *Blueline, Vol XXIII*, 2002, and (2) *November Song, Vol XLV*, 2024, SUNY Potsdam.

Grateful acknowledgment is made to the following sources for permission to reproduce copyrighted material: Kimberly M. Blaeser, *The Eloquence of Earth*, first appeared in *Mujeres Talk*, 2014.

Atmospherepress.com

PART ONE:

The Science
of Not Caring

"The opposite of love is not hate. It is indifference."
- Wilhelm Stekel, 1921 -

Prologue

A Rough Couple of Years

Jason was back in La Crosse. It was the fortieth anniversary of his father's death in 1983, and he went to his father's grave outside of town and then into the city to trek his dad's favorite hike. As he approached the steep little hill on Crown Boulevard that led to the path, Jason saw a sign. Damn. Was it now posted "No Trespassing"?

It was no doubt valuable property. But when Jason got close enough to read it, to his relief, the sign had been put up by the Mississippi Valley Conservancy. It had been "Protected Forever" for public use. His dad would have been so pleased.

The route went straight up along a sandstone bluff, a trail his late mom had called Peter the Goat Herder's Path. Still, she'd often joined Jason and his brother as his father told them wild stories from his childhood about exploring the caves above them. Stories involving springs and some strangely sympathetic bats that had led his father and friends out when they'd gotten lost.

Jason made his way up to the top where there was a wide view of the river. His father claimed that on a clear day one could see Minnesota and Iowa as well as the sloughs and turns of the Great River snaking its way down the west coast of Wisconsin.

It was a warm November day, sixty-four degrees and sunny. There was still a surprising amount of color, too. There were some stubborn red and gold oak leaves and even some spindly green shoots on the bushes lower to the ground as he made his way up the winding path.

Up at the top, there was a bench, painted in festive, Grateful Dead–style colors. La Crosse had always had plenty of hippies, including his dad. Jason sat there on the bench, missing his father, as well as his mother, Tara, and Camille.

He heard himself say his father's slightly corny prayer: thanks for giving, Lord, but please go easy on the taking away. It made him laugh because it was especially fitting these days. Jason had had a rough couple of years.

His dad had been witty, charming, and something close to (but not quite) a flirt. His mom adored his dad. Jason and his brother, too. His father had died when Jason and his brother, Justin, were just boys. His dad had a lot of personality; too much, Justin had said at one point growing up.

After the hike, Jason went downtown to the Charmant Hotel and paid homage to his lost love, Tara. The hotel was in a redbrick former chocolate factory down by the Mississippi. He and Tara had first made love in this hotel, where Jason ordered a glass of Tara's favorite Chardonnay and a plate of olives. They'd had a "brief but spectacular" (as they said on PBS) love affair as she was approaching her divorce. Just as they were finding their way together, they'd both suffered the trauma of gun violence: Jason had survived, Tara had not.

Now, Jason toasted Tara and let himself revel in his bittersweet memories. Though love had come to him again, the memories still burned like hot coals.

Coal itself was at the heart of the next calamitous turn of events, as it was for the whole planet. Fighting coal had its own set of consequences. The powers that be wouldn't give it up easily. Jason still had nightmares about the coal island, Earl, the boat and, especially, Camille and the dogs.

Chapter One

Organic Foodie Goodness

The sunny September day was perfect for Jason Erickson's drive from Madison to Viroqua to meet his girlfriend, Grace Clarkson. The rolling hills along two-lane Highway 14 were still full of summery life. He noticed a large bird, with the unflapping winged flight and white head of a mature eagle, glide effortlessly from a bluff to the large cottonwood stand along the creek. It settled onto its nest to feed its young.

Jason pulled over and snapped a picture, but it was too distant to keep. It didn't matter; he'd seen it. It was there, protecting its young.

As he pulled into the western Wisconsin town of Viroqua, he saw a few climate protestors, gray-haired organic farmers and back-to-nature greens, out in front of the food co-op with homemade signs. Jason's late father would probably have known some of them—his dad's old hippie buddies who'd settled in the hills of the Driftless Area forty years ago. But there were also three young couples with their kids, including some who'd probably skipped school.

It was touching to see the school-agers. This was their day, the International Climate Day of 2019, organized by Greta Thunberg and young people worldwide who were protesting inaction on the climate crisis. A group of them had even presented a complaint to the United Nations, calling inaction "child abuse." Jason honked his support for the local crowd and pulled over to take a picture when some kids waved.

"Do you mind if I take a picture?" he asked.

"No, that's what we're here for!" one woman replied.

She was a young mom with a baby on her back and another grade school-aged girl peeking out through a cutout hole in a large paper box painted to look like floodwaters.

"How high is the water, Mama? I'm scared," was written on the box.

"Feel free to post it," she added. "That's why we're here."

"Great, I will." Her daughter smiled at him.

Jason still cared that much, at least. He was finding that there was a certain science of not caring. The Dalai Lama said compassion was not a sign of weakness but strength. But then Jason was still a little weak and jumpy from losing Tara and having been shot. His focus bounced from thought to feeling and from feeling to a kind of restless murmur as though some intrusive background music was playing.

The low throbbing hum of loss.

Jason's romance with Tara had gone slowly because she was married when they met, but he sometimes asked himself if he'd gone too fast with Grace. They'd started seeing each other within a year of Tara's death. It had seemed reasonable at the time, especially since they had both lost partners and knew that gloomy terrain. But Grace had lost her husband Jon to a drunk driver twenty-five years ago when they were in law school, and Jason's wounds were still fresh.

He'd fallen into things with Grace, fallen into their routine rather than having chosen the life that she wanted for them. Since Tara's death, Jason was mostly just muddling through. He felt adrift, even driving through the familiar autumn hills of the Driftless Area.

Grace really wanted him to get involved in the fight against the renewal of an enormous coal shipment and storage facility on Lake Superior. She'd sent him a lengthy email. It was a five-year permit renewal. Fighting coal was fighting the climate crisis itself, she argued. Not without reason. Burning fossil fuels for electricity was still the leading source of greenhouse gas emissions that led to climate change. Every ton of coal burned represented almost three tons of carbon dioxide alone and most of the sulfur dioxide in the air.

Though the numbers were down because of the rise of natural gas, ten million tons of coal still went through this plant every year. They shipped Powder River Basin coal from Wyoming and Montana all the way to Europe and Asia via the St. Lawrence Seaway, as well as to local power plants.

The fate of the world was at stake. But was he up to the challenge? Had Tara's death killed some part of him too? The part that gave two figs—that was willing to do more than post pictures on Instagram?

It was clear that Grace was almost counting on him to join her in leading the legal fight against the renewal of the coal facility. For Grace, it was a commitment to fight climate change and a statement that she and Jason were partners of some kind. Grace had lost her husband when they were both in law school, and she'd never let go of her dream of having a professional and romantic partnership.

But that was her dream and not necessarily his. Was he ready to make that kind of commitment? Probably not. Jason wanted to travel and to get in touch with his old English-major self. Read more. Start writing again.

Jason pulled into a prime parking space right next to the Driftless Café, worrying that they might be closed for the climate strike. The Viroqua area was the center of the local organic food movement that supplied upscale restaurants and co-ops from Chicago to Minneapolis. The Driftless Café chef was a local celebrity, the host of a regional public TV show, and famous for his green local fare.

The café was open, but Grace hadn't arrived yet. Jason checked in with the host at the bar and waited in the lobby. Had Grace conspired to meet him here on Climate Strike Day, in this bastion of organic foodie goodness, to subtly influence his decision? She was a savvy lawyer and wasn't above that sort of thing. Her legal mentor and Uncle Ray had apparently been a master at such head games.

Tall, blonde and fit, Grace came striding into the restaurant. She planted a kiss on his cheek. He moved to kiss her on the lips, but she had already stepped away. Grace had a certain coldness, a façade that he could seldom get behind. She was always so focused. That was especially hard because he was so unmoored.

"I can seat you two now," a waiter with inked-up arms said. He led them around the corner to a blue booth under a huge photo of an earnest young farm family, towheads all, one of the restaurant's local providers. "Cypress will be right with you."

"I love that name and these producer photos," Grace put in. "How was your drive, Jason?"

"Nice, though I had to dodge a few climate protestors out on Highway 14." He smiled. "Newlyweds and nearly-deads, as a friend of mine says. Very subtle, by the way, asking to meet me here on Climate Strike Day."

"Thanks. I thought so." Grace grinned disarmingly. "So sue me. People care."

"Me too."

"I know, Jay."

A tall woman with blue hair and green eye shadow approached them. "I'm Cypress. Can I get you a drink to start?"

They ordered the white wine special and looked at the food menu after the waitress had left.

"Beef tenderloin—the only salad topper option—on Climate Strike Day?" Jason asked. He was already a bit grumpy, dreading Grace's sales pitch. "I even thought that they might close in solidarity."

"Don't worry," Grace replied. "I'm going for the falafel with local greens. But for the record, the livestock industry causes twelve percent of carbon emissions and coal is closer to forty."

"Fair point." Could we really get rid of more than half of carbon emissions if we gave up beef and coal? Probably not, but it sure as hell would help. Cypress returned with their wine, and they ordered. They clinked wine glasses.

"What's holding you back?" Grace asked, sipping her wine.

"The law just takes up so much space in one's brain. And you know as well as I do, when you're doing one of these big cases, there's so little room left for anything else," Jason said. That was the closest he had to a rationale. "I've told you that my counselor says that law itself has been anxiety-triggering for me and that I should tread lightly there for a while."

"Yes, sound advice. And thanks for being direct." Grace lined up those big blue eyes with his. "But hasn't that space been claimed already, a long time ago?"

"Maybe," Jason began. "But it's also been nice to visit other long-lost regions."

"Touché. And I get it. I'm not here to guilt you. You've been through a lot." Grace sipped her wine. "Delicious. I love the Central Coast. Have you thought any more about subbing as an English teacher?"

"Yep. I even signed up for training this November."

"I get the appeal," Grace leaned toward him. "But I still want to pitch you the idea of working on the coal plant case with me."

"Go ahead."

"Our client would be a consortium of local neighborhood, environmental, and climate action groups." Grace paused to take another sip of her wine. Was she channeling her Uncle Ray again? "And they've promised to raise a healthy budget for experts and investigations."

"Did I do their old permit?" Jason asked.

"No, Judge Benson did, but you did a similar one with Great Lakes Power and Light. Audrey Benson has this one, too."

"She's conservative but not a hack. She's fair. That GLPL coal case almost got me fired."

The legislature passed a bill saying no one could hold his job for more than ten years, which he'd been doing for eleven years at that point. His boss had said, "They should've just put your position number in it."

"Governor Doyle vetoed it, right?"

"Yes." Jason's stomach gurgled. As a state administrative judge, he'd often felt like he was in someone's crosshairs. "What are the legal issues?"

"There are the same air issues as in your old case. They're blowing coal dust all over the lake and neighborhood. There are several dozen PM-10 and 2.5 air emission violations. There's a water permit, too. And you know where I stand. I'm with Beyond Coal and 350.org."

"I know. You've sent me those links. But your clients are really fighting climate change, right?" Jason asked.

Grace nodded as Cypress brought their beautiful falafel plates.

"That used to bug me when people brought up giant issues outside the scope of the legal case."

"I hear you." Grace napkinned a little yogurt dressing off the side of her mouth. "Yum, that's excellent. But the locals swear they're messing with the air monitors and don't spray down the coal piles with that stuff to keep the dust down. Apparently, that stuff is very expensive, and the neighbors think they're only spraying it on a small portion of the pile." She reached into her backpack and pulled out some photos. "Looking at these, I'd say they're on to something."

Grace handed him the pictures.

Someone had hung out white sheets to dry and taken photos at regular intervals over two days. Over the course of just forty-eight hours, they looked like black-and-white Jackson Pollock paintings with increasingly large black blotches. Jason thought of the young mother on the highway, the baby on her back, and the little girl with the box sign.

"That's obscene. Kids are breathing this air when they

play outside in Lake Superior City?"

"You know the answer, Judge," Grace replied.

"This is all very compelling, but why must it be me?"

"It doesn't necessarily," Grace said. "There's a lawyer in Eau Claire who is interested and has some time."

She handed him another picture. A girl of three or four with big brown eyes was holding some breathing apparatus over her mouth and nose.

"This is Lacy, daughter of one of the petitioners. She's had asthma since she was two." Grace paused as Jason looked at the heartbreaking photo. "Her mom says that she's been to the ER so much she calls it the Ear." Grace looked at him closely and then looked away. "'Do I have to go to the Ear again, Mommy?'"

Chapter Two

Duluth Sunset

Grace got into her car and headed back toward La Crosse. Jason followed her in his. He was right; it didn't have to be him. Why was she so intent on getting him on board? As a former judge who'd handled similar cases, Jason had valuable experience that few others had, but there was more to it than that.

The coal transshipment case would be all-consuming. Grace didn't want to spend so much time away from Jason. Of course. But was she also trying to revive her old dream with Jon—that fantasy of being fun-loving, do-gooding lawyers together? Was she putting that baggage on Jason? She called him.

"Look, I don't mean to pressure you about this whole coal case thing." She could see him smile in her rearview mirror. "You know, my old dream."

"Of course. You and Jon were great together."

"Thanks." Jason and Grace's late husband had known each other in law school, but poor Jon hadn't lived much past that. She and Jason were both fifty now. She'd missed her chance at having kids, but it wasn't too late to have another meaningful partnership or even marriage.

"But it's okay if you are. It's your dream," Jason added. "We both know that grief can be tricky."

"It's not fair of me. And it's not likely to work."

"I was just thinking that the law itself has been triggering for me since the shooting..." Jason's voice trailed off, censoring himself. "Do you know who is repping the coal company?"

"Courtney Sharpe, from Earl Franks' old firm."

"No shit? Audrey Benson won't put up with any of her histrionics."

"You see why I want you? Who else has that kind of insider knowledge? Also, you know how these big trials go—"

"As a judge, at least," Jason finished for her. "It's different, trying a case. All the prep nights."

"Exactly. For the lawyers trying it, it can be pretty much 24-7," Grace said. "I don't want to be away from you 24-7 for four or five months."

"Me either," Jason replied. "Look, why don't we go up to Lake Superior for a long weekend, and we could kind of scope out the coal place."

"By weekend, do you mean, umm… tonight? I have until Wednesday to tell them if I am going to take it. I guess we could drive up tomorrow or even tonight if you want."

"My bag is already packed for your place," Jason replied.

"Should be peak fall color up north."

"I need to gas up, so you go on ahead," Jason said. "I'll make a hotel reservation in Duluth. It's about five hours from La Crosse, I think."

"In Duluth and not Superior?" Grace asked.

"Yes, Duluth is much nicer."

Grace drove over the hills through Coon Valley and saw the sign for Norskedalen. The Norwegian Heritage Center was nestled in the bluffs, where she and Jon had their wedding. So many beautiful photos from that day. It didn't stab her heart the way it used to, but the pain was still there. It would always be there.

She'd been seeing Jason for two years already. They jokingly called themselves Gray-Jay, like a celebrity couple. She'd made a drawing of a Gray Jay, the bird some people called the Canada Jay or Whiskey Jack, and then scanned it to make a logo under the Header "Erickson and Clarkson, Attorneys at Law." She was keeping that one to surprise him if he said yes.

They stopped at her house, she packed, and soon they were driving north. The sun was starting to set by the time they finally made it to bleakly industrial Superior, Wisconsin and then over the bridge to more prosperous Duluth, Minnesota. Both had been gritty port towns, but Duluth had reinvented itself lately to become a regional tourist hot spot.

Jason insisted that they walk down to the pier to catch the lake and lighthouse before checking into their hotel or seeing about dinner. The wind blew Jason's hair around, revealing a thinning patch at the top of his head. They'd both crashed through their forties into their fifties.

The sky was reddish orange over the tourist area along the lake. Lake Superior was cobalt blue, choppy, and forbidding. The lighthouses here weren't just for show; fierce storms could appear on the big lake in an hour.

"Look, there's our hotel, Fitgers." Grace pointed. "It even has a bookstore. Thanks for making us a reservation."

"And it has a good restaurant too. We have a reservation there, at The Boat Club, soon."

"Great, I'm more than a little peckish."

They checked in, unpacked, and had a delicious dinner of whitefish and salads. They also shared a bottle of excellent Chablis. The restaurant was relaxing; it looked out amiably over the Greatest Lake. Formerly blue-collar Duluth was almost posh in places now. There were lots of wealthy tourists from the Twin Cities. Grace would stay here during the coal case if she could, although it might be pricey for her client.

They went back up to their room. Jason was exhausted from driving, and soon he was dozing off in their hotel room. Grace stretched out beside him, listening to his comforting, steady breathing.

They both slept straight through the night.

Grace crept out of bed in the morning and got them coffee from the lobby.

"Thanks, Grace. No one has ever brought me coffee in bed

before," Jason said softly. "But having slept on it, I want you to know that I'm still not feeling any overwhelming desire to get back on the saddle and practice law yet."

"I know. Maybe you could just help me with any questions off the record."

"Of course. Always. For me, the law is sort of like a war zone now. I guess I should talk about it with my counselor—I've got an appointment with her in a couple of weeks."

"Thanks for being straight with me." Grace looked out the window toward the lake. "I want to be straight with you too. I am going to need a co-counsel on this case, and Tim Gergen has let me know that he wants to do it."

"That's the Eau Claire lawyer, that Tim guy that you dated?"

She nodded.

"Ouch."

"It was not a serious relationship. More like two or three dates. Tim is no threat. You know I'm committed to us."

Jason nodded, sipping his coffee.

"But we would be spending a whole lot of time together."

Was she making some kind of gentle threat? They both knew that even opposing lawyers sometimes bonded in complex cases. With co-counsel, there was often shared giddiness from both solidarity and fatigue.

"That's why I want you there," she added.

"Well, you have to do what you have to do to try your case." Jason set his coffee down on the nightstand. "And I have to do what's best for my mental health."

"Of course," she replied, softening. "I know."

"I haven't really admitted that my mental health is what's holding me back," Jason continued. "It's not so much that I've become an ethical slacker—it's that it fills me with dread and anxiety to take on another case with some bad guys."

"Are they bad guys?"

"Well, I dreamed about those coal-stained white sheets

last night." Jason shook his head. "And little Lacy at the ER."

"Shall we walk along the waterfront a bit before heading out?" Grace tried to change the mood.

They held hands and walked along the shore. The scale of the Big Lake was humbling. And the depth. In places, the water was more than thirteen hundred feet deep. The Indigenous people called it the *Anishinaabewi-gichigami.* The Great Anishinaabe Sea. This formidable freshwater sea could be navigated all the way to the salty Atlantic. That's why all the industrial sector, including the coal pile, was there.

"Amazing." Jason looked out at the water thoughtfully. "It's so beautiful and so forbidding at the same time. You can feel the cold, even in September."

Grace still liked his quiet intensity, even if he sometimes seemed a little lost. He was kind and good to her—if sometimes a bit distracted. It would be hard not to see him for weeks at a time. Would their relationship survive?

Of course, it had been way more than two or three dates with Tim. They'd talked about a business partnership and more.

Why had she lied to Jason?

Chapter Three

Not All Gingerbread

Courtney Sharpe had won some significant cases that had helped make her Managing Partner, but she'd long ago learned that being MP wasn't all big bonuses and freshly baked gingerbread. Today was an especially good illustration of how much it could suck.

First, there was the employee-management issue from hell, especially for Courtney. A disgruntled female associate who had not been given partner-track status had filed a complaint against a female partner, alleging that she'd been screwing a handsome young male associate. The young male attorney had recently made partner, while the complaining associate had not, which would potentially cost the young woman hundreds of thousands of bonus dollars over the course of her firm career.

As an ambitious young associate, Courtney had done something similar herself with not one but two male partners at Higgins and Clark. Both of those old partner paramours were gone, but surely some critical people in the firm knew the story of her own ascent at Higgins and Clark? It was a terrible conflict of interest for Courtney as the managing partner.

Would she have to disclose it? How much of it? Could she finesse it by saying something like "due to a personal conflict?" Would that fly? The disgruntled associate would start digging into it either way.

Not good.

Then, Courtney's own associate, Jake Simmons, approached

her enormous walnut desk, looking glum. "We've got a couple of hearing requests on that coal transshipment case up in Lake Superior City, Wisconsin." Jake set them on her desk. "No lawyers yet, but someone's clearly been coaching them."

"Shit." She wasn't thrilled to learn that she'd be spending several weeks in far northern Wisconsin up on Lake Superior. "What do you think?" Courtney asked. She glanced over the papers herself.

"Mostly NIMBY stuff, in my opinion. But there are a couple of real issues. The coal operation had been regularly getting notice of violations on air monitors, and then that suddenly stopped. People are saying that there haven't been any recent violations because they messed with the monitors."

"That's not really a permit issue, though. That's enforcement," Courtney said.

"Well, they've done a good job of making it one. And the other decent issue for them relates to whether they're in fact spraying on the piles the overcoating that reduces coal dust. It's quite an expensive process, apparently. Or, at least, that's what Earl Franks told me." Jake paused and looked away.

Had Jake winced a bit saying Earl's name, knowing he'd gone to prison for trying to bribe a judge? Or did Jake know that Courtney had dated the much-older Earl?

"Don't worry. I miss the big dumb fucker too," she said. "And I still intend to pick Earl's brain on this, whether that ex-con has a law license or not."

"Of course, that's a great idea."

"I'm full of them. That's why I'm running this place." Courtney sometimes still couldn't believe that she was managing partner, regular pains in her ass notwithstanding. "And let me approach Earl, okay?"

"Of course, boss." Was he sucking up? Jake looked as he always looked, so sincere.

"Look, our biggest problem is not even in this petition," she began. "There's just one thing that scares me."

"What's that?" Jake asked.

"It's coal itself. It's not a legal standard. It's just a gut-check thing. People are just sick of coal."

Jake nodded. Courtney liked working with him. For a third-year associate, he always had his ear to the ground and often made creative arguments.

Courtney and Jake started mapping out a strategy.

"People say that Grace Clarkson, who won that groundwater contamination case, is coming in," Jake said.

"And possibly bring Judge Erickson in with her?"

"Yes, or that Gergen guy from Eau Claire."

They would both help the already capable Grace Clarkson. She was top-notch but hampered by her small firm's lack of resources. If Grace was going to have her boyfriend Jason Erickson as an advisor, then Courtney was sure as hell going to reach out to Earl Franks.

She pulled out her phone. Earl was living on Blue Lake with that preacher's widow. She tried the old number she had, but there was no answer. She tried it again first thing in the morning, and this time left a message. Then she went to see Sydney, her therapist.

The personnel case and contacting Earl would give them plenty to talk about.

Chapter Four

On Pink Lake

Earl Franks started up the ultra-quiet Endura trolling motor on his Mercury fishing boat and set off for Farnum Bay on the other side of Blue Lake. It was more like Pink Lake, the way the sunlight set off the waters. The sun had just begun to rise. Gloriously. Earl loved being out in the morning fog—enjoying the September chill and stirrings of color along the shoreline.

The smallmouth bass were practically jumping into his boat. Fall was his favorite season, and he still couldn't believe his good fortune after twenty-five months in the dark prison. He'd bought the boat a couple of weeks after he got out. There was a story there, though one he'd only told Betty.

It involved Sam the Snake.

His brother Sam hadn't come to visit Earl even once in prison but had instead seized the opportunity to have Earl's ninety-three-year-old mother sign payable-on-death notes that stripped Earl of his inheritance. After Earl got out, an old friend who did probate had helped Earl investigate it a bit. It turned out that Sam had also been using his new power-of-attorney powers to systematically steal from their mother while Earl was in prison. Earl and the attorney sent a letter confronting Sam about the theft, threatening to go to the police.

That's how Earl had recovered enough to buy this boat. It was a beauty and even had a little pull-up portable cabin for bad weather outings. The boat was Earl's refuge. Piloting it was freedom itself.

Earl had wanted to christen it the Double-Edged Swordfish,

but Betty said that was too clunky. He'd settled for Betty's own suggestion: Brother's Keeper. "That boat's definitely a keeper that came from your brother! And people will think that you're religious," Betty said.

"If they only knew," he'd deadpanned.

Prison had also kept him from his mother's funeral. He tried, but the approval to leave had arrived too late, and Earl had had to watch a recording of his mom's funeral. Watching his brother's hypocritical religious posturing had been literally sickening, and Earl had thrown up. Not a great idea in prison. Cell neighbors bitched, and the stench of his own reaction to his brother's perfidy had hung in the air of his cell for a week.

Now, the lake air was as fresh as it had been fetid in prison. And going out on the Keeper was his life now, this pink-dawn sky, fishing Blue Lake several days a week. Not sucking up to sleazy clients in Chicago, and not helping his fellow inmates in prison. No. This pink sky and the equally rosy lips of Betty Franklin, the woman he'd left sleeping inside his house, were his life.

Yesterday, he'd reached his bag limit of five smallmouth and a dozen or so bluegills and was back before Betty had even stirred in bed. He brought Betty her coffee and fried up the bluegill with some eggs for their breakfast—something Pastor, as they both still called her late husband, had never done.

"What a treat," Betty gushed. She was pleased. When they were finished and had cleaned up the kitchen together, she gave him a sly smile. "Want to do some other things Pastor never did for me?"

Earl couldn't believe his good fortune. Sometimes when he woke up next to Betty, he couldn't go back to sleep. He was so happy. They'd been summer neighbors for thirty years, and Earl had always enjoyed her company. Pastor was a sanctimonious stuffed shirt who "insisted on saying grace before eating cheese and crackers at four o'clock," as Betty said. Earl himself had seen him do it.

They were fresh autumn morning air for each other.

As he pulled in another nice smallmouth, he heard her voice in his head: "When are we going to eat all of these bass?" He released the grateful yellow fish and trolled himself quietly back to his pier.

As he entered the back door, he saw the look on Betty's face. There would be no hero's welcome this time.

"Good morning to you too," Earl said. "What'd I do this time?"

"That's what I want you to tell me," Betty replied, pacing. "Your cell phone buzzed not once but twice this morning, and the second time, it fell off your bed stand."

"Okay, sorry. Kind of dumb of me, but not worthy of this kind of greeting. I told you, I've been leaving my phone inside so that I don't take five hundred photos of the sunrise."

"That's not what I'm mad about," Betty said. "When I picked up your phone, I saw that both calls were from your skanky ex-girlfriend, Courtney."

"Courtney Sharpe?"

"Yes, what other Courtney is there?" Betty's arms were crossed and her lips tight. "What's going on, Earl?"

"I have no clue." Shit. Did Courtney have HIV or something? "I haven't spoken with her since before my sentencing."

"You swear?"

He nodded. "Probably just some old file." He was touched that she was jealous. Earl was crazy about Betty. "Nothing personal, I'm sure."

"Okay, I'm sorry." Betty came toward him and gave him a glancing kiss on the cheek. "How were they biting this morning?"

"Really nice bass today, and so was the sunrise. Very pink."

"I saw it." She mustered a slight smile. "But call her back. Now."

"Yes, boss."

"I don't want us sitting around dreading it all day. I'll make you a cup of fresh coffee."

The phone was ringing as Betty brought his Earl-the-Pearl mug.

"Courtney, why the hell are you calling me?" Earl blustered, trying to reassure Betty.

She smiled, full throttle this time, and slipped back into the kitchen.

"Very professional greeting, Earl," Courtney replied. "I can tell you've been out of office life for a while."

"My girlfriend wasn't thrilled that you called. Twice."

"The second time I left a message," Courtney said. "Did you listen to it?"

"Nope. Just stepped off my fishing boat."

"Well, your girlfriend can rest easy. I just want to pick your brain, not jump your bones."

She knew how to jump them too. Damn. Why'd she say that?

"Do you remember working on a coal processing plant up in Superior, Wisconsin?" Courtney asked.

"Sure, of course." Earl accidentally slurped his coffee. Courtney couldn't contain a cruelly candid laugh.

"I've got a similar case," she said. "And their permit is up for renewal."

"And this concerns me how?"

"I was hoping to talk through a couple of things with you. I'd be happy to send you a consulting fee," Courtney purred. "And, of course, we could even do that in cash."

"Let me think about it," Earl said.

"Sure. I need some time to formulate my questions anyway. You know I value your opinion, big guy."

"Call me the same time next week, and I'll think about it in the meantime."

"That works. How are you doing anyway?" Courtney asked.

"Just fine and dandy." It was true. Every day out of prison, every day waking up in the sunlight next to Betty, was a gift. "You?"

"Me too. Got my loans paid off, and I'm the head honcho over here now."

"Heard that, congrats. And I'm glad you're out of hock too," Earl said. "We'll talk again."

"Thanks for considering it. It might be fun to work together again."

Earl attended to nature's morning necessities, as his ex-wife Maggie was known to say. Shite, shower, and shave, as he thought of it. Then another phone call? What the hell? His cell phone was sometimes silent for whole weeks. His daughter wouldn't be likely to call now.

"Yes, this is Earl Franks the lawyer," he answered. "Former lawyer now. Who's this?"

"It's Tim Gergen, a lawyer from Eau Claire. I'm wondering if you would be willing to give me some background on a couple of cases you've worked on. Full disclosure: I might be representing some neighbors who are opposing a permit renewal."

"Go ahead," Earl said, pleased to be back in demand.

Chapter Five

Dead Ends and Guard Dogs

"Google says we're close," Jason said, pulling into yet another dead end.

They were having a surprisingly hard time finding the massive coal processing plant. There wasn't a whole lot of the facility that was open to the public.

Most of the coal was stored out on a private, man-made peninsula abutting the bay, where the huge ocean-worthy boats were filled. Railroad cars led to conveyors that transferred the coal either onto barges for local domestic shipping, or onto the huge island-like pile beside the lake that served ocean-going vessels. Jason did a quick U-turn out of another dead end.

"I'm sorry we can't find it from shore," Grace replied.

"The coal plant bought up these properties, no doubt. They don't want to be found."

"It's going to be tough to get a look at this, except from the water," Grace replied. She looked at him closely. "Sorry I dragged you up here."

"No worries. Let's stop at that convenience store and ask them. The locals sometimes know public footpaths for lake access."

"Hopefully they have a bathroom too." Grace smiled.

Jason pulled over. The neighborhood was as bleak and gray as the sky. The rundown convenience store was called Al's. As they approached the entrance, Jason put his arm around her.

"I'll buy something," he said softly. "And maybe you can casually ask."

"Don't worry, I'll smile pretty too," Grace replied. "At least if they have a bathroom. Otherwise, I'll keep grimacing."

They went in. "Restroom?"

The clerk pointed straight back.

"Beer?"

"Right next to the john."

Grace made her way into and out of the bathroom, and Jason took his turn. They picked out a six-pack of Bent Hop IPA and went back up to the clerk.

"Do you know where we could get a look at the coal shipment plant?" Grace asked sweetly.

"Well, you could take a decent picture from the Duluth bridge," the clerk said. "Or just get a little fishing boat. There's a path, but the best way to reach that is by boat. Otherwise, you might run into one of their guard dogs."

"No thanks!" Grace shook her head. "Jason here is more comfortable with guard dogs than I am."

"Jason Erickson," he said to the clerk, extending his hand.

"I'm Al Hendricks."

"Not sure how you feel about the coal processing plant, Al, but Grace and I are lawyers thinking about opposing the renewal of their permits."

"The plant has ruined my life and business," Al said quickly. "Those guys never spend a dime in here, and no one lives in the neighborhood anymore. All I get is beer sales. That's a good one you've picked by the way. It's $9.53 with the tax."

Jason gave him $10.

"I'll make you a little map drawing, but don't blame me if that dog takes half your ankle." Al scrounged for a scrap of paper. "You can walk from here."

They made their way back out to the car, and Jason put the beer in the back seat. "I'll go alone," he said. Grace had been knocked down by a large dog as a teenager and was still afraid of them. "But please keep your phone ready for my distress call."

"You don't have to do this, Jason. Maybe we should see if there are any boat rentals first."

"I'll just get a few pictures, and then we'll go back up to the bridge."

"Okay. I'll google boat rentals nearby," Grace said.

Jason tried to make sense of Al's squiggly hand-drawn map. After a couple of misfires, he found the dead-end alley that led to the lake. The city had probably helped the company hide it by making it an alley rather than a street. The end of any street that abutted public water was open to the public, and it led to what looked like a longtime public access trail along Lake Superior.

As he headed down the path, he could smell the rotten-egg, sulfur-scent of the coal pile. Then it quickly came into view. Behind a high fence, there was a massive black mountain of coal. Small parts of the pile were being sprayed with an expensive treated water spray to hold and keep down the dust. He snapped a couple of photos on his phone.

It appeared that the anti-dust treatment only hit the front edges of the pile that were closest to the lake, so Jason took a brief video. This angle might be valuable if Grace returned with an expert. As he was putting his phone away, Jason heard the barking dog. The German Shepherd frantically ran to the fence. It growled and bared its teeth.

"It's okay, boy," Jason called to it as calmly as he could.

But then the dog nosed its way under the fence. Jason snapped a picture of it as it made its way toward him. The huge dog stopped four feet away. Jason backed up, giving the dog its territory.

"It's okay," he said, still backing up. "If you want me to leave, I will. Good dog."

The dog snarled aggressively as Jason slowly backed down the trail. When he finally mustered the courage to turn around, he saw the dog find its way back under the fence.

It was clear that there was something the company didn't want people to see.

Chapter Six

A Coal Pile Beside the Lake

Rather than random googling, Grace decided it was better to go back into the store and ask the owner, Al, if he knew someone nearby with a boat. "Know anyone like that?"

"How about someone who especially hates the coal pile?" Al asked. "I know a guy. Jerry's a grad student and fisherman. When are you talking about?"

"Now, if possible," she replied. "I can pay in cash."

"He's always broke," Al said. He dialed Jerry up and then turned away, mumbling.

"He says he'll meet you out front in fifteen." Al asked Grace, "That work?" She nodded. "Twenty-five bucks plus gas?" Al continued.

"Forty," Grace replied, knowing she had plenty of cash.

She went back outside to wait for Jason. He'd texted her that he'd found the path. Five minutes later, Jason came jogging up the alley. His goofy, skipping stride was unmistakable.

"They're up to something!" he called. He shook his head. "And check out this pic I got of the dog."

It was a German Shepherd. Its teeth were drawn wide apart, ready to draw blood.

"Yikes! Glad I stayed here," Grace said.

"He's just marking his territory, but the odd thing is that he's trained to go under the fence outside their property. And I think I know why."

"Keep people off their end of the path?"

"Yes. There's a huge area where the treated water never

sprays. Maybe a pile of friable coal ash. That sub-bituminous stuff has lower sulfur, but it breaks apart easier."

"I know." Grace tried to nod politely at his mansplaining. But it was good to see him engaged. "I found us a guy who's willing to take us for a view from the water."

Jerry, the grad student, was already waiting at the convenience store. He was tall with long, sandy hair and in his mid-twenties. Jerry squeezed them into the front seat of his truck and then backed into a little boat launch six blocks away.

They got the tiny boat off the trailer and into the choppy water. Jason held Grace's sweaty hand as they started out into the enormous black water. Jerry caught what must have been her look of fright.

"Don't worry," Jerry assured. "We're in a mostly protected bay. And I'm not going far from the shore."

The scale of the massive coal transshipment plant came into view. There was a long loading machine that Grace knew lined fifteen hundred feet of shoreline. Behind it was a pile that could hold up to five million tons of coal. Jason pointed to two giant aerial lawn sprinklers spraying the front.

"Do you notice how little of the pile is actually getting sprayed?" Jason asked. "If it's a timed setting, it's been on the same cycle for over a half hour."

"There's still an unhealthy shit-ton of dust," Jerry put in. "Right around here." Jerry slowed the boat to a crawl. "Probably the best spot to take pictures."

Grace and Jason quickly obliged. It was like a large coal mine had been imported from the hills of Kentucky or the prairies of Wyoming and then plopped down here, right next to the great freshwater lake. Absurdly, she thought, this far into the twenty-first century.

"Where does all of this coal come from?" Jerry asked. "Why is it here?"

"Most of it comes by train from the Powder River Basin out west," she answered. "And then they ship it by train to power plants in the Midwest and Canada or by water via the St. Lawrence Seaway. There's a joint US/Canadian pathway that goes from here to Quebec. From there, they can ship it anywhere that still uses coal for electric power. Ten years ago, they used to ship out twenty million tons a year."

"She knows her stuff," Jerry said.

"She does; Grace won the only case she ever did with me."

"Well, true, but Jason was the judge, not my opponent. That's why I'm trying to get him to help me."

"Oh my god." Jerry stared at Jason. "Are you that Love Judge from the famous murder case?"

Jason nodded. He'd always hated that tabloid moniker, which he felt somehow diminished his feelings for Tara.

"Cool!" Jerry said with youthful enthusiasm. "I mean, I'm sorry for all that."

"Can you take us out a little way so I can get a photo of the eastern corner?" Jason quickly changed that painful subject.

Grace thought about the recent past as they trolled along the shore, snapping photos. She had been a minor witness: she'd seen Earl Franks in La Crosse, corroborating Jason's testimony that Franks had tried to bribe him.

It'd all been an exhausting time for both, and it created a lot of baggage for them now. Two-plus years later, Jason was still licking his wounds. Grace wondered if he'd lost his passion for justice, the trait she'd found most attractive in him. Or maybe not.

There he was, trying to keep his balance on this rocky little boat, taking pictures to help her and all the kids who lived within miles of there. Grace was pretty sure that Jason had walked through a door. But where would it lead?

And were they going there together?

Chapter Seven

Selling a Timeshare

Courtney was home by six thirty for once and, since it was a beautiful fall day, decided to take a walk with Ben down to Kathy Osterman Beach on Lake Michigan in Chicago. It was about nine blocks from her condo, and then they'd probably stop for dinner at one of the nearby neighborhood restaurants.

They held hands, like old-fashioned sweethearts. They were. He even asked her how her day had gone.

"It's done. I just need to make one more slightly awkward call tonight."

"To your old flame, Earl?" Ben smiled.

"I think he could help us on the coal transshipment case."

"Yes, you told me," Ben said, smiling. He was too secure to be jealous of Earl or anyone from her past. "I hope the old guy will come through."

"How was your day?" she asked.

"Productive. I found a very relevant UCC case from the Western District of Wisconsin and my case is in the Eastern District there."

"Awesome. It sure is a beautiful day."

They were approaching the lake, and there was the usual interesting and diverse group of beachcombers: several wrinkled, older, sun-worshipping couples, some mostly naked gay men flirting, and a coed volleyball game of young people. The sun was shimmering its silver light on Lake Michigan.

The September sand was still warm enough for Courtney

to take her shoes off. Ben did the same. They pretended to dance barefoot and left their shoes where they dropped them.

"Why don't you go make your call now?" Ben wriggled his toes in the sand. "And then we can just enjoy the rest of this beautiful evening?"

She found an empty bench and called Earl. A nearly naked man on rollerblades came by in a flash. You never knew what you were going to see by a Lake Michigan beach.

"Hi, Earl. There are two reasons I'm reaching out to you—"

"Full disclosure," Earl replied. "You're not the only one."

"I'm not surprised. Not only do you know the most about the coal shipment and storage operation, but you're also the best one to counter what I call the Coal Itself argument because that's what you did with DDT."

"That wasn't my idea. I was just a couple of years out of law school."

"I know; you told me. You just took credit for it and then used it to become AG. But the point's the same." She saw Ben expertly skipping stones down by the lake. He looked like a happy little boy. "I'm afraid that they're just going to try to drill down to the truth about coal and say it's time to be rid of the nasty stuff."

"That's what he said too."

"He? Jason Erickson? The judge who got shot?"

"I'm not sure I can say." Earl paused. "But no, not Jason. There's this other guy out of Eau Claire on their side already."

"Damn, they're on top of it if they're talking to you already."

"Seem to be. There's one more problem though, Courtney."

"What's that?"

"I think I'm on their side in this one. I'd like to be able to eat more of the fish I pull out of this lake. I don't want people to be flooded out all over the world. I want to climb on some glaciers before they all melt away."

"And don't forget the polar bears!" Courtney laughed, a

little unconvincingly. The truth was that her trademark cynicism was starting to wear thin. Ben. It was hard to be both cynical and in love.

"Laugh all you want," Earl fumed. "I have my reasons. Did you know Laurie is pregnant? Almost ready to pop, even."

"Well, good luck with that then, Grandpa. You can't work for them, though. It's a huge conflict."

"Nice try, but I'm not a lawyer anymore. And I never represented this facility anyway," Earl said. "Come on, Courtney. It would even *help* my old client to have this competitor shut down. Now that I think of it, maybe you're the one with the conflict."

"Nice try yourself, Earl. They know and they see the existential threat to coal."

"They should; the climate has changed. Why do you think those kids all over the world are skipping school—"

"Because it's fun and exciting?" Courtney parried. "And because it makes them feel important for playing hooky?"

"Sure, but it's their planet that we're fucking up, not just the polar bears'. All the more for little Emma, who's still in Laurie's womb."

"Christ, not another Emma!" Her voice sounded more authentic. "Does every girl have to be called Emma?"

"We're done talking—"

"Wait, are you saying flat out that you won't even let me run a few ideas past you for four hundred dollars an hour?"

"Yeah, that's what I'm saying."

"And I was going to propose meeting at the Edgewater Hotel in Madison to discuss it." She looked to make sure Ben was out of earshot. "Remember our night there?"

"Of course, I remember." Earl seemed to soften a bit as he continued. "But Courtney, we can't go back to that time. I'm in love with Betty. You have to keep moving forward in life; otherwise, the past just eats you up. That's what I learned from not seeing the sun for two years."

"I'm not trying to go back in time. Don't flatter yourself; I've got a nice new man in my life." She waved to Ben as he motioned for her to hurry up. "I'm just trying to give you a surefire side hustle. Come on. This is a no-risk bet."

"I'll hear you out, but not at the Edgewater. And not in Madison."

"Okay, then. How about meeting me somewhere closer to you? Somewhere with no history. What about Wisconsin Dells? And you let me make my pitch over lunch?"

"You sound like you're selling a timeshare," he joked.

But Courtney was pretty sure that meant yes.

Chapter Eight

Courtney's Pitch

A couple of weeks later, Earl slid his RAV4 Hybrid into a parking spot at the Dells Resort, where he was to meet Courtney. His old Lexus had saved his life by thwarting his closed-garage suicide attempt with its battery, so he'd bought another hybrid, albeit a more downscale model better reflecting his more modest circumstances in his retirement.

Betty was having a minor cow about this meeting, so he texted her to say that he had arrived but there was, as of now, no sign of Courtney.

That little shit is going to stand you up, Betty replied.

Maybe, but she's the one asking for a favor. Earl was genuinely touched by Betty's alarm and jealousy. *Thanks for keeping your eyes on me!*

She replied with an upside-down smiling face emoji—the meaning of which Earl had no clue. Then, *Remember your priest, Earl*, she texted.

That would be Father Jacob, the prison priest. He'd started Earl on the hard path of considering the consequences of his own actions in the case that had sent him to prison. Earl was by then a trustee, wearing blue, not orange, pajama coveralls. Jacob was a bit of a hippie, maybe gay, but so what? He was real with Earl. He cut through Earl's BS with his own—or was it even bull? Jacob seemed to believe it.

"You know, Earl, a Jesuit priest taught me how to think these things through," Jacob declared. "He'd listen carefully as students pondered his Socratic questions. There would be a slightly dramatic pause before he'd ask, 'What are the implications of saying that, or of doing that?' That was all. That was enough."

"I get it; you can't have people bribing judges, or the winners are always those with the most money to bribe," Earl replied. "That already happens in the state legislature. But what do you do when someone has a gun in your back and tells you that you have to?"

"It's your answer that matters." Jacob shook his head. "Maybe ask for help?"

Now, Earl saw Courtney, in a powder-and-navy-blue pinstripe suit, sliding out of her shiny black Beamer SUV. She was three years more alluring than the last time he'd seen her. What was she now, thirty-seven or so? A real woman.

She's here, he texted Betty.

Betty replied immediately. **Be good.**

"Hey, Big Guy." Courtney smirked. "How's life on the Outside?"

"Beats the hell out of the other option. You're looking very Managing Partner from where I sit." Earl looked down at his phone, making sure that he hadn't accidentally butt-dialed Betty getting out of his car. He always flirted with Courtney.

"Thanks. Let's go claim our table; believe it or not, the food is pretty decent in here."

Courtney went up the stone stairs first, rocking those pinstripe dress pants. He tried not to remember the erotic joys they'd shared together. But what made this working-class Minnesota woman so special to Earl was not her beauty; it was her way of being. Unlike so many of the younger lawyers, she was not full of either shit or herself. That was uniquely attractive. Courtney was always authentically engaged in whatever she was doing, and she did a lot of things well.

"Looks like you're still running," Earl observed.

"Thank you, Mr. Justice. Still running about twenty-five a week." She turned around to greet him at the top of the stairs.

"Look, Earl, we had a ton of fun together, didn't we?"

"We did, until you took the party to another destination."

"I was right to see the shit about to hit the fan with Calandro," Courtney returned.

"You were," Earl replied. Tommy Calandro had had Earl over a barrel and forced him to try to bribe Judge Jason Erickson. That had put Earl in prison for a couple of years while Tommy C had retired somewhere in Italy. "I understood that part."

"I told you all of that was not my deal. But my point is that we could still flirt and have fun if you helped me on this case." She smiled and then quickly knitted her brows. "But I'll be straight with you: I'm not going to fuck you to get your help. I'm in a serious relationship."

"I'll be honest with you: I'm loyal to Betty." Though flirting with Courtney sounded fun. And Earl appreciated her not leading him on. "We're talking about getting married."

"Congrats." She offered him her delicate hand. "And by the way, lunch is on your former employer."

Courtney made her pitch. Ten thousand bucks down and a flat $500-an-hour rate after the first twenty hours. All he had to do was honestly alert her to any flaws in the opponent's case. The old Earl would have had the check cashed and put five K down on a horse, but post-prison Earl snuck to the bathroom to text Betty. She'd already texted him twice.

I'm in the john, honey. It's just lunch.

That's another name for a date, Earl.

Nothing like that; she's just dangling our new pier before me. Ten K now and five hundred dollars an hour to babysit.

It's your decision. Your conscience.

I know.

The old pier is fine with me, Earl.

Nice of you to say.

Though she was lying, Earl gave that text a thumbs-up. He knew how much she wanted to replace his decaying old wooden pier. Even her underpaid late pastor husband's pier had been better, but Betty had sold it with their highly mort-gaged house. They'd always been pressed for money. Who knew that God paid slave wages?

Betty had only cleared a little under $100,000 after the Realtor, and that was just because of appreciation. And the church had only provided Pastor with a $50,000 life insurance policy. That was all she had in the world.

Betty never spoke ill of Pastor. But one time, when she was a little tipsy and full of afterglow, Betty told Earl that he'd given her the sex and security that she'd been longing for her whole adult life.

Thanks, honey, Earl texted her. **Gotta go!**

He made his way back across the sunny dining room, just as their salads were arriving.

"Yum, that's a real Niçoise," Courtney said.

"Besides money, why should I work for you?" Earl asked. "I mean, I still have some kind of long-shot chance at becoming a model citizen again."

She winced a little at the prospect. "Well, that's kind of like saying, 'Other than for the air, why should I keep breathing?'"

"For you, maybe; not for me."

"Not what I heard. They say Judge Jason took most of your savings off your hands."

"There was some personal contribution, but most of it was insurance money," Earl replied. Courtney had done her home-work. He'd had to kick in $150,000 for the settlement. He was maybe a little strapped, but not *flat* broke. "The guy was shot, and he lost someone he loved."

"That wasn't your fault, Earl."

"No, it wasn't. I'm at peace with all of that." He paused a minute, staring at his green beans. Was he? "So basically, what I hear you saying is that there's no reason other than dough that I should work with your team? You might not believe this, Courtney, but since my... retirement."

"You mean prison?"

"Okay, sure, since prison, I've only tried to do things that I care about, things that will make a better world for my grandkids. And coal isn't it."

"That's very laudable. Seriously. But what about doing it for old time's sake, for your former girlfriend?" she purred. Then she added, "Just cut the crap, Earl. So why are you here then?"

She had a point, the same one that Betty had been making. "Well, I'm not saying that I'm totally immune to the idea of old time's sake."

"So I've got a shot then?" Courtney leaned closer to him. She still smelled like fresh-baked bread.

Damn, her. Damn, him.

"What, exactly, would be involved? I will think about it, but I'm not making any promises."

Chapter Nine

Grand Marais

After their night in Duluth, Grace had surprised him with a two-night reservation at a rental cabin in Grand Marais, up near the Canadian border. It was a two-hour drive. Jason and Grace made their way up beside the slate-black water of Lake Superior north of Duluth.

It was nearly lunchtime when they made the turn down the gravel road toward their cabin. Google Maps was spotty and there were no street signs. Jason was driving and Grace was reading the owner's instructions, trying to navigate.

"What does it say we do after the road to the National Forest again?" he asked.

"Turn right for two miles and then look for N67756. Take a hard left when we see it."

"Okay." Jason found himself thinking about Tara again, about that time they'd gone out together to see the world-record pine outside Blue Lake. When they'd found it, the majestic pine had been brutally sheared from a lightning strike. "Can you read that number?"

"N67750. Our cabin should be next."

"Yes, hooray, we made it!"

After an awkward struggle with the lockbox, they made their way inside. It was a classic rustic loft-style A-frame with twisting stairs that led to the loft bedroom. The cabin was pleasant but smelled a little damp.

"Oh, look, Jason," Grace said, opening the refrigerator.

"They left us a nice bottle of wine, a baguette, and a cheese-and-fruit plate."

"Very thoughtful. If we go out for lunch, we won't have to go back out for dinner." That sounded relaxing after all the car travel.

Jason brought their bags in and soon they were back out, exploring picturesque downtown Grand Marais. They had a delicious lunch of local whitefish at a place called the Angry Trout, and then stopped at a bookstore called Drury Lane Books.

Jason bought a copy of *The Overstory* by Richard Powers, and Grace bought *Walking the Old Road*, a local history of native people written by Staci Lola Drouillard, a member of the Lake Superior Band of Anishinaabe. "Great choices," the bookseller told them. They put their books in the car and then walked out to the nearby rock formation they both remembered called Artist's Point.

"The names here are so evocative," Grace said as she headed out the zig-zaggy trail toward the water. "Pincushion Mountain, Sawtooth Bluff."

"Artist's Point," he replied. "These rocks look like tablets; they're so square and perfect."

"Probably sheathed off and pushed up by the glacier."

The waves had picked up, and the wind was bracing but not brutal. From the far end of the path, you could see the row of hills that framed the Superior Shore. Rivers sent waters crashing down waterfalls toward the inland sea. All of this was worth fighting for, worth saving. But he wasn't anyone's savior.

"Look, I thought you might like to know that I've made my decision." He grabbed Grace's hand, and then turned to face her. "I'll help you, as much as I can, but I'm still going to be in Santa Barbara for all of January."

"Oh, that's great. Can I list you as my co-counsel?"

"How about Of Counsel?" Her smile shrank. "And I promise to understand if you feel the need to bring Tim in."

"I will have to." She nodded. "I can't take this all on myself."

"I'll help as much as I can, but…"

"So, you're not going to go to Lake Superior City for the pretrial conference?"

Of course not. "No."

"Okay." From her slumped shoulders, he could tell that Grace was disappointed.

She'd been saying for a while that it was time for them to either move forward together or step back. But moving forward for them meant one of them moving because Jason lived in Madison and Grace in La Crosse, two hours away. Grace had a thriving practice there, and it didn't make sense for her to leave it. When they'd started seeing each other, the drive over the hills had been a calming routine for him. Jason loved visiting La Crosse but wasn't sure if it was big enough for him to live in. He did know that it made him miss his dad.

They were out until after seven, lost in their own thoughts. Grace didn't say much at all until they got back to the cabin, and she put together their little dinner. Jason opened the wine and poured them each a glass.

"Cheers," Grace said, clinking glasses. She was trying. "Here's to our adventure today and to not talking about the case for the next two days."

"I'll definitely drink to that!"

They had the bread and cheese with grapes and olives and a couple of glasses of wine. It was after ten when they made their way up the steep ladder. The loft consisted of a massive king-size mattress surrounded by built-in shelves and reading lights on either side.

"Sweet, it's like that teahouse we went to in Chicago," Jason said.

"I loved that place," Grace replied.

She was crawling around on her knees in her underwear, pulling down the blankets with her backside facing him. Jason took the opportunity to give it a playful pat. She turned around to kiss him on the lips, but it was just a dismissive good-night kiss. They were both tired, still the fire seemed to be going out between them.

"I'm sorry that I'm not going to—"

"—It's okay," Grace said, her voice trailing off. "Goodnight."

There wasn't much more for either of them to say anyway. Grace was soon snoring softly beside him, but Jason's thoughts crashed through his head like the waves above the rocks of Artist's Point. That dog the day before had come teeth-first under the fence. What were they hiding? The air in loft area felt close and claustrophobic.

He quietly got up to crack the window more open. Grace looked angelic and peaceful. It was always so easy for her to fall asleep. Would he ever love this sleeping beauty with his whole heart? He knew that he wasn't ready to sleep, so he crept his way stealthily down the ladder and into the bathroom.

There he was in the mirror with his messy hair and his shirt off. But who was he now? Though he'd kept up his law license, was he even still a lawyer?

Jason had tried working for the Democratic governor as a senior advisor on environmental policy. He'd had plenty of ideas, but few had gone anywhere, given the do-nothing Republican legislature. Jason had quietly agreed to have his position eliminated after just six months. The truth was that he'd been relieved; he hadn't been able to muster a whole lot of intellectual energy, even for this dream job. Maybe he'd tried to go back to work too soon?

He was financially secure for the first time in his life. Two lawsuits had resulted in two middle-six-figure settlements for Jason. Then, the state gave Jason a pension buyout that provided him with a decent monthly income and health insurance until he was eligible for Medicare.

But survivor's guilt came with this new wealth. He'd suffered, too, as his therapist was quick to remind him, but he was here, and Tara was not. And that was grotesquely unfair. It also felt unjust to Grace that he hadn't gotten over losing Tara.

What did he really want?

He wanted to go back to spend January in Santa Barbara as he had every year since Tara's death. Lately, he'd had that old urge, that strong gust of thought and feeling, that made him want to write. His grief counselor encouraged him to keep a journal and use his new freedom to reconnect with that part of himself. He would text himself sentences or fragments of a poem.

Jason went to the refrigerator and found some Spanish olives and the wine. He poured himself a glass of the Chardonnay, put some of the olives on a plate and sat down at the little kitchen table. He pulled out his phone and wrote himself an email, sorting through his own jumbled thoughts.

What did he want to say?

Chapter Ten

Timothy James

A week after her trip to Lake Superior with Jason, Grace was meeting Tim Gergen to discuss bringing him in as co-counsel. She was excited about the idea. Tim was a nuanced and very pragmatic lawyer who would stay focused on the case. Jason was still licking his wounds and lost in a daze. She understood, but it was sometimes exhausting to be around.

Instead of her usual morning run, Grace walked with a cup of coffee down to Riverside Park, noticing the brisk morning air and steamy autumn dew. The bluffs down the river were already starting to change color. Fall was everywhere now, gently warning of what came after it.

Then she went home, showered, and walked to work. The morning flew by, and then Tim came to her office punctually at one o'clock.

"How are you, Grace?" He swooped in to kiss her cheek. He was a bit chubbier than when they'd dated before, but he still had a fine head of graying blond hair. "Ready to rid the world of coal?"

"Oh, is that what you're planning to do with one case in Lake Superior City?"

"Well, we have to start somewhere."

"You're right, and please have a seat. Do you want some coffee?"

"No, I just want to figure out where we're at on this."

Why had she and Tim not made it the first time? At the time, Tim was in a rock band called Slow Pedestrian that was playing almost every weekend. She could either go and watch the same show or just skip seeing him. There was this bit he did about how popular the band was becoming because you saw signs for them popping up at intersections all over the country.

Back then, he was a little full of himself. A friend of Grace's had seen his band play in Winona, and she had told Grace that she'd seen him kissing a fan near the bar's bathrooms. Tim said that it was just a persona that went along with being onstage, but it was a bit much for Grace. Especially because she just didn't think he was that talented.

More significantly, they lived in different cities, and neither was interested in moving. Grace's La Crosse Central high school basketball team, where she had been the backup point guard and sixth woman, had played the Eau Claire teams, and she remembered those long rides home after a loss. But Eau Claire and La Crosse were only an hour and a half apart. Madison was over two, and yet she'd taken Jason, and not Tim, on.

"Did you hear me, Grace? What did your boyfriend decide?"

"He's out, though he's willing to help us strategize as best he can from California."

"Do you want to try this case together, Grace Elizabeth?"

"Yeah, and we're going to kick ass," Grace replied, stalling. Yes, she still remembered his middle name, too. "Timothy James."

"Tell me about those kids who have to keep going to the emergency room."

It was exciting to be working with someone whom she knew so well, someone who had some enthusiasm about the project. He even had some ideas about the coal case.

"There will be an in-person pretrial conference. Shall we drive up together?" she asked.

"Yes, that sounds wonderful. We can strategize."

Chapter Eleven

A Confidential Memo

Courtney was up and, on her treadmill, listening to Taylor Swift's "Style" by five forty-five. She wasn't exactly a Swiftie, but the treadmill was humming along to it and the song fit. She'd read somewhere that Swift had written twenty-one songs about her exes. Whatever worked. Courtney admired Swift's business success and energy, even if her music didn't move her personally that much. Taylor was a boss.

Since seeing Earl in Wisconsin, Courtney kept thinking about her time with him. He had met some of her needs at the time. It wasn't just about her making partner, even though that had been her primary motivation. She liked Earl, that blustering fool. He was all Id and no filters. There was something appealing in that.

It had been fun and easy between them until he was forced to offer a bribe to a sitting judge. Earl hadn't seen the need for the bribe. "I swear they forced me into it," he'd told her. "I can win this fucking case without it."

Courtney hopped off the treadmill and showered. Then she sat down at her iMac to check her email. Courtney was going to a therapist, trying to finally deal with her many layers of shit. She'd found a good therapist with a Google search, so now her computer feed was full of those *Psychology Today*–type lists about your attachment type or other feel-good salvos about getting away from a narcissist. Courtney usually avoided them, but she was click-baited into one about Ten Personality Traits of Family Trauma Survivors.

High-achievement or perfectionism. Check. *Avoiding relation-ships or getting close to people; jumping from relationship to relation-ship.* Double check. *Too rigid or too loose boundaries.* You people do know your stuff, don't you? *Feeling of shame or guilt.* Did deeply buried, unacknowledged shame count?

The achievement syndrome had taken Courtney a long way in her career, and it was almost worth all the other crap. She'd paid off her student debt and was looking to buy a condo outright. Later today, she had an appointment at a sweet two-bedroom, two-bath apartment in the Edgewater area of Chicago that she loved. She could walk to the lake, or to a couple of sleepily charming restaurants and any number of great date bars.

Now it was dates with a kind of settled routine with Ben. Every other weekend at each other's place and plenty of shared flirty office time, too. Ben's office was just six blocks away from hers. He was three years younger than her. It was the healthiest relationship that she'd ever had. There were many mutual kindnesses. He understood about her thing with Earl and was seldom judgmental into the bargain.

Her mom would have said that Ben was a catch. But Courtney still wasn't sure that she wanted either to catch or be caught. That was the real legacy of her childhood trauma. She still had some self-protective need to feel like she could flee at any moment.

It was still only six thirty in the morning, but she made herself look at her work email. A strange email address. Should she open it? Supposedly their security system kept out viruses and worms. It was oddly formal looking and addressed only to her. The subject line was her awkward personnel case.

Confidential Memo
This case is about ethics and disclosure and whether there's a double standard for women partners accused of doing some-thing that male partners have taken as a rite of passage since

the founding of the firm. The first partners divided up the sec-
retaries and paralegals, many of whom both had law degrees
from the same schools as their overlords. As recently as the past
five years, a young woman associate made her way all the way
to the top by the exact same practice that is at issue in this case.

The memo went on, at length, to discuss the specifics of the case at hand. Courtney's stomach swirled. She was only the second woman to be named head of the firm and the first had been twenty years ago. They knew about her and Earl and, later, James. Who was it from? Had anyone else received the memo other than her? Where did that leave her? She fretted about it all day long. It was a grueling workday, trying to clear out a space to just work on the coal case.

After the day that she had, Courtney had thought of canceling her appointment, but now she was drooling to get inside this elegant brick three-flat. The street was pretty, full of trees, and she had no problem finding parking for her five-thirty showing. That wouldn't be true in either Uptown or Rogers Park.

Courtney loved Chicago. It was calmer than New York, in part because it was full of homey little neighborhoods. She'd first lived in Avondale, a sweet little, mostly Latino northwest neighborhood full of brownstones, trendy shops, and beautiful churches. It was diverse and vibrant but also calming. She'd loved walking its tree-lined streets.

Next, she lived in laidback Uptown, not far from Montrose Avenue Beach. She didn't even like jazz that much, but she'd started hanging out at Le Piano there and listening to old Miles Davis standards on Spotify. It had such classy vibes, and she hadn't felt odd there, even when she was single. Now, she was looking hard to buy a condo in affordable Edgewater, a small little Northside neighborhood that abutted Lake Michigan.

"Are you Courtney?" a young woman asked. "I'm Jasmine, working with Kim. Are you ready to be delighted?"

She was. "I love the classic brick look of the building. This is the one with two bedrooms and two baths, right?"

"Yes, and that's rare. A new kitchen, too," Jasmine said as they made their way to the second floor. "This one will go fast. It's not even officially up yet."

There was a dignified entryway, and sunlight throughout on the old oak floors. The current owners had plants in the living room and both bedrooms. The kitchen appliances were new and called her to make a delicious dinner. Her therapist had been telling her to find a place of refuge, where she felt truly safe.

"Are you living on your own?"

"Yes, though my boyfriend and I are talking about him possibly moving in. But don't worry; I could pay cash on this one."

"It's $385,000."

"I think that I'm going to make an offer," Courtney gushed. "I love it!" There was more to it than that: it felt like home.

When Courtney got back to her office, her associate Jake came in immediately and dropped a Notice of Pretrial Conference on her desk. "Why is the judge holding a live pretrial in Lake Superior City?" he asked, shaking his head.

"One of the quirks of the environmental permitting process is that if the permit impacts water, any member of the public with an interest can become a party," Courtney explained. "This is mostly an air permit, but there were a couple of issues that impact Lake Superior, so we must go up there to identify the parties. When do we have to go up?"

"The Monday before Thanksgiving. She wants us to name a preliminary list of our principal experts and consultants by then too."

"That's your job and why you're flying up with me," Courtney said. It was good to be a boss. She had to get an answer from Earl soon. She tried calling him, but he didn't pick up.

Chapter Twelve

A Promise in Bayfield

Just before loading up the car, Earl noticed he'd had calls and emails from both sides about the coal shipment case. The emails both included draft contracts for his participation. Courtney was paying five times more than the opponents, and it wasn't clear that Jason Erickson would want to work with him if he was working with Grace and Tim. But all of that could wait.

Earl and Betty had planned their long weekend excursion to the Apple Festival in Bayfield for a couple of weeks, but there was a significant detail that Earl had not shared with her. He would ask her to marry him that night at the Pier Plaza Restaurant, where they stayed. Knowing Betty, Earl had a fake ring so that she could pick out her own if she said yes. He was pretty sure that she would.

They spent a glorious sunny fall afternoon at the Big Top Chautauqua, listening to their Blue Canvas Orchestra and drinking apple cider. Then they went back to their hotel to get ready for their eventful dinner. Betty had a strange look on her face.

"Earl, you're wearing a jacket and tie," she quizzed. "Just to go downstairs?"

"I've got to look at least halfway decent to be seen with the most beautiful woman in Wisconsin."

"Get out of here, you," she replied. But she was humming to herself as she put on her shiny gold dress.

Betty was liberal and fun as hell, but she was a Christian

woman. Ironically, that seemed to be his type. His first wife, Maggie, was a little saintly, too.

Earl had recently made the mistake of joking to Betty that they were "shacking up," and it had landed like the proverbial fart in church. "Don't even joke about that, please," she'd said with a wounded look. "We're making a home together, not shacking up."

Now, Earl fretted that the restaurant wasn't fancy enough. He'd warned the waitstaff and secured the best table looking out on Lake Superior. But it was "rustic Northwoods" rather than marriage-proposal romantic. Oh well, you had to play the cards you were dealt. Besides, the sunset was cooperating, casting a magnificent golden glow over the water. The windows were open, and the air was as fresh and autumnal as the Dudley heirloom apples that they'd bought that afternoon.

"This is perfect, Earl." Betty clinked his glass.

He'd planned to wait until they were well into their fish dinners, but he instead took her hand and looked into her eyes. "You're perfect, darling."

"No one is, Earl."

"Yes, you are, for me. So there's something that I wanted to ask you." He heard himself getting choked up. He pulled out the dummy ring and looked into her eyes. "Betty, would you marry me?"

Her thick eyebrows went up and her eyes widened. He'd caught her off-guard. "Do you promise to be a loyal, faithful husband who doesn't gamble and who always has my back?"

He could do that or die trying. "I do."

"Then, of course, I will, Earl." She smiled. But then, looking at the ring, she wrinkled her nose and frowned a bit.

"Don't worry, sweetheart, that's just a placeholder. You can pick out your own ring."

"Thank God, Earl, because that one is pretty lame."

Betty kissed him. Some of the restaurant staff and patrons burst out into applause. "So where should we do the deed?"

"Back in our room is fine, ladybird," he teased.

Betty couldn't keep from smiling. "You know that I meant the wedding ceremony!"

"Wherever you want is fine with me."

"Oh, Earl," she said. "You're so sweet."

Everyone was still staring at them, some also wiping tears from their eyes.

Chapter Thirteen

Rooting for the Turkey Baster

Jason drove up to Minneapolis Tuesday afternoon to have Thanksgiving with his brother, Justin, and his wife, Sunny, on Wednesday before having it with Grace and her mom on Thursday. It was a four-hour drive from Madison, but the sun was shining, and it was forty-eight degrees. Jason was filling up his car in Black River Falls when Justin called him.

"How's it going? What's the weather like in Minneapolis?" Jason asked as he put the gas nozzle back and hopped back in his car. "I'm pumping gas in northern Wisconsin in my shirt-sleeves."

"I think it's like forty-five; not bad. Do you remember the time it snowed so much that we couldn't make it to Grandma's house in La Crosse for Thanksgiving?"

"Of course," Jason said. "You pretty much saved my life with your brake-tapping skills. Everything set for tomorrow?"

"Yeah, I just wanted to run something by you before you got here."

"What's up?"

"I just got some discouraging news, Jason."

"Oh, I'm sorry. What's up?" Jason found himself grinding his teeth, bracing for the worst. It had been a problem for him after he'd been shot, and he'd even got a mouthguard that he didn't use much to keep himself from doing it all night.

"We just got our test results back, and we both have some issues," Justin said.

Justin and his wife had been trying for some months to

have a child. "What's next?"

"We get three tries spiking her hormones up at the appropriate time and then special delivery with a turkey baster."

"Well, that's hopeful."

"After that we can try IVF with my juice or find another turkey-baster donor." Surely, he wasn't going to ask Jason. "The IVF is really expensive, and it might not work, either, given some of our possible issues."

"Wow, that's a lot to take in." Jason was relieved that he hadn't been asked.

"Look, I know that you'll have to think about it, but if it comes to it, would you consider being a donor? We've talked about it. It's the closest that we could get to having my genes."

"I will think about it." He'd be rooting for the turkey baster or the IVF. "It would be a little awkward for all of us, no?"

"Of course, but..."

"Don't worry, buddy. I'll give it some serious thought."

"It probably won't be necessary, but if it came to that, it would be nice to keep the Erickson genes in the mix."

"I understand."

"But look, I know that you and Tara had talked about having a kid, so if it's too hard for you, no worries."

"Thanks. You're right; we did."

"I feel better just talking about it all."

"Call anytime."

On the drive up, there was that old ache at the loss of Tara. He'd never fallen so hard and fast. They were going to move to Blue Lake, make babies, and live happily ever after.

Now, he thought of their visit to Minneapolis in the weeks before they were both shot. Could he have done anything differently? Mulling all of that over for the millionth time passed the hours, and he was soon sitting in his brother's cozy house near the Seward Co-op.

"I forgot to ask. How are things with you?" Justin queried.

"Okay, but I'm a little confused about both Grace and this coal case that she roped me into helping her on."

"The last time we talked, you said you didn't think that you guys were going to last," Justin said. "But I think you were a little buzzed."

"Did I?" They both laughed. "Well, it's been kind of trending that way for a while."

"What makes you confused about the case? Can't you separate out your issues with Grace and trying to shut down the North American coal industry?"

"Yes, but I'm still going to California for January. Get this: Earl Franks may help us out with it! It's Grace's idea. She's also brought in Tim, her old boyfriend, as co-counsel."

"Okay, your path is clear. Dump Grace and fight the coal industry with your new frenemy, Earl Franks. Now, can we just watch football?"

"Are there any games on Wednesday?"

"Sure. College."

Justin went on about the games, but Jason was thinking about Tara, about their plans for a life together in Blue Lake. About the little girl with Tara's brown eyes who would never be born. He was missing them both.

Chapter Fourteen

A Bittersweet Thanksgiving

Grace had been excited about Thanksgiving at her place, with her mom and Jason as guests. She'd put in her order for the precooked turkey and stuffing from the People's Food Co-op before Halloween. But now that Jason had decided to go to California rather than be her co-counsel, the gathering at her house had a kind of bittersweet character to it. Also, Grace was feeling a bit conflicted.

She had driven to the coal case pretrial with Tim.

They'd stopped for dinner at a bar that Tim knew in Rice Lake. It was the first of many meals that they would share trying the coal case. Now she found herself thinking about Tim more than she should be. Tim looked every bit the seasoned trial lawyer in his blue suit and white shirt at the restaurant the other night. They were a formidable team together.

What would her mom think if they wound up together? Grace remembered that her mother had seemed to genuinely like Tim the handful of times that she'd met him. But after Grace had ended it, her mom had confessed that she'd never quite trusted Tim.

Grace hadn't told her mom anything about working with Tim because her mother was all excited that Jason was joining them and had made mashed potatoes and baked both her pie specialties, a pumpkin and a pecan. Jason arrived with a beautiful autumn flower centerpiece, a bottle of Nouveau Beaujolais, and a huge plate of precooked green beans from his organic CSA.

"Smells amazing," he said by way of greeting. "Beautiful day for a drive!"

"Oh, this is lovely," Grace replied, taking the centerpiece from his arms.

"Happy Thanksgiving, Connie," he called to her mom.

"Oh, Happy Thanksgiving to you, Jason." She darted over with her walker for a kiss, wearing way too much White Linen, her preferred perfume. "And a new Beaujolais, too! Come and see the beautiful turkey Grace has made for us."

"Mom, the co-op prepared it, not me." Her mom was still always trying to sell her.

They drank a glass of the fruity red wine and remarked again on all the past Thanksgivings, which were so much colder. When they sat down to eat, her mom made the three of them hold hands for her to say grace.

"Thank you, God, for thy bounty, for our health, and for letting us share this day of gratitude together. Thank you for sending us Nancy Pelosi to keep an eye on President Trump. And thank you especially for bringing these two beautiful souls together as such a dear and sweet couple, Amen." Jason squeezed her hand with this last, and Grace felt both relieved and a little guilty. She'd been flirting (more or less) harmlessly with Tim almost every day this week, even as she felt Jason backing away from her as they approached their January apart. "And wait, one more thing, Lord, keep them together in the next year," her mom finished.

The three of them laughed, and Grace quickly changed the subject. "Do you guys still want to drive over to see the Rotary lights later? There's no Packers game."

"Yes, that sounds perfect," her mom said, her mouth full of stuffing.

"Of course," Jason said.

"The turkey is delicious, dear. Everything is just grand," her mom said. Then, trying to appear nonchalant, she added to Jason, "I hear that you might be going off to California soon. Or have you decided yet?"

"Yes, I'm still going to help Grace as much as I can, but I'm spending January in the foothills above Santa Barbara."

"Oh, you are?" She wiped her mouth with one of the Thanksgiving napkins that she'd embroidered and given to Grace shortly after her ill-fated marriage to Jon. "Oh, that's nice if you can afford it, I guess."

"I'm hoping that Grace can join me for at least a long weekend or so."

"That's going to be hard with that coal case up on Superior," Grace replied.

Of course, she could fly out for a long weekend, but it would throw her off. Grace had always thought of herself as something of a grind. She'd managed the 3.96 grade point that got her into law school by rarely going out on weekends.

She and Jon were married and did all kinds of grinding together in law school. She worked even harder after Jon's accident and through her grief over Jon and her uncle, who died only a couple of years later. Her uncle had left her both the building and his practice. Then she almost accidentally became an environmental law hero after taking on the Big Dairy CAFO and winning. She just needed to bear down and keep working; that had always been her way of coping.

"I'll try," she added.

"Sounds good," Jason said blankly. "Can you pass the stuffing?"

Shortly after dark, they loaded her mom and her wheelchair into Grace's new Nissan Leaf EV and joined the line of cars waiting to see the La Crosse Christmas lights beside the Mississippi River. People came from all over the area, from the small towns in Iowa and Minnesota. The line of cars was at an almost complete standstill.

"Connie, it's still warm out, would you like me to get you into the lights up close and personal in your chair?"

"Oh, that would be very gracious of you," she replied.

Jason loaded her into the chair, and Grace watched them

for a minute, a bit wistfully, as she sat in the line waiting to catch up to them. The multicolor neon lights made them both look a little like Christmas cartoon characters, as Jason zigzagged her mom through the crowd.

He was such a decent guy, but that only went so far. The odds were not great that they would be together another year, her mom's prayers notwithstanding. Jason went back to Madison later that night.

The Friday after Thanksgiving, Grace got a call from her client, Ellen Smythe, the mother of the little girl with asthma. "We had a terrible turkey day; Lacy had a severe episode late Wednesday night, and we had our Thanksgiving at the hospital in Duluth."

"I'm so sorry to hear that, Ellen. Is she all right?" Grace said, trying to think of anything she could legally do to help.

"She's out of the hospital, and they prescribed a new medication, but who knows?"

"Do you have any idea of what might have triggered it?"

"It was windy on Wednesday, but the girls had an extra day off from school, and I stupidly let them play outside."

"Don't blame yourself, Ellen; just take good notes and, as we discussed, keep a record of every severe asthma flare-up. Send me that information, and I'll have my paralegal see if he can find a pattern with wind speeds and directions." That was a long shot and may not even be relevant to the permitting case. "I'm sorry, that's all we can do with the permit application."

"Could we sue them?"

"Probably not. In most cases, a valid air permit acts as a shield against litigation."

Ellen choked out a little laugh. "They've got it all figured out, don't they?"

Grace put down her phone, took off her clothes and got into bed. Then she heard her phone buzz again. Ellen had sent a photo. Little Lacy was lying in the hospital, connected to her breathing apparatus. Grace started to cry.

How could she help her? Whatever it took to win the case, she would do. Grace lay there crying until she finally fell asleep. It had been a very long day.

60

Chapter Fifteen

A Christmas Sorry

As usual, Courtney was dreading the holidays. She'd been estranged from her father for many years and was just barely in touch with her mom. Courtney sent her mom birthday and Christmas cards, and they would usually get together once over the season. This year she and Ben were planning to go to his family for Thanksgiving and to her mom's house on Christmas.

Thanksgiving at Ben's parents' house in South Bend, Indiana, had gone splendidly. Ben's parents were welcoming and fun-loving. His mom, Carolyn, had made a traditional turkey dinner with all the usual extras. Courtney's pumpkin pie, just her third ever, had been a success. Carolyn served it with homemade crème fraiche.

As they were enjoying this feast, Courtney found herself wondering how Ben's father, Russ, could have done some of the things that Ben had told her about. Would this gentle man complimenting her on her pumpkin spices turn violent again under different circumstances? What level of frustration could have led him to attack little preteen Ben with the buckle end of a belt?

People were always such a puzzle. How could her uncle, her father's twin, have taken an interest in her own vulnerable little body when she was so young? It was still a dark mystery.

After dinner, they all walked around the Notre Dame campus, taking selfies together in front of Touchdown Jesus and the other landmarks. Ben and his father had had a lot of conflicts, but you'd never know it now. Carolyn hugged her and said, "Come again, dear," when they left. It was all heart-warmingly wholesome and upped the feeling of unease for Christmas.

She'd told Ben the broad outlines of her story. Her mom's drinking problems and volatility; her many stepfather figures after she'd divorced Courtney's father. Her complete estrangement from her father after Courtney had spoken about his brother, his twin. Her father had accused Courtney of playing the victim to get attention. Her mom had believed her but, in her alcoholic haze, hadn't done anything. "Just push him away and give him a knee in the groin," she said. The twin had come on to her mom as well, but Courtney had been a preteen.

"You never know which Rose Sharpe is going to greet us at the door," Courtney said as she and Ben approached her mom's third-floor apartment.

Juggling the Christmas presents, Ben put his arm around her and nodded.

"Hi, Ben. I'm Rose," her mom said, smiling. "I've heard so many nice things about you."

"Me too," Ben said.

"Hah," her mom laughed. "I doubt that. Courtney, Merry Christmas. You've got a good one here, one that will lie for you."

"Merry Christmas, Mom." Courtney gave her mother a perfunctory hug and made her way in. The apartment was clean, decorated for the season, and smelled like turkey. Good signs that her mom's drinking was under control. "Your place looks great. I love your tree."

"Yeah, I sprang for a real one since I knew you two were coming."

The whole visit went surprisingly well. Her mom didn't drink the whole afternoon. The meal had mostly come from a local grocery takeout, but Rose made some of the home-made dinner rolls that Courtney had liked as a kid. The crust of Courtney's third pumpkin pie was a little bit overdone, but they all enjoyed it anyway.

Her mom flirted harmlessly with Ben, and he flattered her back.

"I see where Courtney gets those beautiful eyes," Ben said.

"And her nice figure, too?" Rose twirled around with the coffee pot in her hands.

"You're both lovely women," Ben replied.

"Very diplomatic." Rose poured the coffee.

When it was time to leave, her mom got a little choked up. "Oh, sweetie, thanks for coming and bringing your handsome fellow, too."

"Of course, Mom. We'll be back soon."

"No, you won't." Rose wiped away a tear. "But I'll still love you anyway. I'm sorry for everything that I helped put you through." She'd never said that before. "I want you to know that I just got my hundred days pin, and I'm really hopeful this time."

"I love you, too," Courtney said. "And I'm proud of you."

For all the shame Courtney had felt about her family, it was true.

Chapter Sixteen

Christmas at Blue Lake

Betty was in one of her moods, and she and Earl passed Christmas Eve morning in bed. She'd brought him coffee and the *New York Times*, then let her intentions be known, and there he was in the sunshine of her love. Jackpot.

Pastor had been a once-a-month guy. If that. Not Betty. Earl was the lucky beneficiary of three decades of pent-up demand. It wasn't just sex, either; it was full of passion, tenderness, and vows of love. Earl and Betty had chemistry. There was one sex-crazed twenty-four-hour period when the two of them had made love ten times. The senior division champions, she'd joked. How could he cheat on a woman like that?

"Have you decided what you're going to do, lover boy? What side are you on?"

"Yes, honeybunch."

What were the sides? Courtney or Grace? Coal versus the sun? Betty would be proud of him if he fought the coal plant. He wasn't going to let Courtney play him.

"I'm going to help the people opposing the coal plant."

"Oh, Earl. I'm proud of you."

"They can only pay me a hundred bucks an hour."

"We have all we need. We have each other. Our health. This beautiful house. Money in the bank."

"We have a lot, Betty." He kissed her.

"What's next?"

"I guess the first thing is to try to make peace with the judge. I hear he's not keen on working with me."

"Can you blame him?"

"Nah, but it doesn't have to be awkward."

"It'll always be awkward, Earl, but Bud used to say that it takes courage to walk out of the shadows and into the light, and that's exactly what you're doing."

Earl thought of a wisecrack about the late Pastor but bit his tongue. "Father James used to say something similar: that change meant walking naked into a land of uncertainty. The Courage to Change and all of that is part of AA, NA, GA, and all those groups."

"Did you go to the one on gambling much, Earl?"

He shook his head.

"Still feel that urge?"

"Not much," he lied. It was way more than that. But it was best not to think about it. "So, your kids are for sure coming tomorrow for Christmas? Laurie is in."

"Gabe and Marcy are coming, but Martha is still deciding."

"Do you think it's me, or is it because Laurie's coming?"

"Honestly," Betty replied, "I'm not sure."

"I think the way we did Thanksgiving might be better."

"I know. You're probably right." Betty paused and ran her hand through Earl's hair. "But Christmas in Blue Lake is just so special."

"In all my years here, I've never experienced a Blue Lake Christmas."

"Well, you're going to tomorrow."

Earl's daughter Laurie and her husband, Mitch, arrived first. Earl, despite himself, hovered over them a bit nervously, worrying about the blending of families. He got them both a glass of what used to be Laurie's favorite wine, a hearty Malbec from Mendoza, and they clinked glasses a bit awkwardly just as Betty's son, Gabe and his wife, Marcy, arrived.

"Dad," Laurie cautioned. "I can't drink this!" She pointed to her just slightly protruding midsection. "What are you thinking?'

"Of course not," Betty called. "I've got sparkling grape juice for Laurie and Gabe." Like his Pastor father, Gabe never drank. Meanwhile, Marcy had one of the Dark and Stormy rum drinks that Earl and Betty had made.

"Thank you all so much for coming, and Merry Christmas!" Earl said before the six of them toasted. His mind went back to several holidays that he had spent alone after his divorce from Maggie. And the even lonelier two years he'd spent at the Portage correctional facility.

Which was worse, Earl wondered, Christmas by himself or in prison with the crew? A close call. He'd gone to the chapel, and Father Jacob was in good form, singing familiar carols that had everyone smiling and joining in. But there you were, stuck, when it was over.

Earl looked out at the white pine trees that lined the lake and felt again the sweet lightness of being out of prison. He'd longed for Blue Lake every day he was there. He'd never missed the condo in Skokie that he'd sold. But he would day-dream for hours about this lake. You could be part of the air, the sky, the weather out here. Inside, you could only be part of the cold concrete and metal that kept you locked up. You were as gray as your surroundings. What had he been thinking? Prison was far worse than just being alone in Skokie.

"Christmas cheers!"

Betty had put together a fabulous spread, and the two younger couples seemed to be hitting it off, yammering on about a couple of TV series that they'd both streamed: *Handmaid's Tale* and a cartoon, *Bojack the Horseman*, or something like that.

"We watched *Handmaid's Tale*," Betty said. "Chillingly appropriate for our times but not exactly Christmassy. Maybe we could all watch something together?" This suggestion lit-erally seemed to suck the air out of the room. "Or not," she quickly added.

This old Pastor's Wife was very apt at reading the room.

"I thought we could take a little walk on the lake path,"

Laurie offered, trying to find common ground. "It helps relieve the pressure on my back."

"That sounds great," Gabe replied.

"The ham is delicious, sweetheart," Earl said.

"Oh my gosh, yes," Marcy said. "And the scalloped potatoes, too! Betty is amazing."

Earl loved Betty's simple fare. Nothing fancy, but just right. That was the irony of his lifelong quest to be one of the swells: he almost always preferred the less pretentious. How many chef-foraged meals had he paid a small fortune for and not even enjoyed? Gone home to raid the fridge later for something familiarly edible. He did his best thinking with a belly full of simple food.

"I've got some news," Earl said. Everyone at the table looked at him, expecting a wisecrack. "I'm going to help out some environmentalists with this case up on Lake Superior."

They talked about it a bit, especially him possibly working with Jason.

"He was pretty hostile when I saw him at the prison," Laurie recalled. "But that was a few years ago. Maybe he's mellowed by now."

Earl's face must have shown his discomfort in remembering that prison visit, because sweet Betty quickly changed the subject.

"I got that CD that you told me about, Gabe," Betty said. "That Anais Mitchell one about the myth of Orpheus."

"*Hadestown?*" Laurie asked. "I love that!"

The six of them sat there on Christmas afternoon, listening to it play on the Bose. From the first note, Earl felt the music. A poverty-stricken couple was going to let nature and the trees set their wedding table. Now Earl was going to marry Betty. He looked at her, shining in her red dress beside the wood fire.

And then along came baritone Greg Brown, one of Earl's favorites, belting out "Why We Build the Wall." Gabe mentioned that Mitchell had written it long before Trump. Laurie said something about poets being the antenna of the species and Gabe agreed. Those two got along well.

"The next two are perfect for your decision, Dad," Laurie said.

She was right; the songs that gripped Earl by the throat were the next two about trying to make a better world, even though nothing ever seems to change. The music and being with his blended family soothed him and made him feel even better about trying to oppose the coal plant.

Later the six of them took a moonlit walk along the Blue Lake path. It had been a warm December, and the lake was still open. It was just above freezing, and there was a mystical cloudy mist above its dark indigo water.

Earl squeezed Betty's hand and she squeezed his back.

Chapter Seventeen

Below Mission Canyon

Just after the holidays, Jason, in Santa Barbara, got a call from Grace after her coal case meeting with Tim. She told him about their proposed legal strategy.

"One of us will be hitting the standards, and one of us just arguing against coal," she said with excitement. "Jason, are you there?"

"Yes, I'm listening," Jason replied. "It sounds like something that could work."

"But?"

"Well, we should also be arguing for some very specific permit modification, a reduction in the total volumes that reflects and builds on projections on the decline in the demand for coal over the five years of the permit. That would also reflect the reality on the ground of air violations. We give the judge a compromise of modifying the permit from X million tons to something way less than X million tons."

"That's why we need you; you think like the judge. How are you feeling about it?"

"What part?" He had lots of feelings.

"Any, all."

"You mean about you working with Tim?" He was trying to sound nonchalant. "I guess I'd prefer that your co-counsel was not someone you slept with for two years." He wanted to add, "Especially since you lied about it only being a few dates, and you couldn't say why you two broke up." But he didn't.

"Please, Jason, don't worry about Tim—I have no interest

in him other than having him help us win this case."

"You asked me how I felt."

Silence. Intentional, like everything Grace did.

Finally, she added, "I did."

"How about you? How are you feeling?"

"I was feeling really stoked, but now I'm worried that you're going to be a pain in the ass about Tim. I should have been honest from the start. In fairness, I know it's not the best situation."

His turn to pause. "No, it's not."

"But I have to ask you, do you really even want to be involved?"

"Are you trying to ditch me already?" Part of him would welcome exactly that.

"Please. Give me some credit. We've been faithful to each other for the past two years."

"I'm sorry. One of my ill-advised jokes." What was bugging him? That he really didn't want to go back to Wisconsin to fight off German Shepherds on a massive nineteenth-century coal pile? "I will be out to help in a couple of weeks." Or was it more serious—was he just too full of doubts about Grace, too? "And I will keep sending you my weekly strategy texts, too."

"Thanks, those are really helpful." Their romance had started off as so healing and sane, but was it running out of gas? "There's one more thing that you could do that would be helpful, and it doesn't even require legal work."

"What's that?"

"My paralegal is swamped, but I was having him see if he could create a spreadsheet comparing when the girl with severe asthma—"

"Lacy?"

"Yes, just a simple looking at when she's been admitted to the ER or hospital and when the air permit violations have occurred. Also, if he had time, I was going to have him look at weather data, especially wind speed. I hate to pay my expert until we know if there's anything there."

"Sure, send it to me."

"It's a mess, just pictures of calendars that her mom has kept and our chicken scratch about the violations. Hopefully, we'll get Interrogatory Answers about the violation notices sometime soon."

"They'll object first, so send me what you have to make sure that there's a there there."

"Thanks so much. So what are you doing right now?"

"I'm sitting in the grass by the Spanish Mission, talking to my hardworking girlfriend."

"That's right, Jason. And I'm talking to my brilliant-but-lazy boyfriend, and all is well."

"We can talk later." Lazy? Nah, he felt energized. Growing, even, like he was losing some of his Rust Belt parochialism.

"Okay, thanks for your input."

Jason looked through the unwieldly data that Grace had sent him for a few more minutes. He felt bad about the little girl, Lacy, and her family spending Thanksgiving in the hospital. He was trying to make sense of photos of her mom's calendar with X's on it for other visits to the ER over the past four years. He found another match between a windy day, a Notice of Air Violation and a severe asthma episode. This was the fourth!

All of this would have been extremely promising evidence if this were a simple civil nuisance case against the coal shipper, but it was unlikely to matter much in the permit renewal. But, of course, an air permit was a shield from such litigation. It was depressing to think that the most important information of all, the real-world impact on a child living nearby, was not likely to be admitted in this case. Jason was feeling gloomy anyway to be heading back in a couple of weeks to the Wisconsin winter.

People always asked him why he kept going back to Santa

Barbara, and he gave them his stock reply. *Because I love it!* It was the climate, the history, the easy mix of Spanish, Mexican, and American influences. It was the food, the wine, and the olive oil.

Of course, California had its own challenges. Foremost, the homelessness crisis. There was an encampment they were scheduled to break up of over one hundred unhoused people in a park north of here. Some were slated for tiny houses, but most had nowhere to go.

One night he talked to a woman who said she was saving for a new sleeping bag.

"I had one that was good to twenty degrees, but I got robbed. And I literally pissed my pants when he threatened me with a knife." She pulled a pair of carefully rolled jeans out of two plastic bags. "Have to get them washed." She smiled, showing a tic tac toe of missing teeth.

He gave her a ten-dollar bill and wished that he could have done more.

The homeless in the motel parking lot, like guests with their backpacks strapped over their UCSB sweatshirts, like guests until their overly solicitous "sirs" and smiles hit you up for gas money even as they pushed decrepit bicycles. Some parks were full of them, too, lonely souls hoarding plastics to keep off rain, carpeting to soften the hard ground, and endless layers of clothes. Something about their plight upset Jason in some deep, visceral way that he just didn't feel about the coal plant.

But the planet was in trouble here, too. He'd gone to hear a climate change speaker at UCSB, and she'd done an experiment with audience reactions on their phones. What scares you most about the climate crisis? Texted answers were then scaled to a screen showing the proportion of replies. The word FIRE was at least ten times bigger than any other answer. That was a reasonable fear here.

Santa Barbara was no paradise. But it felt good to sit in

the sun below the canyon, to be away from Wisconsin, from the gloomy state where Tara had been murdered. He loved sitting here, soaking up the past and present. The Spanish Franciscans who'd founded it in 1786 had picked both a beautiful and a strategic spot. The mountains framed the white and pink Mission structures, and from inside there was a view of any approaching ships in the bay. That was Jason's problem; he was no longer thinking strategically.

What did it mean that he was having second thoughts about Grace and him as a couple? Or was it more about where and how he wanted to live? He'd grieved Tara far longer than he'd known her, but there was still some lingering trauma there, too. There was an almost existential sense that happiness would always be just out of reach for him.

Now he noticed a woman about his own age sprawled as he was, maybe twenty feet to his left. She was discreetly smoking what smelled like marijuana. It was a not-uncommon smell in California in 2020. He nodded to her, and she invited him over.

"Want some?"

"It smells great. Thanks, I will." He moved over to where she was lying. "I feel like a high school kid again."

"And I feel like a degenerate teacher."

Jason laughed. "Are you?"

"No, but I have a very responsible job." She had large sunglasses and a hat on, a sort of elementary disguise. But her long dark hair spilled out of the hat, and he could see thick eyebrows and the very top of her green irises.

"Well, I won't narc you out." He smiled, taking another drag. "I'm Jason."

"I'm Camille," she said, offering her hand. "Another perfect day in Santa Barbara."

"Yes, perfect. I always feel so at home here. But I'm just here for January." He handed it back to her. "The last couple of years I've come out here from Wisconsin in winter. I say

I can't afford to winter here, but I can at least January here."

"Hah! I just moved back here myself. I was an undergraduate at UCSB, so I jumped at the chance to come back here."

"I didn't know it when I came to visit, but I'm kind of thinking of relocating here myself."

"It's chill here. Old and very *au current*, too. I'm done," she said, handing him the pre-rolled cone.

"Me too. But would you like to get a glass of wine?"

"Now, or ever?" She pulled down her sunglasses. The Mission Park grass made her eyes a shining green.

"I meant now, but ever works, too. At least if it's in January."

"Okay, now it is. Do you know this place called the Uptown Lounge? They have all my local favorite wines, and I'm getting to be a regular there."

"I'm putting it in my phone now."

Chapter Eighteen

The Proximity Principle

Grace was getting frustrated with Jason. Damn him. She could understand wanting to spend the winter on a beach in California, sipping wine instead of helping her fight the coal industry in Lake Superior City. But did she respect it? No, of course not. She also felt a little abandoned, though maybe that was selfish.

Meanwhile, Tim.

"What's happening in California, Grace?" Tim asked as they made their way down the elevator to the hotel bar. They'd spent the day together, going over the coal shipping case.

"Beach, sun, wine," Grace replied. "And, likely, some legal weed."

"Must be nice." Tim smiled, rolling his eyes. He'd been known to party to excess when he was in his band.

Grace loved being lost in her work, concentrating on some detail, and then looking across the room to see Tim similarly engaged, with his tortoiseshell readers dangling above his fleshy face on his nose. There was something about his absorption in his work, his *indifference* to her, that she found appealing.

Tim was a few years older than Grace and Jason, a youthful fifty-four, and had a daughter, Luna, who had just graduated from college and was a teacher in the Minneapolis public schools. Grace and Tim had dated for almost two years. But because they'd lived in two different cities and Tim had Luna every other weekend when she was a kid, they hadn't spent that much time together.

Nothing like the weekly shuttling she'd recently under-taken for Jason. Five hours every other weekend. Did he even appreciate it?

Retired and financially secure, it might have been harder for Jason to understand what it involved for her. She some-times felt stretched too thin, pulled in too many directions. She didn't spend quite as much time with her mother as she had before their relationship. Her mom loved Jason and never complained, but Grace felt some guilt.

About everything.

"So can I buy you a glass of wine, Grace?"

"Yes, if I can buy you one. Long day."

Grace took a seat at the crowded bar with Tim. There was some social psychology term she couldn't remember about how being close together over time cemented relationships. Putting in long hours together, prepping and taking depo-sitions, ordering Chinese takeout or thin-crust pizza, work-ing together for a common purpose. *The proximity principle.* That was it. Humans like things that are familiar to them. Seeing someone every day created a kind of proximate intimacy.

"I like drinking wine with you after a hard day's work."

"Me too, Tim," she said simply. Normally Grace would reply with some observation about some legal issue or event from the day, but tonight she was too tired. She was too ticked at Jason. "We work well together."

Grace was feeling a little buzzed already from just one glass of pinot noir. Excited, too. Prepping the coal case with Tim was kind of intoxicating. The ideas flew back and forth with delicious speed and symmetry. They thought alike, in law and life.

Why had they fallen apart the last time they'd dated?

Because she strongly preferred La Crosse to Eau Claire and didn't want a partner who lived almost two hours away? Or was it because things had moved so fast and Tim had started talking about both a professional and personal partnership? The only problem that they'd ever had was that Tim had pushed a bit, and Grace had withdrawn back into her lonely little lawyer life in La Crosse.

She still admired Jason, but she was taking stock of things. Where were they headed? Grace wasn't married or living with Jason, after all. They were both fifty, but after two years they'd never even glancingly discussed marriage. But did she even want that anymore, from anyone?

"I agree; we did a lot of things well together."

"Yes, lots of things." Damn it, she was flirting, too. Damn them both. "Do you really think that they're not adding the surfactant agents to the water spray?"

Jason was convinced that most of the pile was barely receiving any water, much less the crusting agents required by the permit.

"Well, they are both expensive and time-consuming," Tim replied. "And one thing that I've learned from twenty-six years of practicing law is that corporations will always do the easiest and cheapest thing possible."

"Yes!" Grace exclaimed, noting her own odd enthusiasm. "Would you like another glass of wine, Tim?"

A couple of days later, there was a Zoom conference, and of course Jason and Tim got into it. It started when Jason suggested a surprise Motion to Enter the property with an expert to quickly grab some coal samples.

"That's great advice, from on high." Tim shook his head. "But they'll immediately seek an Order to Protect."

"Of course, but we'll get it decided by phone with the ALJ that same day and pounce."

"It won't work," said Tim. "Come down into the trenches with us, Jason."

Grace was looking away from Jason and toward Tim sympathetically, in agreement.

But she said, "It might if we had some insight into her calendar. Of course, it might just mean we're spending money on our expert if it doesn't work."

"I can get her calendar," Jason said. "It's just one idea. Really, the only one I have to deal with the fact that I'm convinced that they're not really spraying that whole pile. Somehow, we've got to prove it. Can we agree on that?"

"Of course," Tim replied. "I apologize, Jason."

"No worries."

"Just probably a little jealous of you coming in from California and telling us how we messed up."

"I thought it was a strategy session."

"It is, but some of this looks differently from Eau Claire."

"Well, not everybody wants to be in Eau Claire in January, bro."

"I suppose you're too good for that."

"It's not a judgment; it's just a different choice," Jason replied. Tim and Grace looked at each other, and then at him. "But I'm here, and I'm trying to help."

"Yes, let's get back to that, to why we're here," Grace said. "Any other thoughts about our overall strategy, Jason?"

"Did our expert get you a number for a reduction based upon the decline in overall coal shipping that he has some rational basis for?"

"No," Tim replied. A little chippy again? "I'm not going to ask mine for one. I'm going all in on No Coal."

"You and I can talk about that later, Jason," Grace said, nodding to him quickly. Twirling her hair in little circles. "It's not clear what expert could give that kind of opinion."

"Maybe an economist or MBA who has looked at the numbers? And then get your air modeler to talk about how much of a reduction that would be to coal dust dispersion. I've seen that done and accepted by higher courts."

"It's expensive and risky," said Tim. "What if the judge rules it's not coming in?"

"You cite the *Stregland* case; that was my case. There's a Court of Appeals decision."

"That case says you could do it, in your discretion, but doesn't say that the next person would be required to do it," Grace argued.

"True," Jason conceded. "But I think the judge will. You have to gamble a little."

"We see No Coal as our best gamble." Tim nodded to Grace.

"We?" Jason asked. "Grace?"

"That's why I wanted to talk to you privately about this. I haven't made up my mind, but I kind of agree with Tim on this. To do a complicated, two-expert opinion to propose a reduction that our clients won't be that happy with seems risky to me as well."

"It's not really, in my experience. Just have your modeling expert run a few different scenarios, so that's already in anyway."

"That we can do," Grace offered. "That makes sense."

"Well, aren't you planning to have any numbers guy also weigh in on the declining demand for and use of coal?" Jason asked.

"I'm not," Tim said immediately.

"I'm not sure," Grace said. "I'm still thinking that one through. Have you had time to look through the hospital and air permit violation data?"

"Yes, I've found a couple of correlations, five I think so far," Jason replied. "And three or four were on very windy days. It's promising if you can get it in the record. I'll have a nice little chart for you by the time I get back to Wisconsin."

"Great, thanks again for that."

"Okay, well, those were my only suggestions." Jason looked into the camera straight through to Grace's eyes. "So I guess we're done."

Somehow the last phrase felt like a double entendre, though Grace wasn't sure he meant it that way.

Chapter Nineteen

Closing Time

Courtney was so excited that she could barely sleep. She had the day off and was doing the closing and getting the keys to her new apartment tomorrow. As she shifted from her back to her side, she thought of how she'd arrived at this exciting new place.

It had all started with a productive session with her therapist, Sydney. Courtney had been sitting in the now-familiar blue leather reclining chair, going over what had happened to her with her uncle, her father's twin brother. "He looked just like my dad, so that was especially creepy. Most of the time, I was so tense that I couldn't keep food down. But what has troubled me is that sometimes I liked the attention."

"Both feelings are completely understandable under those circumstances." Sydney looked at her closely. "Liking it is sometimes a very healthy way to get some control back. It's a common coping mechanism."

"It's always made me feel guilty, even if I know intellectually not to slut-shame myself." Courtney took a deep breath and closed her eyes, stretching out in the comfortable chair. Sydney was convinced that it was often in the moments between words that much of the growth in therapy occurs. "Just so you know, I've never told anyone that before."

"I'm glad that you've trusted me with it." Sydney leaned in and then gave a lingering look away. Finally, she said, "Courtney, you also know intellectually that there's absolutely no reason to feel guilt. You were eight years old when all of that started."

"I know, just a little girl." That's when Courtney started tearing up.

"Please, give your adult self the break that that little girl never got."

"I just got hard, cynical," she managed through her tears.

Then Courtney sobbed, for the first time in years.

"That was a healthy coping mechanism, too." Sydney got up and came over and held her hand.

"My childhood was the worst. I used to be afraid to go to sleepovers because I was still wetting my bed when I was fourteen."

"That's a common side effect of stress, especially but not only in children." Sydney let go of her hand and knelt to look into her eyes. "Maybe it's the body's way of coping with trauma, like grinding your teeth."

"I did that, too. My whole life has been some kind of coping strategy."

"And you have." Sydney put her arm around Courtney's shoulder. "You have coped. But now you can set yourself free of all that coping, of all those feelings. I want you to just put them in a box called my Unfortunate Childhood. Now you're free to be the Fortunate Adult that you deserve to be."

"Is it really that simple, Sydney?" She'd composed herself.

"Of course not, but that's the broad outline. For you, those two boxes might be helpful." Sydney went back to her chair. "What would make you feel safe and secure and free enough to make some new choices?"

"I'm not sure. Maybe that's why I'm thinking of buying a place, having that refuge?"

"Maybe think about other things that make you feel safe. That's your homework for next week."

There were several other things, including the scent of Ben's sweaters, but she couldn't remember them now as she lay on her back and drifted off to sleep.

The closing was at a slightly seedy title company near her apartment. The sellers had already signed everything and moved to Arizona. The closer was named Brittney and wore too much eye makeup.

"It's pretty rare for a person of your age to pay cash for a place in a nice part of Chicago," she said. "You should be proud of yourself."

"Thanks, I guess I am," Courtney said, finally grabbing the keys.

She drove there immediately and pulled her new blue yoga mat out of the backseat. She went up the stylish staircase and opened the door to her second-floor apartment. Then she lay down on the mat in her new living room. The oak floor smelled of Murphy Oil, which reminded her of her grandma—her mom's mother. The sun was shining in from both the front living room and the side kitchen windows.

She meditated for a couple of minutes, then she started thinking of what she'd need to spend the night here. Her bed topper, a coffee cone, a bottle of wine, some nearby take-out. And, of course, Ben.

Chapter Twenty

Wedding Planning

"What kind of wedding did you have in mind, sweetheart?" Betty asked over morning coffee. It was the first and last topic of conversation lately—wedding planning from dawn until dark. But it was worth it because it made her so happy. "Can we have it in a church?"

"Sure, but hopefully not in Pastor's old church," Earl replied, taking a bite of his bagel.

"That's still my church, Earl!"

"I know, but honey." Earl paused. "That's a little too close for me."

"Okay, thanks for being honest; we'll rule out Blue Lake ELCA Lutheran. But where then?" A large bird, possibly a Great Blue, rose like a swimmer out of water with a big fish in its beak. "Was that a heron?"

"I think so, looked like a Great Blue. You asked what I had in mind; I was thinking something very simple in a beautiful place, just the two of us. I don't want to get wedding planners involved."

"Sure, but I'm not getting married by Elvis in Las Vegas!"

"Oh, darn," Earl teased. "There goes my big plan."

"Not Vegas, period."

"Of course not." Earl was doing his best to avoid all forms of gambling, since that had been his undoing. "That's a place that I don't even want to think about anymore, much less get married in. I was looking at the US Virgin Islands."

"Nice, but isn't that really expensive?" Betty was shining,

as he called it, with happiness.

"Yes, but we're both getting married for the second and very last time, so who cares?"

"What kind of churches do they have down there?"

"It just so happens that I have that page up on my iPad."

He showed her the screen titled "Chapel Weddings in Saint Thomas and Saint John."

"Oh, Earl, they all look just so sumptuous." That was her preferred word for something special. "Just sumptuous. And I agree that looks too romantic to even invite the kids."

"I agree; why drag them into it?" Earl was relieved. "They know that we love each other and live together."

"We can just enjoy ourselves on the beach and in the hotel!" Betty exclaimed.

"Yes, we can," Earl replied.

That had gone well.

Later that day, Earl booked a hotel, an officiant, and a chapel for March 19, the first day of spring. That was Betty's idea, too.

Chapter Twenty-One

Uptown Lounge

The Uptown Lounge was a nondescript place on the outside, but festive and full inside at 4:30 p.m. There was an almost movie-size large screen TV and rows of seats for watching sports. Fortunately, there was no game on now, as Jason and Camille entered.

"What's happening, Rev?" The bartender asked. "The usual?"

"Yes, Janet, and please pour one for my friend Jason here."

"What are we drinking?" Jason asked as they found an out-of-the-way seat on two plush chairs.

"Qupé, a local Chardonnay. It's the Chumash word for poppy."

"Cheers, and one more question. Did the bartender just call you Rev?"

"Cheers," Camille beamed. "Yep, she called me Rev. But I'm a harmless Unitarian."

"Go figure. I'm a lapsed Unitarian myself."

"Of course you are." Camille nodded. "What do you do?"

"I'm an attorney, though I'm kind of lapsed at that, too."

"I started off at Vet school, but I liked smoking weed with the Divinity School crowd better, so the next year I dropped out and joined them."

"Quite a vocation." Her earthy laugh, full of surprise, made him think briefly of Tara. "But I guess now it's me smoking pot with the Divinity crowd," Jason joked, sipping the wine. "And figuring out my next move."

She got him to tell her the whole story—the bribe, Tara, Earl, and Grace's pressure to join her in fighting ten million tons of coal a year.

"And I thought people wanted *me* to save the world." She stood up and gave him a lingering hug.

The hug felt good. More than minister-adjacent. Was he reading Camille correctly? She was coming back from the bar with two more glasses of wine.

"This is another one of my favorites." She handed him a glass. Her hair was long, like so many women in California. Her green eyes now looked blue. "A couple of women run it."

"So, are you married?"

She shook her head.

"Partnered?"

Same response. "No. It's not complicated." She put the wine on the table and moved toward him. She smelled like pot. Her thin face made him think of one of Modigliani's beauties. "I moved here this summer, but he was already out of the picture. He lives in Spain. You?"

"Been seeing a woman, the Grace I mentioned, for the past two years. We live in two different towns, too, but they're only two hours apart."

"Likely to last?"

"You answer first. What about you?"

"No, we both agreed that that ship has sailed a long time ago. You?"

Jason took a minute to think about it. "I honestly don't know anymore."

"Why is it a mystery?"

"We're at different stages of our lives. She's really into her job, trying to be a super lawyer. I respect that and Grace tremendously, but that's not really calling to me anymore."

"So what does call to you now?"

"Don't laugh."

"I'm a minister," Camille said. She took a dramatic sip of

wine. "I know when not to laugh."

"For the record, you're cute." And extremely clever. "And funny."

"Thanks, but you're dodging my question."

"Writing. I've been making notes for a novel. I've got the plot from the personal tragedy connected to my legal career. You know, being shot and losing the woman I loved."

"That's a lot." Camille held his hand. "Of course, write."

"Yes, I'm still a bit shell-shocked."

"Oh, and please let me know if you ever are free, will you?" She kissed him on the lips.

Later that night she asked him, "So what do you believe as far as the spiritual?"

"I don't think that it matters as much what I believe as what I do. But I guess I'm sort of a pro-God agnostic."

Camille laughed. "What does that mean for you?"

"I don't know, and I don't pretend to know if there's another life after this one, but I hope so. I've had some experiences that you could describe as spiritual, so I try to stay open to that larger life force that seems to tie everything together. I try to be kind and be influenced by other people."

"So it turns out that you're still a Unitarian, after all!" she teased.

That same Sunday, Jason found himself going to a church for the first time since Tara's funeral. It was a beautiful white Spanish Colonial Revival church built a few years after its predecessor had been destroyed in the 1925 Santa Barbara Earthquake. Jason was early but hung out in the garden across the street until he saw Camille's head through the open doorway.

She was wearing not quite a robe, but a flowing blue-and-gold sash of some kind that gave her a certain majesty even from this distance. He darted across the street to catch her.

"You made it!" That smile.

"Some insatiable spiritual hunger, I guess."

"Thanks for coming." She held his hand. "You picked a good week, especially for the music. I've got to run, but want to meet me for lunch at one at the Los Agaves on De La Vina?"

"Sure, perfect."

Jason had a few minutes before the service began and planned to go back outside in the sun, but something about the church held him. He sat there in the austere white sanctuary, with its rustic wooden beams. Meditating. In/out. Letting/Go. What was on the other side of this calm? Letting/Go.

The service served up conga-powered, Latin-flavored music and then more service. So many ways to get involved in the lives of others, in the lives of the community. Was Camille looking at him, or was that his imagination?

Now, she was above her congregants at her podium, looking powerful and beautiful in her flowing blue floral sash. He hadn't noticed before that her hair was going a bit gray on the sides. She was probably a little older than him. Her sermon, which the bulletin modestly called Thoughts, was "How to Cope in the New Year."

How, indeed, with Trump in office, impeached but unbowed, threatening so many of our shared values? This is what worked for Camille. Look for the Good Things. Act. Action provides hope, the only sure way. Act.

What was it that gave Camille's simple exhortations such power? Was it the sincerity with which she acknowledged her confusion and grief about the state of the world in January 2020? There was also her dignified humility and the authority conferred by her perch above them. Or was it just his crush on her, which Jason now found as compelling as her words?

He liked her candid interest in him and wanted a happy ending for her story. He wanted one for himself, too. So far, his was more meh.

She moved him; that much was clear.

Whatever it was, Jason felt more confused. Her words called him back to a coal pile on Lake Superior, but her very presence begged him to stay. Jason thought of the data that he'd been working on trying to tie that little girl Lacy's hospital trips to the coal shipper's air violations. Yes, he would go back and help Grace with the case. He would act.

Jason enjoyed the service. There was no mention of God, only of the generic good, but the vibe was still religious. Whatever humans made of it, this was still the same cosmos—God or no God. Tara had been a believer. Had her spirit survived her? Who knew?

It seemed like a less pressing question than how best to serve what is good. When he'd been working, he felt he had that opportunity every day. Just listening to every point of view, treating people with respect, and trying his best to be fair. But how did he contribute now?

And why was he so ready to let his legal skills go to seed? Already. He was fifty-one years old. Grace, the same age, was in her professional prime—while Jason walked the midmorning Central Coast beaches with the tourists, the surfers, and the wealthy retirees.

Just as he arrived at the restaurant, his phone buzzed. A text from Camille read, **Do you mind a change of plan? Can you meet me at my place?** Then, there was a screenshot of Google Maps.

Later, he rang the doorbell, and she buzzed him in. Camille stuck her head out the door. She was still all dressed up but had lost the sash. Her apartment was very small, a tiny two-bedroom in a crumbling white stucco building.

"Welcome," she said in greeting. Then she kissed him on the lips again. "I wanted to do that throughout the whole hour."

"Me, too," said Jason, taking her into his arms.

Chapter Twenty-Two

Loveless at Lovechild

Grace was hustling back to her office after a fundraiser at The Breakfast Club, a downtown restaurant with an 80s theme. A group of cool local people had come together to make secret payments for kids who were behind on their school lunch arrearages. These were typical La Crosse people—quietly decent and empathetic.

January was almost over, and Grace always remembered her Uncle Ray. The days were getting longer. *Just making it through January* was one of his keys to surviving a dark Wisconsin winter. There was *way more light coming in February.* She missed him; he was such an optimist.

Grace had a typically busy day. She had a video meeting with Tim later that afternoon and a dinner date with Jason, just back from California, in the evening.

Jason and Tim! It was confusing. Would she be with Tim if she hadn't been committed to Jason? Their law practices would fit together well. Yes, that thought was never far from her mind.

Now what? She was treading water with Jason, at best. Sometimes, it was more like she was struggling for air, trying not to go under. The truth was that Jason had become a drag. He was lost. Grace couldn't believe that Tara would have wanted him to just retire at fifty. For herself, Grace still had mountains to climb in the law and in her life!

She'd felt closest to Jason early in their relationship. After one early date, they'd wound up in bed but only to hold each other and cry. She'd confessed that she'd never gotten over losing Jon, and he poured out his love for Tara.

Grace had been twenty years in on getting over her grief, and Jason's was still fresh. Too fresh, and sometimes his distance brought hers back. Maybe they'd started dating too soon after Tara's death? They'd tried to take it slow—months of sexless date-equivalents.

Losing Tara had withered him to the point that he was still finding himself again when Grace knew perfectly well who she was and what she wanted. She wanted to have a strong partnership and keep growing as a person and in her profession. Jason wasn't even sure that he wanted to be a lawyer anymore, while Grace felt her professional powers growing and that she had the exact set of skills needed by the world in its moment of climate crisis.

Tim felt that way, too.

And Tim, to his great credit, had never gotten over her. Jason had never gotten over Tara. Tara was some distant, long-lost light that beckoned to Jason, and he was a lost ship. That was understandable. She'd been the same way about losing Jon, but now it reduced her to a shadow figure.

Jason was a dreamy thinker, an intellectual like Tara, and Grace was a do-er who knew how precious every moment in a life was. She found herself wondering if they had ever really been in love. It had been such an accidental romance.

The video conference with Tim was late in the afternoon and lasted almost two hours. They were strategizing about the coal case. Tim was oddly animated and more than a little flirtatious.

"Do you remember when we went to see your Uncle Ray in that play in Winona?"

"Of course; that's one of my favorite memories of Ray, in his Rosencrantz costume!"

"I thought he was Guildenstern?" Tim asked.

"Maybe he was."

"I was so in love with you then, and I thought we were solid because your uncle and his boyfriend both liked me."

"We were pretty solid then, but now we're supposed to be talking about the case." She wanted to sound vaguely encouraging. They'd gone back to the hotel room in Winona that night, drunk a bottle of wine on the balcony and made love a couple of times. She was in love with him, too, then. "Anything else on the case? I'm supposed to meet Jason at six."

"No, but I'm glad that you remember that night in Winona."

"I remember." She tried to give him her most alluring smile. "Good night, Tim."

Grace was feeling slightly nauseous and dreading the date or meeting with Jason. Maybe it would be better to just have him say no and let things take their course with Tim? Being around Tim was so much easier, and that was pretty telling.

She was to meet Jason at Love Child, her favorite local restaurant. It had won many accolades as one of the best and 'most romantic' restaurants in the Midwest. It had high ceilings rising above elegant brick walls and lush velvet seating. But now she wished they'd chosen somewhere else. Their relationship was anything but romantic at this point.

Grace made it first and waited in the entry for Jason. Jason came in, sporting a fresh California tan and sun-streaked, wavy hair. He was prettier than Tim, but so what? He gave her a perfunctory hug.

"You're looking fit," she said, as the hostess saw them to their table.

"Thanks, it was nice to get some sun. And I did a lot of hiking."

"I've been running fast on my treadmill," Grace replied. "It's been a life saver."

They were both making small talk. She noticed that his hands seemed to be trembling as he took a sip of his water.

"So, what does the case need?" Jason asked.

"We're still lacking proof that they're not spraying the whole pile."

"We have to do an Order for Entry Upon Land to get some samples."

"Didn't I tell you?" No, Grace remembered, she'd told Tim. "I've already drafted that up."

"You guys are going to have to grab some unsprayed samples. They'll probably spray everything the night before."

"'You guys,' not us together?" That said a lot.

"It is your case. Yours and Tim's."

"What about us?"

"How are you feeling about it?" Jason asked back.

Grace took a sip of her water. They were both much more comfortable asking questions than answering them. One of many occupational hazards.

"I'm not feeling as certain about us..." She would leave it there.

The waiter came and they placed their orders.

"I understand. Not as certain and ready to take a break?"

"Maybe. What do you want? You're the one who is so distant." She paused a second. She looked away from him toward the open kitchen. The chef, who was the co-owner, was joking with the waitstaff. "Did you meet someone in California?"

"Yes."

So why hadn't he told her? "Okay, I think we should take a permanent break," Grace said. She noticed herself twirling her hair in the girlish way that her mother used to chew her out for. "I'm not going to lie; I'm pretty disappointed with you."

"I'm sorry." Jason looked at her and then averted his eyes.

"And you should know that there's still some chemistry between Tim and me."

"I knew it. It's not surprising." He tried to take her hand, but she quickly took it off the table and out of his reach. "There's a familiarity, and you both seem to want the same things."

"There's a comfort in that, for sure. Just so you know, I haven't acted on those feelings. I'm not like that."

"I'm sorry to say that I thought I wasn't like that, either."

That was a confession, as much as she could bear. "A hard break it is then," she said, surprised by the crack in her voice. "Where does that leave us on the case?"

"I'm still all in, if you still want me."

"Yes."

"It's important."

"Good."

"I'm very sorry, Grace." He tried to take her hand.

She moved it quickly away. "Me, too. We were healing each other. We had some good times. Whatever the timing, we've been drifting apart."

"I want you to be happy."

"Same here. What's her name?"

"Camille."

"Is she a lawyer?"

"No, a Unitarian minister."

"Oh, for fuck's sake, Jason," Grace managed. She was both laughing and tearing up. "You're gone a month, and you bedded down a minister?"

Chapter Twenty-Three

A Fortunate Adult

Courtney's move went smoothly. Her furniture fit snugly into her new condo apartment, and there was way more room in the updated cupboards than at her rented place. The movers set up her new king-size bed and installed a new high-efficiency air conditioner.

Thanking her for her cash tip, one of the movers commented on what a sunny place she'd bought. "It is," she agreed. She was so excited and wanted to add, "I own this sunny place outright," but that would have been rude.

If only she didn't have to spend two weeks in Lake Superior City on that stupid coal transshipment case. The events with Earl left her with a bitter feeling about the case. The date for him to sign the contract with her had expired. And was she a bad guy, as Earl seemed to suggest?

Deep down, maybe she wanted the world to be done with coal, too. Whatever it was, it contributed to losing the competitive fire that had always fueled her in litigation. She gave her associate Jake more witnesses to depose and then present at trial.

At bottom, she didn't really care that much about the case one way or the other. She just wanted to stay home in her remarkable new place and binge-watch some soapy TV series with Ben. The second night, she called him right after dinner.

"Ben, I've got a completely virgin mattress over here that's really comfortable for sleeping, but I'm not sure how it will be for other activities."

"That sounds lovely! Are you getting settled in?"

"Yes, this place has such amazing light and lots of storage space."

"I'll be over in twenty-five minutes," Ben said.

Courtney sat watching the early evening sun dance across the wood floor in her living room. Her parents had always had carpeting and linoleum, and she loved the look and feel of grainy wood with the sun on it. It was real and yes, Sydney, it felt homey and safe.

Ben arrived and they made their way into her new bedroom.

"I love the color of this room," Ben said.

"Me too," Courtney said. "It's royal blue. Come and try out the new bed."

They lay down together and snuggled. "I like it," Ben said, kissing her. "But I like you more."

Courtney pulled back a bit and took her shirt and jeans off, as Ben did the same.

"Look, Ben. Really, the symbolism of this bed is meaningful for me. I've never been with anyone else on it, and if things keep going the way they are . . ." She paused. "I don't want to ever make love to anyone else on it. It's my new start."

"Our new start. I don't want anyone else, either. I just want to be your lover boy," Ben said. While looking directly into her eyes, he'd managed to get them both completely naked.

"You're doing fine so far." She ran her hands through his wild hair as he kissed his way down her body and set her on fire. "Come up here and make love to me," she said.

Though it was exquisite, afterward she cried.

"Did it hurt?" Ben looked baffled. "You seemed to be into it!"

"It was lovely," she said. "I'm just feeling a little emotional about my good fortune."

She told him about her discussion with Sydney.

"I want you to be a very Fortunate Adult." Ben held her close.

"You've got me starting to feel like maybe I am already."

Chapter Twenty-Four

Just One of the Guys

Earl went to a funeral for a cousin just outside La Crosse. He was meeting Grace Clarkson about the coal case in La Crosse afterward. The funeral was in the little white Lutheran church in Cashton, where he'd been confirmed. He felt self-conscious as he made his way from the parking lot inside.

He'd long been the star of the Franks family. First, in sports, winning a Class B State Title in football and then a scholarship to Michigan. Then, of course, in his legal career.

His mother had kept a scrapbook of every time his name had been mentioned in *The La Crosse Tribune.* He'd been the superstar boy wonder attorney general elected because he'd helped ban DDT and then was appointed to the Wisconsin Supreme Court. He'd lost all of that with his gambling and debt to Chicago mobster Tommy C, and then the conviction in the bribery case.

Now, his big-mouth cousin Tony gave him some not-so-good-natured razzing about going from the Supreme Court to the maximum-security prison. "Look who's out of the slammer, His Honor Justice Earl."

"Shut up, Tony," his cousin Rob, of all people, said. "Earl's here to show his respect for Jimmy, just like everyone else. So show him some, too."

"I was just teasing him, Rob."

Earl changed the subject. "How about those Packers?"

Everyone laughed and then weighed in on Rodgers and Adams and company. Earl felt his body relax, feeling pleased now that he'd had the guts to show up. And maybe now he could just be one of the guys instead of the annoying super-star they all resented.

The funeral commenced with familiar hymns that seared him with their hopeful sentimentality. It was the culture he had grown up in, even if it no longer felt like his own. "Amazing Grace"; did he truly believe in it? The answer was not straightforward. Religion, like the hymns, was a mix of hope and sentimentality that Earl had never quite been able to let go of despite his doubts.

'God is love' had always made some sense to him.

Earl said his goodbyes and headed over the hills toward La Crosse. His plan was to meet Grace Clarkson and her col-league at her office in downtown La Crosse. Even though he'd always liked it, that town had some bad juju for him now, since Grace had ratted him out there and it had been part of the case against him.

Clarkson Law Office was in a fine old building right down-town. A well-dressed guy showed him where to wait for her. It was a classy little place—cool old leather sofas and chairs and a picture of her uncle Ray Clarkson who'd founded the firm years ago.

Grace came out and introduced him to her co-counsel, Tim Gergen. He was a balding, fifty-something, slightly chubby dude with thick glasses.

"Thanks for coming in, Earl," she said, leading him back into her big corner office.

"Beautiful place you've got here, Grace. Like how you honor your uncle."

"Thanks, Earl." She seemed taken aback by his kindness. "I'm glad that you're not holding any grudges against me."

"Nah, you just testified to what you saw. The only thing that ticked me off was your description of my legs." They both laughed. This was going to be okay. "I'm here to fight global warming."

Tim frowned. "We mostly talk about it as the climate crisis. The newspapers in Europe and the UK have been using that term for years."

What a smug little prick. Earl stifled a snark. "Well, I'm sure that I can learn a lot from you two, and I can tell you everything that you want to know about Lake Superior coal transshipment."

"Yes," Grace said. She was smoother than Gergen. "And we really appreciate it."

They spent an hour talking about opposing the permit. They were shocked when Earl said that his client hadn't sprayed the whole pile either.

"I would try to get my hands on their spending for it. If it's a publicly traded company, that should be in their financial reports."

"We thought of that, too," Tim said. "But it's a family-owned private company."

"You can still try. They'll say it's proprietary and confidential, but the judge can look at it in camera. What's the first thing you guys want me to do?" Earl asked, warming up to the project. It was good to feel like one of the guys here, too.

"We'll pay you for your time today, but before we can sign a contract, there's something that you need to do."

Were they going to try to make him be bonded or something? "What's the big mystery?"

"It's no mystery, just a little awkward," Grace replied. "Jason Erickson has been consulting Of Counsel with us, too. And it would be nice to know that he has no problems working with you."

"He's still angry with me," Earl replied. "I get that, but I will try."

"I thought it might be best if I called him and then handed the phone over to you."

"You want me to talk to him right now?"

Chapter Twenty-Five

A Familiar Gruff Voice

Driving back home to Madison, Jason found himself taking Grace's scenic route along Highway 14 as a sort of homage. Or was it a penance? Grace belonged to these hills and had been married up one of these winding coulee roads many years ago when they were both in law school. Driving over the hills that his father loved, Jason felt a little guilt, but there was also some relief.

He'd fessed up, at least. Grace hadn't seemed all that surprised or even wounded. But she could be hard to read.

Jason had been so focused on confessing and breaking up with Grace that he'd barely thought about the surprise Camille had given him shortly before leaving Santa Barbara.

"This is unreservedly a very good thing," she'd said that day at lunch.

"It sure seems like it," he'd replied. It was very early days, but it seemed possible that together they were more than the sum of their parts alone.

He loved being with her and, when he wasn't, thinking about her. Something that she'd said was often still on his mind days later. And, of course, her beauty brought its own light and intimate texture. There were her green eyes, her long and thick dark hair, and what she called the "constellation" of moles on her chest.

He thought he knew her reasonably well after their long walks and hours of candid conversation and making love for two weeks, but he didn't understand her at all until she invited him to dinner at her apartment, and there were three places set.

"Micah's back and he's going to join us tonight."

"Micah?"

Camille smiled. "My son, he's been away at camp, but he's coming back this afternoon."

"That's a surprise; you never told me."

She nodded a little awkwardly. "Don't worry, he's ten and a lot of fun. Maybe a little on the precocious side. And he doesn't have a father to trouble us. The guy in Spain is not his dad."

"I'm sorry. When did you lose his father?"

"Can't lose what you never had." Camille's lips curved upward, and she raised her nose a bit, too. A sure sign that a wisecrack was coming. "His father was a withdrawal from a sperm bank."

"How brave of you." Camille was fifty-two, so a late pregnancy ten years ago as a single mother was both courageous and risky. "Is he named after the prophet from the Bible?"

"Yes, of course." She leaned close to Jason and kissed him. "You're the first person outside of a church function to ask me that."

"I know Micah." He took her hand. "Act justly, love mercy, and walk humbly with your god."

"Exactly. I've even done a homily on that last point."

But should he meet her kid already? "It seems a little too soon to meet your son."

"I'm sorry, I should have given you more warning. We were just having so much fun."

"Yes," Jason replied. He felt his heart rate kick into overdrive. Why did she trust him already?

"If you're going to join us, we have to go downstairs to meet the shuttle bus."

Was he? "Are you sure that you want me to meet him already? Especially if he's been away." It seemed too soon and a bit rash.

"Micah insisted on it. He wants to check you out to make sure his mom's okay."

Jason laughed as they made their way down the stairs to the street below. The orange sun was just beginning to move farther west, into the Pacific. He was always still so pleased to go outside and experience the beauty of Santa Barbara. Like a hopeless tourist, he sometimes still took pictures of the mountains from grocery store parking lots.

"I'm a little nervous," Jason confided.

"With Micah, we'll soon know if he likes you."

"What did you tell him about me?"

A small green Ojai Adventures minibus with kids in it approached and then stopped. "Saved by the bus," Camille replied, running to greet it. A slight boy with long, curly hair ran to hug her. He was wearing a light blue T-shirt that said Try Kindness. "How was it?"

"Really fun, but I'm tired."

"Do you have everything?"

Micah nodded and then stuck his hand out to Jason. "Are you Jason?"

"Yes, Micah, nice to meet you. I like your T-shirt."

"Well, a couple of kids made fun of it," Micah replied, looking at his mother.

"What do they know?" Jason asked.

"How to punch really hard!" Micah smiled. He had Camille's impish grin.

Jason laughed out loud. "Do you know how to block punches?" he asked.

"Not really."

"Well, you're talking to the east side Milwaukee Junior Golden Gloves runner-up, and I could show you sometime if you want."

"Sure, and show me some punches, too!"

"I will, if it's okay with your mom."

"What do you say, Camille?" Micah asked. He called her Camille?

"I'd rather have you teach him Spanish, but I guess that would be all right with me. Try Kindness, and if that fails, a little self-defense is just fine too."

Yes, that had all been a surprise. There was a lot to process, too. But it had all gone well.

Now, Jason felt some new, more insistent guilt as he made his way over the hills and back to Madison. What had he done? He'd never cheated on anyone before in his life.

No more Saint Jason. But he trusted his instincts and his feelings for Camille. It was probably a little reckless, but he trusted Camille, too.

Was he ready to be in Camille and Micah's lives? As Jason hit the Beltline around Madison, he was thinking about his childhood, and especially being Micah's age. Jason had grown up three blocks from Lake Michigan in Milwaukee.

One of his fondest memories was regularly riding his bike along the lake up to Atwater Park in Whitefish Bay. White Folks Bay, some called it, but it was just a modest inner suburb featuring the park with its steep bluffs and stairs leading down to the lake. Now, he lived in Madison, three blocks from Lake Monona and regularly walked there to settle himself.

The next evening, he found himself doing exactly that.

The last pink light of the sunset was still lingering above the linden trees. A couple of kids were still shooting hoops in the winter darkness, as Jason had himself done at that park near Lake Michigan. He and Justin used to shovel the snow off outdoor courts and play in the freezing winter.

Life went by fast, and change was at the very heart of it.

Grace had so much dignity, but she'd made it clear that they were done and that she was likely to move on quickly with Tim. Good for her. Maybe Tim could give her the kind of all-consuming partnership that she needed. Jason needed something with a bit more freedom.

The sun was setting in earnest. Pink as usual, as almost always on the two lakes that formed the Madison isthmus.

Lake Mendota, too, had those bright pink sunsets. The pink-and-blood-orange sky danced off the silver lake, and above it was the majestic white Wisconsin State Capitol building. It had to be lowered a couple of feet to comply with federal law that no state could erect one bigger than the national capitol in DC.

It'd been built by Fighting Bob La Follette and the Progressives early in the last century. Back when the government took an interest in making life better for the little guy with new ideas like unemployment insurance and workers compensation for on-the-job injuries. The pseudo-populism of Trump, despite its winks and nods to the non-college working poor, was at its core a deeply cynical, almost nihilistic, vision of government. Government was there to richly reward its deep-pocket supporters with lavish tax cuts and other perks and to put a thumb in the eye of many others. Maybe the new Democratic House could moderate both sides of that equation, even if ever so slightly.

Camille thought so. Grace wasn't as sure. Grace was a hard-headed lawyer and widow who knew that life didn't always turn out how one wanted it to go. Camille's steadfast optimism, sometimes bordering on the Pollyannish, was welcome but sometimes a little bewildering.

Still, it was something that Jason needed. Missing Camille, he snapped a photo of the capitol sunset with the caption "a couple of blocks from my house."

His phone rang again. Jason was relieved to be distracted.

Camille? No, it was a Wisconsin number from north of Madison. For some reason, he called it back. The gruff voice, "Hello, Jason?" was familiar.

Oh shit, it was Earl Franks.

PART TWO:

A Lover's Quarrel

"The injuries we do and those that we suffer
are seldom weighed on the same scales."

- Aesop -

Chapter Twenty-Six

Somebody That You Trust

The meeting was pretty much "take it or leave it." Earl decided to take it, even though it was a four-hour drive from Blue Lake to Milwaukee. Jason Erickson had finally agreed to meet Earl at some new arts hotel downtown where Jason's friend was having an art opening. Betty encouraged him to go.

"Don't forget, he's got good reason to never want to speak to you again, Earl," Betty reminded him as she put on her makeup in their master bedroom bath. "That's a bit of a trek. If you need to stay over, that's just fine."

"Would you want to come with me?" Earl asked, spitting out his toothpaste. "We could make a night of it, stay at the art-hotel place, and then go to the Rep or the museum?"

"Yes, that's a lovely idea," Betty replied, smiling that big smile. "That's a Friday night; let me see what play is on!"

She was always up for almost anything. Sure, part of that was being retired, but there was also something fundamentally upbeat about her that Earl loved. She was such a good sport. About everything.

On the way down, Betty played that *Hadestown* CD that Earl was already getting a little sick of, but she nonetheless had him singing along to a couple of songs with her beautiful former choir director voice. The theme of the story seemed to be to grab on to someone if you loved them. Earl had learned that same lesson the hard way, with his divorce and stretch in prison.

Saint Kate, the arts hotel, was impressive. They served

you champagne when you checked in and there was already a bunch of people gathered around the bar and lobby that looked out on a busy city street. A middle-aged Black guy played the guitar and sang an Al Green song, *Love and Happiness.*

Earl got them registered, and then he and Betty sat sipping the cheap champagne for a bit before they took their bags upstairs. Earl kissed her and went back down to the lobby. He was five minutes early. Betty's influence again.

He grabbed a beer and sat at a small table. An older woman in a striped dress was also waiting for someone at the table next to him. A man with an oddly colored, almost gold toupee introduced himself and joined her. A first awkward date.

Earl had never had to go through that after Maggie divorced him. He'd gone from Courtney to prison to Betty in short succession. How lucky Earl was to have Betty upstairs waiting for him. Now, there was Jason coming out of the main art gallery up a staircase from the lobby. They nodded.

Earl offered his hand as Jason approached him. To Earl's surprise, Jason took it and gave it a quick shake. A good sign.

"Thanks for meeting me, Judge."

"You look better than the last time I saw you," Jason replied. It landed like a punch to the gut.

"Nobody looks great in prison," Earl said a little defensively. "And now I live year-round on my cabin on Blue Lake."

"Must be nice." Jason frowned. "That's exactly what Tara and I had talked about doing."

"Oh, that's tough." Dammit, Earl hadn't known that Blue Lake was still a touchy subject for the guy he'd tried to bribe. "Tara would be proud of you for everything since then, including taking me and her killers down. And this coal case, too."

"Thanks, Earl." Jason's face softened. "What did you want to talk to me about? Some kind of Twelve-Step Amends?"

"Nah, coal. That plant." Twelve steps, did Erickson think he was a drunk, too? Oh, maybe he knew about Earl's former gambling problem? Probably that, Erickson had gone to Earl's sentencing. "Grace Clarkson and that Tim Gergen guy want me to help them out, informally, on that coal transshipment plant permit."

Jason looked perplexed. "Did Grace call you?"

"No, Gergen did. But I called you from her office."

"Well, it's a free country. Going to do it?"

"I want to, but I know it may be a bit awkward for you, so I was hoping to get you to greenlight the idea."

Jason looked him in the eye and gave a sort of half smile. "Frankly, right now I'm at amber. Caution. Let me get a glass of wine."

When he came back, Jason sat down rather brusquely. "I'm trying to make sense of this kinder, gentler Earl Franks. Or are you going to try to mess with me again?"

"Ouch." What a cheap shot. "No, I'm not."

"Look, I don't want to rehash things or even give you a hard time. Why don't you just give me your pitch? I'll take it under advisement and head home."

Earl did. It was kind of a long and winding path. He'd done a couple of similar cases and remembered some details. His old client had skimped on that coal-encrusting spray stuff because it was pricey. He no longer had his law license, but he could be an asset to the team. He'd stick to his lane. Earl genuinely wanted to see the world use less coal for his grandkid's future. Did he resort to the polar bears again? Maybe not, but something almost that hackneyed.

"Nice pitch, Earl. I'll say this for you, you still have your lawyer chops."

"But?"

"I didn't have a but in mind, but if you want one, why should Grace or I trust you? How do we know that you're not secretly in the tank for your old flame Courtney?"

"Flame?"

"Come on, Earl." Jason sipped his white wine. "I thought you were going to level with me."

"Okay, Courtney and I may have once been an item, but that's not relevant." Earl took a sip of his beer and shook his head. "My girlfriend, Betty, who lives with me on Blue Lake, would either leave me or kill me if that ever started up again."

Jason laughed. "I suspect that's true." He'd seemed to have mellowed a bit, too. "Look, Earl, I'll level with you. I still have a sort of a mental health thing going on about having been shot and losing the love of my life. Can you understand that?"

"Yes, I do understand." Earl instinctively put his hand on Jason's shoulder and to Earl's surprise, Jason didn't remove it. "I did two and a half years in prison, in that hell hole at Portage where they kept Jeffrey Dahmer, at your specific request."

"Tough duty. Did you learn anything?"

"Yes, and I think you're sharp enough to understand that I wouldn't have driven four hours to ask you for your... forbearance... if I hadn't?" His voice had risen loud enough for the guy in the gold toupee to give him a look. "And did the old Earl give two shits about the polar bears? He'd probably be off playing the ponies in Vegas instead."

"Well, here's the deal, I'm spending a lot of time in California these days, and I'm not even as much as a second chair on that coal case. You don't need my permission. Talk to Tim Gergen."

"I have and I will." The prick wasn't going to want to work with Earl, whatever he said. He tried another tack. "What do you know about Tim Gergen? Is he a decent lawyer?"

"He's kind of a trial lawyer gym rat." Jason's brow furrowed, and he glanced around the wide room. "Gergen's savvy in court but not exactly a genius. A little plodding. Not a great strategist. Grace has the big picture better."

"Yes, she's sharp." Erickson clearly didn't like Gergen. Maybe Gergen was moving in on Grace? "Do you mind if I ask, are you and Grace still together?"

"Nope," Jason responded, grabbing his wine to change the subject. "What do you think they should argue on the coal pile?"

Now they were just two lawyers discussing a case. They spent the next fifteen minutes discussing strategy. Jason was incisive and quickly got to the very heart of it.

"Earl, it was odd, when I went for a walk by the coal facility, there were several German Shepherd guard dogs that seemed very anxious to keep me away."

"Attack dogs?" Earl asked. Jason nodded. "The company I represented never did that. These people are hiding something."

"Yes, and I have a hunch what it is. I don't think they're spraying that whole mountain of coal with that expensive sealer. Did your people?"

"Sure, a couple of days before and after the inspectors came for their annual site visit!" Earl shook his head. "Even the State had to give Notice before they could do a compliance inspection. It makes it hard to catch them out of compliance."

"But other than that?" Earl shook his head and finished the last dregs of his delicious East Side Dark Lager. "Damn them, that's the most significant condition in their whole permit for particulate mitigation." Jason leaned toward him. "How would we be able to prove that?"

"We've got to get some of the coal that's not being sprayed," Earl replied. "That won't be easy, because if you file a Notice of Entry to inspect, they'll spray the shit out of the whole pile the night before."

"I was just thinking that we'd have to send somebody out on a boat under the cover of darkness," Jason replied.

"It would have to be somebody that you trusted with your life, or at least your law license, because they would have you over a barrel. You'd also have to get an expert to fudge the chain of custody." Earl felt his temple throbbing, a sign that his blood pressure was rising. "Take it from the guy who was blackmailed into trying to bribe you."

Jason gave him a look that was almost sympathetic. Maybe Erickson wasn't such a bad dude. Just then Betty came down, looking like some aging movie star, in her fluttering bumblebee floral pants and her blue moto jacket. Earl introduced them.

"Earl just wants to help, Judge. He's grown so much and still has so much to offer. Can you see your way forward to work with him?"

"Aww, Betty, I already gave the man my pitch." How Earl loved that woman!

Jason stood up and put his black wool winter coat on. He offered his hand to Betty. "It's nice to meet you, Betty." He paused and looked directly at Earl. "Your boyfriend here will never be my best friend, but I think that everyone deserves a second chance. There's no reason we can't stay in our own lanes but be on the same team."

"That's wonderful to hear," Betty observed.

"You gave me your number, Earl; I'll be in touch."

Betty looked at them both with that smile that you could take your shoes off and walk around on.

Chapter Twenty-Seven

Strategy Session

It took Grace a couple of days for it to sink in. She'd been dumped. Sure, she'd been thinking about doing the same thing to Jason, but still. She'd never been dumped before. It was more embarrassing than hurtful. She was fifty-one years old. Would she tell her mom about Jason's infidelity? It might be the only way to get her off her back.

Grace lost herself in her work, as always. She had an ample retainer for the big coal case and had cleared out the space to work primarily on it. She and Jason were law school classmates, precisely the same age. Jason, retired and with all his baggage, was already on to the next phase of life. But Tim still loved being a lawyer as much as she did. She loved working with Tim and sometimes felt like a teenager when they worked together at her office.

One night a week or so after her breakup, they were sitting in her uncle's old conference room with a pile of papers and boxes of Chinese take-out all around them. She decided to tell him.

"Tim, there's something I wanted to tell you."

"Uh-oh. Are you and Jason getting married?"

She laughed out loud. "God, no!" Tim's instincts on matters of the heart were sometimes a little off. "Actually, no, he broke up with me."

"I'm sorry, Grace." He grabbed her hand and held it.

"Are you really?"

"Selfishly, no. I meant for you. Breakups are always a little disruptive even when they're right."

"Yes. It was a week ago when we went to Lovechild. He's started screwing a pastor in California."

"Crazy."

They both laughed, and then managed to get back to work. There was an ease between them that had a slight hint of the erotic to it. They'd been lovers in the past, it had been lovely, and they were both free now.

Later that week they had another video strategy session, which included Jason. Jason had finally given his consent to have Earl come in on the case. After discussing their legal theories of the case, they immediately started talking about a wild plan the two of them had hatched to catch the coal plant red-handed by grabbing some of the unsprayed coal.

"We'd have to send somebody we trusted out on a boat and be prepared to neutralize the dogs," Jason said.

"Neutralize?" Tim asked. "Wouldn't that be obvious?"

"Maybe not," Jason replied. "We could just try tranquilizing them for the evening."

"Interesting," Grace admitted.

"What about a simple Notice of Entry Upon Land?" Tim asked. "Why not try a basic Discovery tool first?"

"Obviously, that would be best, but Earl says that they would spray the heck out of the pile the night before," Jason replied.

"Of course they would," Tim observed. "The bastards."

"But who could we trust enough to keep this whole thing under wraps?" Grace asked, knowing the answer. "Are you saying we'd have to do it ourselves?"

"If Superior freezes, we could just walk out there," Jason replied.

"The water is still open," Grace said. "I just read that only ten percent of Lake Superior is frozen. And the trial is set for the week of March ninth." Grace's hands were trembling. Jason had thought about this already, but Grace was surprised, intrigued, and slightly terrified by the idea. "It's very risky." She looked into the camera. "Do you think it's really worth it?"

"No," Tim replied firmly. "Our licenses would be toast if we got caught."

"Yes, they would be," Jason agreed, swooping his hair back like he did when he was nervous. "And I admit that that probably means more to you two than me right now. Maybe we should try to think of some less risky way to catch them by surprise."

"Could we just buy some of the coal?" Tim asked.

"Not unless we want to buy literally a whole boatload of it," Jason said. "Remember, the coal comes up on trains and then is loaded onto cargo ships to head out the Saint Lawrence Seaway."

"Oh, right," Tim replied.

Grace felt bad for Tim for saying something so stupid. It was going to be awkward working with Jason and Tim at the same time.

"They have all of those notices of violation for a reason," Grace said. "Maybe we do have to think outside of the box a bit. Some corporations do this kind of thing all the time."

"Earl has a small eighteen-foot fishing boat that he's offered to use as a near-shore lookout if the Coast Guard or County boats are out," Jason said. "But we'd need a bigger boat to get to the coal pile on Lake Superior."

"I've got a bigger boat that I've taken out as far as the Apostle Islands," Tim said. "But not in February. We'd need wetsuits and other water-resistant clothes."

"Good point," Jason said. "We hadn't thought of that."

"Are you sure that you'd want to get that involved, Tim?" Grace asked.

"No, of course not," Tim said. "But you could use my boat."

"Thanks for considering it," Jason said. "There are also the dogs. Did you tell him?"

"No," Grace said, reaching for her phone. She showed Tim

a picture of the German Shepherd that had come under the fence toward Jason.

"Yowzer," Tim replied. "Someone else is going to have to go out on that island."

"Tim was attacked by a dog when he was a boy," Grace explained. Another thing they had in common.

"I could drive Earl's boat along the shore as a lookout, or even act as a diversion if the patrol boat was out," Tim offered. "But no way in hell that I'm going out on that island."

"I hear you, Tim. Camille, the woman I've been seeing, was in vet school several years ago and has some tranquilizing stuff available."

"You talked about this with her?" Grace asked.

Jason nodded. "She's willing to help us. I know that would be awkward for you, Grace. And there's one other problem that Earl and I discussed. And maybe the hardest part, even if we could get the samples, is that we'd have to find an expert willing to switch them out after we got them," Jason continued. "That's not a sure thing."

"So, Jason," Tim asked. "You and Earl are asking us and an expert to commit a crime to catch them in the act?"

"I'm not asking you to do anything," Jason began. "I'm just telling you what Earl and I discussed. It's a longshot and a gamble because we'd have to convince an expert to fudge on the chain of custody as well."

"It kind of scares me how good you are at criminal thinking, Jason," Grace said with a little bit too much gusto. "And even if we got the samples, how could we get them into evidence?"

"Yeah, how would we say that we got them?" Tim asked.

"We'd have to do a lawful Entry Upon Land through Discovery. Maybe a day or two later, so that we could explain it. Earl told me that big corporations play those kinds of games all the time."

"He would know," Grace said.

"I agree," Tim said. "There are lots of companies that just ignore environmental regulations altogether because it's cheaper to pay the fines."

"Yes, Earl Franks was as dirty as they come," Jason said.

"So why should we trust him now?" Tim asked.

"Great question," Jason said, stalling. "I sensed that he was sincerely concerned about the climate crisis; he's going to be a grandfather soon. You guys met him; what did you think?"

"I agree that he seemed sincere," Grace replied.

"I couldn't read him fully, to be honest," Tim said.

"Maybe Tim's right and the whole thing is too risky," Jason said. Tim nodded, looking like his elementary teacher had just given him a gold star. "Besides, do you think that we could find an expert to go along?"

"I'm not sure. But it really comes down to whether we think it's worth the risk," Grace answered. "It would be compelling evidence if we could corroborate it another way."

"Earl had some ideas on that, too. One thing we could do, whether we try to get the unsprayed coal samples or not, is get copies of their billing records of how much they've spent on the crusting chemicals."

"That's a great idea," Grace admitted. "But that might lean a little bit on the side of being an enforcement issue rather than a permit expansion issue."

"They could fudge those, too," Tim said. "I'm still not convinced that any of this is worth the risk."

"That's a question for the two of you to answer as co-counsel," Jason said, looking at his phone. "Meanwhile, I've got to."

Grace felt something like a gas pain in her stomach. Was he going to go get some individualized spiritual counseling from his new lady friend? No, he was back in Madison. Tim took her hand as Jason got off the video.

"Personally, I would just say no," Tim said. "But I agree that it could be a gamechanger, so I'll go along with whichever way you decide."

"It sucks that we'd have to resort to borderline illegal stuff to catch them doing really dastardly stuff to the air of the children."

"What Jason and Earl are suggesting isn't borderline," Tim said. "It's just plain illegal."

"But so is the company not spraying a million tons of coal," Grace heard herself saying. "I'm torn. You should have heard the fear and disappointment in Ellen's voice when I told her that we couldn't do anything about Lacy's hospitalization!"

Chapter Twenty-Eight

A Light Feeling and
a Great Parking Spot

"Should I just admit I slept with Earl Franks and recuse myself?" Courtney was discussing her work troubles with Sydney, her therapist.

"Would you have to give up being the Managing Partner?" Sydney asked, as always getting to the heart of things.

"Yes, probably."

"Could they fire you?"

"No." Could they? Unlikely. "I mean, I don't think so."

"Well, good." Sydney smiled. "How much does being Managing Partner mean to you?"

"It had been a long-time goal; it took me eleven years. But now that I've done it, it doesn't mean the same thing."

"That's very healthy, Courtney." Sydney set her pen down and looked directly at Courtney. "You seem more confident in your own instincts."

"Thanks." Sydney's Socratic questions, especially the delicate way she'd handled Courtney's childhood abuse, had made an enormous difference. None of it had been her fault. Later, carrying on with old men was part of her healing. Courtney's success should be its own reward. People who'd never been poor couldn't understand what it meant to own even a modest place without a mortgage, to be debt-free. Knowing that the lifelong battle to come up with the rent was behind you was a singular feeling. "You've helped me get there."

"That's a nice moment to say that our time is up," Sydney said, standing up. "When would you have to decide?"

"In the next week or so."

"I won't see you before then, but I know that you'll think things through and make the right decision based on where you are now in your life."

As Courtney got up to leave, she wondered if Sydney was subtlety trying to influence her with this last comment. One of her major themes was that Courtney had let her past drive too many decisions for too long. Was she finally getting free of those demons? What were the implications of that if it were true?

Some kind of lightness. Ben was part of that feeling, too. It was one of the first times that she had felt a sort of freedom in connection. Courtney made her way back downtown to her office and found her parking spot. If she stopped being Managing Partner, she'd miss that prime parking spot as much as anything.

It was a Thursday, which meant that it was a date night with Ben. The plan was to meet at seven o'clock at the Chengdu Chinese restaurant near her apartment. They had this amazing Sichuan Boiled Fish with napa cabbage that usually fed her twice. Ben would probably end up staying the night.

How much was she going to tell him? He knew the rough outlines of her affair with Earl, but she'd never told him about her brazen dumping of Earl for another old goat, Jack Singleton, who was running the firm at the time. That one *was* sleazy. Courtney regretted it, even if Jack had been the catalyst for her making partner.

She'd really had no feelings for Jack. She was mostly just trying to get away from Earl amid his bribery thing with Tommy C. Jack's skinny and soft old body, his bright pink nipples, had repulsed her then and now. He'd only managed to get it up a couple of quick times, but it had left her feeling nauseous. Cheap.

Sydney had helped her see how different that was from her time with Earl. She'd genuinely cared for him. Earl had a manly vitality and brains at his core, and, despite everything, he was somehow loveable—a big bear in need of a hug.

Now her handsome boyfriend Ben arrived, as always, promptly and with a flourish. Ben was almost always the coolest guy in the room. He was tall and already distinguished looking at thirty-six. He had a beautiful head of longish black hair. Courtney loved the way he dressed and smelled and cared for her.

"Hi, sweetheart," he said, sitting down. "How was your day?"

"Kind of sucky. I want to talk to you about something that happened with that personnel case."

"Sure, let's have a glass of wine and then take a go at it."

She showed him the Confidential Memo and he held her hand. "Will you still love me if I'm not a big shot?"

"Oh hell, yeah," Ben replied, raising her hand to his lips to kiss it.

They ate in silence, nursing Dumplings, Flaming Noodle soup, and then the fish boil. Ben was clearly thinking it all through.

"What are you thinking of doing about it?" he asked at length.

"I'm going to ask to step down as MP for vague personal reasons. I don't think that they can do much if I do. My case isn't directly relevant because the formal policy changed after that. It might be a relief to just have cases to try."

"Yes, maybe we could take that long-discussed trip to Portugal?" Ben deftly slid some Lo Mein into his mouth with chopsticks.

"Before I do, I want to tell you everything that happened on my way to making partner."

"Courtney, I'd really prefer if you didn't." He held her hand and looked her in the eye. "I trust you completely. And you've told me that all of that is behind you."

"It is, Ben." She heard her voice crack. "I swear."

"That's good enough for me," Ben said. "Let's go home and fuck like banshees."

"Sounds like a plan." She kissed him. Then she added, "I love you, Ben."

"Love you too, Court."

Chapter Twenty-Nine

Old and New Acquaintances

The tiny Duluth International Airport was calm and almost deserted. There were just a couple of people in the arrival lounge. Jason was nervously pacing the lobby, waiting for Camille's late flight. Camille had managed to catch a direct flight from LA to Chicago and then into Duluth.

It was still hard to believe that they were going through with this whole scheme, and it was even crazier that Camille had agreed to help them. Jason had been a little tipsy when he first agreed to the boat plan. Camille had quickly agreed to join him.

"I could do it," she'd said. "I still have a ton of dog tranquilizer samples."

"It might be a crime," Jason countered. "Criminal trespassing or even felony animal abuse for endangering the guard dogs."

"It wouldn't be the first time that I was arrested for doing what I thought was right."

"Really?"

"Criminal trespass and I are old acquaintances, though animal abuse would be new for this vet school dropout." Camille was so matter-of-fact about everything. That was one of the things he had already come to love about her. "There was this pipeline thing."

The flight was scheduled to arrive at ten, but it was ten-fifteen by the time the plane landed. Jason's heart fluttered upon seeing Camille in an enormous green parka that made her look like a Packer fan at Lambeau Field in January. She was chatting with an older woman who smiled at him.

They embraced through the layers. Camille shivered. Jason thanked her for coming. "Are you feeling any better about all of this?" she asked.

"So long as we don't drown, the worst thing that could happen is that I lose my law license. Not that I've used it that much lately anyway." They made their way toward the baggage claim. "Did you have any problems with the knockout drugs?"

"I'll feel better when my bag comes through." Her flirty little smirk was just then coming into view. "It kind of took me back to my days smuggling coke from Bolivia."

"You are kidding, aren't you?" he asked.

"Hah, had you for a minute boyfriend!"

She'd started calling him that after the third time they'd made love. It was strange that she was so sure of herself, of his love. Strange especially that she was right. They had the chemistry of confidence.

"Tomorrow night has pretty calm winds," Jason reported.

"Great. My return is booked for Thursday afternoon, so let's hope tomorrow or Tuesday works."

Her bag arrived on the baggage cart with no problem. They had dinner and a couple of glasses of wine. Then they went back to their room. It was oddly intimate and touching to share the hotel room with Camille. Their first time out as a couple.

The woman getting into their king bed occupied so much of his thoughts, yet they'd been together so little. She was so new and yet so familiar. Camille slid under the covers in her sensible, matching white bra and underwear.

"Get over here," she said, throwing off her bra. I've missed you."

Camille was so direct and unpretentious. Confident and genuine. How he'd ached for her.

"Do you have any idea how much I'm in love with you?"

"Yes, I'm in love with you, too," she said, taking off her pants.

Chapter Thirty

A Fool's Errand

Driving across the barren February hills of western Wisconsin, Grace regretted following Jason and Earl's dumb plan to gather the unsprayed coal samples. She hadn't slept well. Her Fitbit had charitably given her a sixty-two score for three hours and forty-six minutes of sleep. Now she was biting her nails with one hand and driving with the other, an unbecoming skill she'd mastered after Jon's accident.

What if Jason and Camille were discovered out on the island? It was criminal trespassing, for sure. An overzealous prosecutor could even charge them with theft for a few hunks of coal. It would depend on the judge and prosecutor how hard they came down on her and Tim as the lookouts. Maybe even some kind of criminal conspiracy?

But one thing was clear. Grace and Tim would likely both lose their law licenses. Twenty-five years of skills they would have lost. They were both still in their prime, while Jason had stopped practicing law after Tara's death.

Grace felt guilty that Tim hadn't wanted to do any of this but had graciously deferred to her and Jason. It might all be for naught if they couldn't get the samples into evidence. She heard her mom's voice. It was *a fool's errand*. Grace thought of her attorney mentor, Uncle Ray, too.

For Ray, ethics trumped everything. He kept a handwritten list of sandbaggers, liars, and other dishonest lawyers taped to the inside drawer of his stately walnut desk. The desk that she still used in his old office in La Crosse. Would this stunt to get evidence have landed her there, on Ray's list of sleazebag lawyers?

He had another quote taped there. Carl Sandberg. *Hear how the hearse horse snickers/Hauling away another lawyer.*

Grace arrived at Tim's big, redbrick house by midafternoon. He seemed pretty wired up and was pacing in the driveway as she pulled in.

"You're right on time, Grace." He managed a smile. "I've got the trailer all loaded."

"How far is Lake Superior again?"

"About two and a half hours."

"Think I better use your bathroom," Grace said.

She'd never been inside his house. She liked the stylish artwork on his walls, an eclectic mix of abstract and nature scenes. Mostly blue and earth tones. His bathroom was an attractive gray and spotlessly clean. Tim had always had good taste.

Would she ever spend the night here? It seemed to be inevitable. But she appreciated how he allowed her the space to make any first move.

"Would you like a cup of coffee or water to go?" Tim asked.

She shook her head. "I've got my water bottle and am already buzzed."

"Are you ready to head out?"

She got into his Jeep with the boat trailer behind them. He'd already backed it out and onto the street. As they made it to the interstate, she noticed that people were giving them looks. Yes, it was a mild winter even this far north, but going out in a boat at this time of the year? She texted Jason to let him know that they were running about ten minutes late.

"How are you feeling about all of this?" Tim asked. "Any second thoughts?"

"Second and third and fourth thoughts." She told him about her uncle's list of sandbaggers and other untrustworthy lawyers. And Sandberg's hearse horse. "He would be disappointed with me."

"No, he'd have lots of respect for you, same as I do."

"Even with this?"

"We're doing it for a reason. We're trying to catch the coal plant in a lie that hurts kids and the planet."

"I know, but still. Part of me wishes you hadn't offered your boat."

They drove quietly together for another hour. The sunny day and rolling hills were surprisingly cheerful and discordant. Finally, Tim looked toward her and spoke.

"Look, Grace, we don't have to do this."

"I know, but it kind of looks like we are," Grace replied. "There's a large boat on your trailer in February in northern Wisconsin."

"I was thinking that we could feign engine trouble and keep a distant lookout from the shore. Let Earl, Jason, and his new girlfriend take the risk. They don't care about their law licenses the way that we do."

"Your boat is better suited for Lake Superior."

"I know. Earl's boat is only eighteen feet."

"And we promised them," Grace said. She wanted to just go home. Why was she arguing with him?

"We did promise, and I'm grateful for all of them helping. We're lucky that Camille was a vet school dropout."

"Yes." The name of Jason's girlfriend irritated her, but Tim was right. "And that she held on to drugs for the dogs."

"I don't think we would lose our licenses if we were on the shore. Though you're right; the boat itself is kind of incriminating."

They both laughed. As they got closer to Superior, Grace got more and more worried. This was all kind of nuts. There had to be another way.

"You know what I keep coming back to?" she asked. "What if we could prove the lack of spraying some other way?"

"Sure, but how?"

"What if we sent up a little drone to film a couple of days

of what and how they spray?"

"Could we get that into evidence if we did it surreptitiously?"

"Maybe." Probably not. It would be hard to establish a foundation. "I think it's worth a shot." Just then, a loud siren and lights sounded.

"Shit, it's a cop pulling us over," Tim said.

The flashing red light was not passing. This cop was for them. After Tim pulled over, the cop swerved in front of them. It was a local sheriff's deputy.

"It will be okay." She was talking to her racing heart as much as Tim. "We haven't done anything wrong."

"I know." Tim nodded as he reached for his wallet. "Nothing wrong with taking my boat to my brother's place up north."

"Evening, folks. You've got a trailer light out." The young deputy was tall and thin with close-cropped hair under his absurdly broad hat. "Can I see some identification?"

Tim's hand was trembling slightly as he handed over his license.

"Where are you going with a boat this time of year?" the cop asked.

"Just running it up to my brother's cabin."

"Big boat, it's a beauty," the deputy said. "I'll be right back."

She reached for Tim's hand. It was equally sweaty. Grace felt her gut churning. If they got out of this, she wouldn't go to Lake Superior City.

Meanwhile, they waited.

"What's taking so long?" Tim asked. "I've never even had a speeding ticket."

At last, the young policeman made his way back toward them. "You checked out okay." He handed Tim a small piece of paper. "I'm just going to give you a warning."

"Thanks, officer." Grace thanked him, too.

"How far is your brother's place?" the cop asked.

"Just another forty-five minutes up the road."

"Try to get it up there before dark. You're a hazard." He left and walked back to his car.

When they'd seen the cop leave, Grace leaned over to Tim and kissed him. Then she whispered. "I didn't know that you had a brother."

"I don't," Tim replied, kissing her back. "There's a rest stop in a couple of miles. Do you want me to pull in there?"

Yes, yes, yes. They pulled in and kissed some more and both got out to go to the bathroom. On the way back to the car, Grace texted Jason.

"We're not coming. Cop stopped us. Should be okay. More later."

"To be honest, I'm really relieved," Tim said. "I was scared to death of losing my license."

"Me, too. We're so much alike."

They drove back in silence, holding clammy hands. When they got to Tim's house, she put her arms around him and held him close. She kissed him and felt a tinge of guilt, both for kissing Tim and for bailing on Jason. But Jason had cheated on her and then dumped her. It was time to let go. Her new life was starting tonight.

"Would you mind if I stayed the night at your place?" She was holding him close, and it felt right. "I can't drive back over those hills again tonight."

"Is that the only reason you want to stay, Grace?"

"No, I'm hoping to spend the night in your arms."

"I thought you'd never ask." Tim held her close and kissed her neck in the way that she remembered.

Chapter Thirty-One

No More Kumbaya

Jason and Camille had an early dinner at a pizza place near Fitgers, where they quickly consumed a Pizza Margherita and a couple of cans of Pellegrino. Then they returned to their hotel room and changed into their black O'Neil wetsuits and insulated windbreakers. They added a couple more wintery layers, both because of the cold and in case they did get bitten by a dog. They also had recently purchased rain boots that were just short of hip waders.

"It's going to be a trip walking on the coal pile in these boots," Jason said, as he adjusted his. "Are you ready, Sue?" Camille and Jason had given each other code names in case they were observed or overheard. Tommy and Sue. The code for Earl was just 911 and to not use his name.

"Yes, Tommy, I've already put the meeting site into my fully charged phone," Camille said as they made their way to Jason's car. "And I've got the knock-out drugs, too."

There was very little traffic as they made their way over the Bong Memorial Bridge from Duluth to Superior and on to nearby Lake Superior City. The boat launch site they'd chosen was just a dead-end street in the industrial section near the water. Earl was already there, pacing along the shore when they arrived. A lion in a cage. Hard to imagine him in prison for two years.

"You're late," Earl said by way of greeting.

"Jesus, Earl," Jason replied, looking at his phone. "We're five minutes early."

Earl made a show of looking at his own phone. "Oh, so you are. Who's this?"

"Earl, this is Camille," Jason said. "Camille, this is the guy who tried to bribe me."

"Ouch." Earl made his way into the driver's seat. "But enough chitchat, let's get going, folks. And Camille—be careful with this guy—you're the third woman he's been with just since I've known him."

Camille laughed. "Thanks, Earl. But I know all about Tara and Grace." She and Jason made their way into the boat. "And his ex-wife Madeline and you and Courtney, for that matter. But I appreciate the heads-up!"

"You Unitarians are always singing 'Kumbaya.'" Earl smiled as he started up the engine. "But feel free to say a little prayer for us out there; these waves aren't fucking around tonight. I love my little Mercury, but she wasn't built for the Big Lake."

Jason took in the rocking boat and the white-crested black waves. In his black hooded raincoat, Big Earl looked impressively confident at the helm. "Does Betty know what you're up to tonight, Earl?"

"Kinda, sorta, nada," Earl admitted.

"Well, thanks for doing this, anyway," Camille said.

"We're all a little crazy, aren't we?" Earl replied, as the little boat swayed in the giant lake's waves. "I pulled up my retractable cabin-thing tonight. Feel free to join me up here if you start to get wet."

"Thanks, we will, Earl."

"I'm going to go out with the running lights only," Earl said. "Have you heard from our mothership?"

Jason checked his phone. "Nothing from Grace. About an hour ago, she said that they might be a little late."

"Do we need them before we head out?" Earl asked. "We're kind of conspicuous out here putting in a boat in the dark in February. It will take us about fifteen minutes to get out to the cove."

The plan was to meet up with Tim and Grace in a protected cove that didn't have access from land and then to switch captains and crew. Tim's bigger boat would be better for going out farther on the lake. Earl was to pilot Tim's boat out to the island, while Grace looked out from shore and Tim served as sentry from Earl's boat. Tim would also draw any patrol boat to him if it came to that.

"I guess not, let's head over to the cove," Jason said. "Grace is usually pretty punctual." She was very reliable, and almost a little anal about time sometimes. "A little late" probably meant five or ten minutes, at most. It wouldn't matter so long as they were there before they reached the island. "Go ahead, captain. We'll be less conspicuous there."

It was a very black night. The small boat was doing a constant shimmy, interrupted only by the occasional large black-and-white wave that nearly overtopped them. The little light on Earl's Mercury was also getting rocked in the crashing waves, sending its beam in crazed directions.

"Reminds me of the *Blair Witch Project*," Camille whispered to Jason.

"Think I'd take a witch over those attack dogs," Jason whispered back.

"I'll take care of the dogs, I promise. Your job is to get samples from the unsprayed pile," Camille said, shivering as she did. "It's chilly," she added.

"Freezing." Jason had checked the weather before they'd left the shore. It was a balmy thirty-three F. But out on the water, the wind was cold and searing, as though clothes and air and skin were all at the exact moment of freezing. "I'm glad we thought of the wetsuits."

"Yeah, come up here with me, you two," Earl called. "I paid extra for this little convertible cabin. It's noisy but probably a little warmer."

They did. The wind was noisier but not quite as searing behind the screen. All three of them now had their black ski masks on. Huddling around the tiny cabin, they looked like figures from a seventies heist picture. Another little light seemed to be swaying toward them.

"I wonder if that's Tim and Grace?" Jason wondered, loudly enough for Earl to hear over the engine and thumping of the waves.

"If it is, tell them to come straight here," Earl replied. He was all focus and brute strength, trying to keep his boat on course toward the cove.

"Yes, and when they get to the cove, have them kill their lights," Camille added.

"Another smart one you've got there, Jason. And you better hope that she knows something about attack dogs, too. Tell us your plan, Dr. Camille. Do you have that tranquilizer pistol?"

"Yes, but only as a last resort."

"She's figured out a way to deliver it a little more humanely."

"Let's hope," Camille said. "I've got a couple of tricks that trainers use to get the dogs to chill. And I've got both a syringe and the Tranq Gun full of Xylazine. I'm more worried about the waves than the dogs."

"I can handle the waves if you can handle the dogs," Earl said calmly.

Seeing him up close, Jason couldn't help but be impressed with the guy he'd always seen as a blustering ass.

"Thank you for doing this, Earl," Jason shouted. "Really, thanks a lot."

"You bet. But how about also saying this?" Earl yelled. "That sometimes doing the right thing isn't so black and white."

"Of course not, there's lots of gray," Jason replied as he patted Earl on the shoulder. Just then, the light went off in a different direction, a turn too sharp for these waves. "I think that that was a car from shore and not them." Jason looked at his phone. There was a text from Grace.

"OMG, slow down, Earl, they're bailing on us!"

"What the fuck?" Earl cried, slowing the boat to a crawl.

Jason read the text as the waves slapped against the sides of Earl's fishing boat. It sounded exactly like the Big Lake was spanking them for daring to be out on its waters at night.

"They're talking about getting footage from a drone instead."

"Jesus Hannah Christ, those fuckers tricked me!" Earl fumed. "I bet this whole two boats thing was a ruse."

"Maybe," Jason answered. That part of the plan had been Tim's idea.

"What do you want me to do? We're about two hundred yards from shore!"

"What do you want to do, Earl?" Camile asked. She was impressively clear-headed, too.

"I think we should fucking go for it! On to the coal island!" Earl shouted. "But it's your call, Jason."

"I don't know." Jason was too pissed off at Grace and Tim to think. "Mostly I'm just ticked at those two goodie-goodies."

"Welcome to my world, Judge Jason."

"Camille?"

"Those two had more at risk, but it's not the end of the world for any of us even if we get caught, is it?"

"You know, guys, for the record, I just got off Extended Supervision—" Earl began.

"What they used to call parole," Jason added, stalling.

"About two weeks ago."

Was Jason the only one who thought that they should call this thing off?

"I admit I'm conflicted," Jason said. Was he doing exactly what he'd done with Tara's death, just avoiding a decision and letting events take their course? He didn't want to be responsible for the others. "Earl has the most at stake; I think it's his call."

"We're going to go grab some coal samples," Earl cried, revving the motor a bit.

"No more Kumbaya!" Camille shouted.

Earl turned the boat around back toward the mountain of coal. It was freezing even in the cabin on the way out in the open water. As the waves rocked them, Jason and Camille huddled together for warmth. They were planning to tie up briefly and then let Earl know when to come back for the pickup.

Soon they were only a couple hundred yards from shore. Earl killed the lights, and the motor, too. Was there a surveillance camera anywhere nearby? It seemed unlikely and wasn't in any of the plant drawings that the company had disclosed as part of trial discovery.

Earl got them as close to shore as possible. Camille and then Jason stepped gingerly off the bouncing boat to the shore. Their boots were just high enough to keep them dry. When they'd made it safely to the island, Jason called out to Earl. "Please stay glued to your phone in case we need you."

"I will. And you know what it's like out here," Earl whispered. "Get the dogs, get the coal, and get your ass back to the boat."

No lights came on, and no dogs were seen. They had landed, as planned, at the corner they thought was the edge of the unsprayed part of the coal pile. The air, even at night, was full of black dust. He'd been reading about coal for months, but now here was the filthy stuff itself. A million-ton mountain of it. The ski mask kept some of it out and some of it in their mouth and eyes. They should have remembered the N-95 masks. Jason could see his breath in the chilly night air as he slip-slided up the hill in the bulky rain boots.

Jason's father often talked about the sight and smell of black coal dust on fresh snow, as everyone used coal for heat when he'd grown up in La Crosse. Lots of the old houses had basement doors where the coal would be dumped.

"Let's hope that the dogs are sleeping," Camille called. Her flashlight flickered ahead. "Our scent might wake them up, though. Dogs can smell stressed humans."

He'd read everything from the Pope's climate Encyclical to a left-wing book about how indispensable coal was to the rise of capitalism. The English King Edward had banned coal because of the soot in the Thirteen Hundreds, but steam power brought it roaring back. In the 1950s, coal-infused bad weather had killed 4000 Londoners, fifty in one park alone, and helped sweep Churchill out of office after he'd led the defeat of Hitler.

"It's like we're miners from a century or two ago," Camille observed.

"It's our flashlights," Jason replied. Their lights on the sprawling coal pile made him think of miner hats and mine collapses and Black Lung deaths in Appalachia and around the world over the centuries. And recently. So many deaths from greedy owners who skirted mine safety regulations.

Both the Pope and the Marxists agreed: this pile was still here, seven hundred years after it had been banned for being a poison, because of the greed of a few. It was the same with this pile and little Lacy, who spent so much time at the ER because she lived three blocks from here.

"The stuff is just so nasty," Jason whispered. "We're right to try to slow it down even a little."

"Of course we are. That's why we're here," Camille replied.

"I'm going to climb over that pile over there and grab a couple of handfuls, and we can be on our way, dear Sue."

"I've got your back, Tommy dear." Jason admired her resolution, and her backside in the tight-fitting wetsuit.

It was awkward filling the bag with his gloves on. The carbon in coal came from dead swamp plants, dirty pieces of death itself, Jason thought as he dug out a few handfuls. He put three or four more glovefuls in his backpack collection bag. Clouds of black dust rose even under just the moonlight.

There was no way that the bonding agent was being

applied on this section of the pile. Greed. Again.

Just then, Jason's ears perked up at the sharp sound of rapid movement over the crunching coal. Shit! Twenty yards ahead, a German Shepherd was hurtling toward Camille.

"Tommy, Tommy," Camille cried out.

The huge dog was nearly to Camille, teeth bared. Jason was farther away from her than the dog was.

"Fire, Sue, fire!"

She did, with no apparent effect. The dog was maybe ten feet away from her. Camille fired again, and the dog stumbled to the ground.

"Damn it, that might put him down past morning," she called. "And those were my only two Tranquilizer Darts. We still have two syringes, though."

"That was terrifying. Let's get the hell out of here." Camille's hands were shaking as they each filled a bag of coal samples. Black dust had gotten through the ski mask and was burning his eyes. "For the record, I love you," Jason said.

"Same here," she said, blowing him a kiss. She shook her head. "Damn, that was a little too close for comfort."

This was all crazy. And what if the samples were really all the same? What if all of this was for nothing?

They started trotting awkwardly over the slippery coal hill back toward Earl. It was pitch dark but for the slightest sliver of moonlight. The coal crunched eerily under their feet: a sound he knew he would never forget.

"Hard to run on this stuff," Camille said. "But there's the boat up ahead!"

Jason slipped and fell to his knees. As he was getting back up, he glanced over his shoulder and saw a streaking shadow. He directed his flashlight toward the sound. Another large dog was charging straight toward Camille.

"Help! Grab the syringe from my bag!"

The dog had knocked Camille down and was mauling her

arms and upper legs above her boots. She'd gone into a protective fetal position with her arms over her head. Jason stumbled toward her and kicked the dog in the head with all his strength. Still, it held on fiercely to Camille's leg and thigh. Jason fumbled in her bag for the syringes.

"Stick them in his shoulder!" she cried.

He did, and then put the second syringe into the other shoulder. The dog gradually let loose of Camille's leg and slid off her. Jason put the flashlight on Camille and caught sight of the gaping wound on her thigh. The cut was savagely jagged and appeared to be nearly down to the bone.

"Can you walk?"

"I'm not sure. But thanks for saving my life!" He helped her up, but she fell immediately back down. "I can't seem to put any weight on it!"

Camille's words were slurred, and soon she'd passed out.

Jason took off his jacket and made a tight tourniquet with his hoodie windbreaker. Would it hold? Even in the dark, it was clear that Camille had been severely mauled. He was shivering uncontrollably as he texted Earl, "Come onto the island, S attacked and I need your help."

Jason held her hand for a second. Then he started gently sliding her limp body down the pile, praying for the first time since Tara had died.

Chapter Thirty-Two

Surfing in the Dark

Storms came up fast on Superior. Earl had even seen a distant flash of lightning. The waves were crashing with increasing violence and frequency. The little boat was like a tiny surfboard on the big lake. Earl was too old to surf, and his left arm was getting wet from the spray. Thankfully, his raincoat was keeping him mostly dry.

But it was fucking cold. The night sky was dark and foreboding. What the hell had he been thinking, surfing the angry lake in the middle of the night on an eighteen-foot fishing boat? Had those other two tricked him? Were they ever really planning to come?

The whole two boats thing had been Tim's idea. Grace was to be a lookout from shore and then Tim was going to pilot Earl's boat nearer to shore and alert the others or be a diversion if the Coast Guard was on patrol. But was all that just a bunch of bull? Earl felt like he'd been played.

Driving north this morning, Earl was feeling excited about this edgy adventure. He'd listened to Springsteen at nearly full-blast, *Fire* and *Dancing in the Dark*. He also felt proud and happy about the opportunity to do some good.

But now those feelings seemed ridiculous. Vainglorious, in the way of sappy young liberals. This was a walleye-trolling boat, not an espionage vessel. He was glad to be done with his legal career. Why was he trying to salvage it now?

When Earl was in law school, students used to say that the people who got As would become professors, those who got Bs would end up judges, and everyone else would be the ones who made all the money. But, somewhere along the line, the big firms (mostly out of snobbery) decided that they only wanted to hire A students. People with limited good sense, a bunch of neurotic professor-types, now ran the most celebrated firms. Earl, a judge-plus law student, never quite fit in.

Then came the gambling debts that had let Tommy C steal six years of his life. What a waste! He'd been forced to use his talents for evil, pure and simple. In prison, Father Jacob used to say, *It wasn't why you did stuff; it was what you did that mattered.* At the time Earl had replied that that was a bridge too Catholic for him, but now it made more sense.

Whatever his motivation, what he was doing was stupid, illegal, and dangerous. Especially for him. For God's sake, he was barely off paper!

Betty would just now be snuggling into their cozy white bed with her book. It was so simple with her. They loved each other, did their best and forgave each other when either of them messed up. Even before he proposed, they'd planned to stay together unless one of them did something *egregious.* It was Betty's term, and though he knew it mostly applied to her fears about him, he embraced that idea from the start.

Was this something egregious? Could she forgive Earl's lies, even in the name of recovering his desire to do good? His phone was on silent, but now it was rumbling in his pocket.

"Yeah, what's up?"

"A dog attacked Sue!" Jason sounded rattled. "I need your help to get her aboard. I just texted you!"

"Sorry. On my way, turn on your phone's flashlight to show me where you are."

Earl held the boat steady through the choppy waters. He had to tie up and get to shore and struggle his way to shore in his hip-waders. Thank God he'd thought to wear them.

When he was maybe ten yards from shore, Earl threw the boat's anchor down. It yanked like an angry dog on a leash as he waded up to the shoreline. The clumsy, squeaking waders kept him dry.

At first, he couldn't see any light against the mountain of coal. Where the hell were they? At last, he saw a flickering off to his right. He put his own light toward it. Camille was at the bottom of a large pile and Jason was above her, tightening a tourniquet he'd fashioned with his jacket.

"Over here! We've got to hurry in case there's another dog out there. We put two of them down."

Earl made his way to Camille. "Jesus, she's out cold," he noted. Then he went over to one of the dogs and put his hand on it to check its breathing. The dog raised its head long enough to bite his hand. "We've got to hurry. The damn dog came to and just took out a piece of my hand."

Earl picked up Camille's legs as Jason held her head and shoulders. Dead weight.

"She's pretty light," Earl said. He stumbled on the crumbling surface but didn't drop Camille.

"Now I really owe you."

"This is where we could have used the bigger boat and a couple more hands."

"Maybe they were right all along?"

"It doesn't matter now," Earl replied.

They made their way to the shore and walked through the waves to lean Camille gently into the boat. She was out cold. Jason ran back for the two bags of coal samples and threw them and himself into the jerking boat. Earl pulled up the anchor and started off in the tiny boat across the choppy black sea.

"Where am I heading?"

"Right back to my car on Seventh Street." Jason was cradling Camille in his arms, trying to protect her from the waves.

"Got it!" Earl shouted. "Is she okay?"

"I think so. I'm wondering if I should take her to the ER here or try to make it to another town."

"Good thinking. Even Duluth might be a little risky."

Earl heard Camille's faint voice over the sound of the waves.

"What did she say?"

"She said, 'Don't risk it.' But we'll see when we get her to the car."

When the bumpy ride finally ended, Earl discreetly tied up where the boat would be hard to see. Camille was mostly conscious and only that wound on her thigh seemed seriously deep. He helped Jason carry-walk Camille to their car, and then headed out.

"None of this ever happened," Earl said. "I'll get the coal samples to Grace and Tim. Good luck!"

"Thank you, Earl," Camille whispered.

"Yeah, thanks, man. I'll check in when we get her to a hospital."

"How far is Minneapolis?" Camille called.

"Probably too far," Earl said, heading out. "Take care of her! At least we got the damn samples!" He was relieved to be on his way back to Betty, back where he belonged.

Chapter Thirty-Three

Why Were We in Minneapolis?

Jason pulled open the wetsuit and carefully looked over Camille's wounds. The bleeding on her thigh had slowed, although his windbreaker was fully saturated. He removed his T-shirt, which was still dry, and tied that around the makeshift tourniquet to reinforce it. The dog had also made gashes on her face and arm that would need stitches. She'd been mostly conscious on their way here, and only that wound on her thigh seemed seriously deep.

"Can you feel your fingers, honey?"

"Yes." She held up her fingers and wiggled them all. "And they still seem to work. I feel better but a little woozy. I may have gotten some of the tranquilizer from the dog's drool. Thought for a minute that he'd severed my femoral artery. But I'd probably be dead by now if he had."

"How about your toes? Can you feel them?"

"Some of them."

"On the left side?"

She shook her head. Her face was a pale porcelain. Almost translucent. He could see her blue veins. Tara had had that same ungodly white pallor the last time he'd gone to see her in the hospital.

"Duluth is just over the bridge."

"Jason, that's not going to work. You must drive me to a hospital farther away, or it will be in all the local papers, and we'll be busted." She was very firm. "You'll lose your license, and I could lose my job, too. How far is Minneapolis?"

"Two hours. Minimum."

"Let's check out of the hotel. I have some amoxicillin tablets and wound wash antiseptic in my bag."

"Let's just go on to Saint Luke's in Duluth, Camille."

"No, dammit! I want this to have been for something. If you wash me out and give me amoxicillin, it won't make any difference other than if I start bleeding out. If I start to bleed heavily again, forget washing out the wound and tie the tourniquet even tighter. Either way, give me two amoxicillin pills. Got it?"

"Yes," Jason said, turning around. Camille managed a little smile. "You're sure?"

"Yes."

Jason ran into the hotel and grabbed a cart to put their bags on. In the room, he threw her things back into her bag and then dumped his own stuff frantically into his large suitcase. The drug supplies were in her backpack, which he put on top. He grabbed a couple of bath towels and hurried out. He almost ran into a guy from the hotel in the hallway.

"Checking in or out?" the guy asked.

"Checking out; something came up unexpectedly."

"Good luck!"

Camille was still awake and stretched out in the backseat. Jason handed her a bottled water for her to take the antibiotics and a Tylenol. She was looking at her face in his rearview mirror. "I think I'm going to need a plastic surgeon, so I'm glad we're going to Saint Paul. Really, I don't think I'm at any serious risk of bleeding out. Wash me out with the antiseptic."

"Are you sure?"

"Yes," Camille replied. "And, by the way, thanks for saving my life."

Jason managed to get the wetsuit off Camille and then very slowly opened a small patch of the windbreaker tourniquet. The wound was scary deep, but the bleeding was mainly staunched. There was just a little blood oozing from the top. She flinched a bit as he doused successive small areas with the antiseptic wash. It was meant to repair skin, too, but the gash on her thigh was too deep. Then he used the hotel hand towels as a fresh tourniquet and wrapped that tightly with the larger bath towels.

"Twin Cities, next. That's the only way this makes any sense."

"Violence never makes sense," Jason said, turning the car back around. "Even from a dog trained by humans."

"The dog was frustrated by my wetsuit and bit me way too deeply. He kind of ripped at it and jerked his head. I'm pretty sure he wasn't trained to kill," Camile said, looking at Jason's efforts on her leg and face. "Good job, nurse. Now drive me to the first hospital in the Cities. Drive fast."

Jason had his Google Maps on the phone and entered hospitals in Minneapolis/St Paul. "Midwest American Hospital, St. Paul, here we come."

"Good boy. One more thing. What's our story?"

"How did this happen? Why were we in Minneapolis?"

"You've always wanted to go to the theater there."

"What's it called?"

"The Guthrie."

"I'll try to remember."

Jason drove at about seventy-five miles an hour to get to I-35 and then drove eighty-five once he made it on the freeway. Camille had fallen asleep and was purring in her regular sleep pattern. Google Maps had said two hours and eleven minutes, but he made it in an hour forty-five.

Jason gently shook Camille awake and helped her out of the car. As they hit the Midwest American Emergency Room, she was able to lift herself into the wheelchair. He wheeled her through the big doors and was greeted by a skeptical male clerk.

"This is urgent; she was attacked by a vicious dog."

"Uh-huh, so a strange dog came up to you two and mauled her, and you're fine?"

"He kicked him off," Camille shouted. "Look, I'm a veterinarian, and I know that I could go into septic shock if the dog hit an artery, so would you please stop harassing the boyfriend who saved me and get me a fucking doctor ASAP!"

The receptionist left to get someone.

"Wow, that was impressive."

"Not very Reverend-like?"

Camille tried to smile, with faint success.

"Was that true about sepsis?"

She nodded. "I'm glad I had those amoxicillin pills."

A young intern came to Camille's aid and told Jason to put on a mask and gown. But then she waved him back in after seeing the wounds. "It's definitely a dog bite. What kind?"

"German Shepherd, like a trained guard dog."

"Before she passed out, she said that you made the tourniquet and gave her three amoxicillin tablets—"

"Yes."

"Good thing," the young doctor said, shaking her head. "If she makes it, that will be why."

"If?" Jason asked.

"Her color. Maybe a sign of liver failure, or not," the young doctor said. "Could be from septic shock. You're going to have to leave."

"How will I keep track of her?"

"Give the desk nurse your cellphone number," the nurse replied.

"Where is the desk nurse?"

"Who knows? Probably called into action. The sky is falling around here." She motioned to the room full of coughing and injured people waiting to be seen. "Bad time for a dog bite."

Jason got up and looked for the desk nurse, not entirely sure who she was. There was some kind of argument going on between two people who wanted to be patients. *I was here first, motherfucker. You waited too long.* Then the charge nurse found him.

"Just give me your cell, I will let you know how the sepsis test turns out and of any changes in vitals."

Now Jason was out on the deserted snowy streets of Saint Paul, walking, wondering what to do next. What could he tell her parents? And dear Micah?

Could he find their numbers to contact them? Should he wait a day until she'd improved? He would have asked her. Unlike him, she would have known what to do.

Chapter Thirty-Four

Big Lake Troubles

After dropping off Jason and Camille, Earl struggled to get the Mercury on the trailer by himself in the dark. Something was messed up with the hoist. He'd also managed to lose a glove. Earl finally brute-lifted the Keeper up and got it securely on the trailer, though he wrenched his lower back in doing so. It was just what he needed before a two-hour drive.

The whole night hadn't gone well, though it wasn't a complete disaster. Camille was lucky to be alive, assuming that she was still alive. They'd managed to get the samples, which Earl was pretty sure would be unsprayed. His right hand was itching from where the dog had nipped him as he started mulling over his whole life driving home toward Blue Lake.

Ruminating, they'd called it in prison. He was a fuck up. It didn't seem to matter if he was doing it to stay alive or to try to do good. Why did he keep messing up?

His prison priest had said that the key to solving his problems was to focus on solutions rather than the causes or consequences of them. But what was the solution to his Big Lake troubles? More time in prison? He hadn't really done anything all that bad.

It was after midnight when he finally pulled into his garage. The lights came on in the house. Damn, he'd woken Betty up.

"Earl Stanley Franks, what the hell's going on?" she shouted. Ticked off. "I wasn't expecting you until tomorrow afternoon."

"They're not going to need me or the boat tomorrow, after all," he said.

"Oh, it's not that Courtney talked you out of it?" Her eyes were blinking.

Aww, she was still a little jealous. "No, of course not, Betty. I wrenched my back a little getting the boat on the trailer and just wanted to get back here and sleep in my own bed. With you."

"Okay." Her face softened. God, how he loved it when the ferocity drained out of Betty's face. Pushing seventy, she still looked so young and innocent when she was content. "I'll be waiting for you in our bed."

"I told them I'd text when I got home, so I'll be right in, honey child."

Earl had a text from Jason: *Sue admitted to Midwest American Hospital St. Paul. Stable. Possible sepsis infection. Dog bite from the street, unknown dog. We came here to see a play. I can't help you guys for at least a few days. Good luck, and just go forward with things as we planned. Keep her in your thoughts. Best, T*

Sepsis? Earl looked down at his hand. Just a minor scratch, but he better go wash it out. He went into the bathroom, washed his hands with Betty's anti-bacterial Dial soap, took a Tylenol, and then went into the steam shower and ran hot water on his back. Then, for good measure, he put a bunch of Neosporin on his scratchy hand.

Before getting in bed, he remembered to text Grace about picking up the coal samples. He wasn't going to Eau Claire to deliver it to those two pikers. She or Tim would have to come over to get them. Period!

By the time he got into bed, Betty was sleeping lightly beside him. There was that gentle face again. It somehow managed to convey both her inner and outer beauty. He leaned toward her to kiss her forehead.

"I'm never doing nothing like that again, my love," he whispered.

She rolled over toward him. "Like what, Earl?"

"Like driving for hours and hauling a boat in February!"

"When I heard you out here, I was afraid that you'd lost your nerve. I would certainly understand if you had, Earl."

"That's very sweet, honey."

"You don't have to be some big hero," she said, her voice husky with sleep. "I love you and our life together, Earl."

"Me, too. Like I said, I'm ready to get out of the hero business." He sighed. "Trust me, I helped your good guys out a lot today. I'm just getting a little old for this kind of late-night adventure."

"That's great, Earl, I'm proud of you." Betty drifted back to sleep.

Earl fell asleep quickly too, and into an uneasy sleep full of troubled dreams.

He was in prison, about to be clobbered, and feeling sickened by the smell of that place as three large young men approached him. Then, he was on a boat full of snakes, tying the boat up to a dock on a deserted island. He was in a war film about the Normandy landings. There were dead and dismembered bodies just above the beach.

That one woke him up.

Earl got up to pee, tossed, and turned for an hour or two. At last, he fell asleep. He slept through the night until nine, when his phone rang.

Betty brought it to him with a cup of coffee. "Earl," she said, handing him his phone, "it's Grace Clarkson."

Chapter Thirty-Five

At What Cost?

Grace woke up at Tim's house in Eau Claire feeling grand. They were both delighted with themselves for pulling out of the coal sample fiasco, and it turned out that they still had plenty of chemistry. Grace was still alight in the afterglow as Tim brought her coffee just how she liked it.

"Thanks, Tim, that's really sweet."

"Last night was... Amazing Grace, how sweet your love," he sang playfully. He still had a solid and soothing voice. "I'm sure you've never heard that before."

Just once, with her late husband, Jon. "No comment, except I agree that amazing sums it up nicely. Are you still singing these days?"

"No, I can't seem to find time."

She gave him a coffee-flavored kiss and then checked her phone. She had a cryptic one-thirty a.m. text from Earl Franks. ***Got something and some news for you.*** She read it to Tim.

"Sounds like everything went well," he said.

"Let's hope." Grace sipped her coffee. "I'll call him in a bit."

She texted Earl back. ***I will call you at nine this morning.*** That gave her an hour to get up and get ready.

He picked up on the third ring.

"Hey, Earl," she said. "Did you guys get some coal samples?"

"Yes, I have them here in Blue Lake. But, more importantly, Camille got mauled badly by one of the dogs."

"Oh my God! Is she okay?" Grace asked.

"Who knows? She passed out and Jason and I had to carry her back to the boat."

Earl read her a text from Jason. Camille had been hospitalized. They were awaiting test results. "Do you know anything about sepsis?"

"That's an infection that's spread to the blood," Grace said. "It can be fatal. I wonder why they went to Saint Paul, two hours away?"

"Probably trying to keep *you* out of the local papers," Earl said, sounding pissed. "When I dropped them off, Jason was heading to Duluth. Camille's a stand-up woman. Unlike some others I know. Were you two ever going to come?"

"Yes, but when it came down to it, neither Tim nor I could go through with it." She bit her tongue and sipped her coffee instead. This convicted felon was advising her on ethics. "Especially after that cop stopped us."

"Maybe I could understand that," Earl began. "But why tell us when we're already on my damn boat out on the big lake literally like sitting ducks?"

"I'm sorry about that, Earl." He was right. It had been spineless of her to bail at the last second, even if it was the right call. "I hear you."

"We had like a minute to decide. The Rev took a mauling for the anti-coal team."

"Let's hope she'll be all right."

"Anyway, the coal samples are here if you want to come and get them."

"I'll come this afternoon. We have the official site inspection tomorrow morning at ten."

"Let's hope the samples are everything that we thought they were," Earl said. "Or this has been one hell of a wild goose chase."

"I'll be over shortly after noon."

"Get those hard-earned coal pieces into our expert's hands, first thing," Earl commended.

"We will."

Earl paused and then said, "My God, Grace, what have we done?"

"I don't know," Grace said, her voice cracking. "But hopefully she's going to be all right." No one was going to die from this permit renewal. "Did we push things too far?"

"We did. I hope we're not all found out and charged with criminal trespass and violating a shit-ton of ethical rules."

"Of course, but right now, I'm just worried about Camille." And feeling guilty for pushing Jason to stay involved in the case.

She filled Tim in on everything she'd learned. He was already googling sepsis.

Chapter Thirty-Six

Of Course She Was

Jason found a room at the downtown Saint Paul Holiday Inn. It was late, and he decided not to call Camille's parents or Micah until the morning. They would probably know more by then. He slept fitfully through terrifying dreams.

Dogs, everywhere. The coal island dogs seemed trained to take Camille down and not go for the jugular. But the dogs in his dreams went right for his neck. Their large teeth and angry eyes woke him up at least a few times. He finally got back to sleep only to be told by a nurse in a nun's habit in his dream that Camille was mortally ill from sepsis. At nine, he gave up and went down to the lobby for coffee.

Jason sat there quietly, drinking the crappy coffee and slowly waking up. Just then, his phone buzzed. He had a text from the hospital.

Negative results on sepsis test for patient #347. Vitals improving, too. Prognosis good. Come in at 10 a.m. this morning for Care Planning. Details below.

Jason refilled his coffee and practically skipped back up to his room. What a relief! He sent a group text to the Superior crew. Then the new reality again. Care plan? Would she have some long-term issues? But she was going to survive; that's all that really mattered.

Now he had to call her parents. It was still early there, but he found their number and called it. Micah answered.

"Hi, Micah, it's me." Jason's heart raced, and he realized his voice sounded funny.

"Everything okay?" Micah asked. "Where's my mom?"

"She's in the hospital in Saint Paul after getting bitten by a dog." Jason set his coffee down. He was pacing around the little hotel room.

"Is she going to be okay?" Micah asked, suddenly sounding very young.

"Yes, it looks like she will be just fine. She might have a couple of scars."

Micah let out a sigh. "Give her a hug for me, will you?"

"Of course, I will. And I'll have your mom call you later today, all right? Can I please talk to one of your grandparents?"

"Hello," a male voice said. "This is Miles Garland. Can I help you?"

Jason explained about the dog bite without going into details about how it happened. "I'll know more soon and call you, as I'm meeting with them in a couple of hours."

"Thanks so much for calling. I know that you're a lawyer; sounds like she'll have quite a lawsuit, too," Miles said.

Camille had said that her dad was something of a money-grubber. Jason decided to trust him, nonetheless. He was Camille's father.

"Actually, no, I don't think she will, Mr. Garland," Jason replied. "Please keep this to yourself, but we were actually trespassing trying to get evidence for an environmental case."

"Of course she was!" Her father even laughed. A little awkwardly. "That sounds like Camille. Give us a call when you know more."

Jason had to put on scrubs and a mask to see Camille. It was a huge relief to find her awake and sitting up on her own power. She smiled as he entered.

"You look great!" he said.

"You mean other than the gigantic bandage on my face?"

It was true, the dog had done a number on her face. "I'm so relieved there's no sepsis." He kissed her.

"I told you we could make it here."

"I called your dad and spoke to Micah."

Camille nodded her thanks. Jason had ten minutes to sit and hold hands with her before the nurse practitioner came in. There was such sweet relief in just being together. Hearing her velvety preacher's voice. She still had her sense of humor and all her faculties.

Hospitals were still a little triggering for him. But this time was different. Camille was going to be okay.

The nurse was a tall Black woman wearing a beautiful multicolored hijab. "I'm Khadijo Mar, and you, Ms. Garland, are a very lucky woman."

The nurse went over everything. There was no sign of sepsis and no fever, but Camille was going to stay one more night and continue her antibiotic drip. She'd had stitches in her arm, face, and thigh. None of these wounds in themselves appeared to be deadly. They'd done x-rays of the wound sites to make sure there were no foreign substances in them. She'd also received half a dozen rabies shots; she'd need three more rabies shots over the course of the next two weeks. It might get black and blue around that area.

"You're a very lucky woman. The dog came within five centimeters of your femoral artery. Just a couple of inches and you would have bled out. But you're going to need to clean and monitor all three wounds over the next few weeks. I probably shouldn't say this, but another way that you were lucky was that we had a plastic surgeon here last night, and he's one of the very best around. If everything stays on its current course, we plan to release you tomorrow at noon. Let's go over the care plan."

The care plan was just about the drains and bandages, keeping her wounds clean, the rabies shots, and considering getting some mental health treatment.

"Can she fly home the day after that?" Jason asked. "She's

got some people in California who will be very glad to see her."

"Yes, I don't see any reason why not."

Camille was going to be okay.

Chapter Thirty-Seven

Two Very Sleepy Guard Dogs

Courtney was in the Billing Zone. She'd worked straight through from seven a.m. to twelve-thirty with no calls, then finally stopped to go to the lady's room. She came back and was pulling out her lunch—Tupperware full of last night's Greek salad and a can of lime-flavored fizzy water—when her phone rang.

"Good afternoon, Courtney." It was Mike Crew, general manager of the coal facility. An easy name to remember because the guy sported a crewcut.

"Hi, Mike," she replied, sneaking a bit of her salad.

"Look, something weird happened at the facility last night," he began. "We had two very sleepy guard dogs this morning. It's odd; they're not hungry and they're usually starving in the morning, too."

"And this concerns me how?"

"Well, do you think we should have them tested to see if someone drugged them or something unusual like that?"

"Why do I care about this as far as the case?" She took a sip of the lime water.

"Well—"

"Wait, don't answer. I asked the wrong question." She didn't want Mike to tell her if they were doing something wrong. Ignorance was defense-lawyer bliss. "Do I need to be concerned about this as far as our case is concerned?"

"Maybe," Mike answered. "Yeah, it's likely that you would."

"Then test them if you can find someone to do it, which I doubt."

Courtney called her associate, Jake, next. He came into her office with a roast beef sandwich, a pickle, and a can of Diet Coke. "Sorry, I haven't had a chance to eat lunch," he explained.

"That looks good," she observed. Especially after her salad. "Um, those guys in Superior are doing something fishy with the coal dump, and someone may have drugged their guard dogs. Any idea of what might be up?"

"It's probably the spraying issue that we've talked about." Jake took a swig of soda. "Their numbers just don't make sense in terms of how much they're spending to cover that whole mountain of coal. The opponents have asked for those figures, but we've objected that it's a confidential business issue of interest to our competitors."

"Yeah, I remembered that you were a little concerned about that," Courtney said. "See if you can find a veterinarian to test those dogs for drugs."

"I'll start making calls around the Twin Cities area." He swigged his Diet Coke.

Jake had Courtney ready when Mike Crew called back about an hour later.

"I can't find anyone to do the test, and the dogs are getting back to normal," Mike said. "Maybe I overreacted?"

"Jake got us the name of a vet in Minneapolis who will do it and who can be up there in three hours."

"How much is that going to cost?" Mike asked. He was a notorious cheapskate and guarded the company's resources like they were his life savings. Or maybe he was fudging the numbers to let him skim a bit? Whatever it was, Courtney had never trusted him.

"Probably be at least five grand," she said. "I think it was somewhere around five hundred dollars an hour."

"If they were drugged, the dogs will probably have pissed

it all out by the time the vet gets up here," Mike said. "Maybe they just ate something funky that came with a load of coal? That happened once before."

"You are there on the ground, Mike, so it's your call."

"Nah, let's not."

"Look, it doesn't prove much anyway to say that the dogs were drugged," Courtney began. "But I have another idea of how we can make sure no one's messing with you, Mike."

"Yeah, what's that?"

"I'm just thinking it through. There's a strict chain of custody on these samples that are evidence." Could it work? "So it should be just their expert who collects them tomorrow and Grace or Tim whose DNA is on them. We can do a DNA test on the coal samples if somebody tries to introduce them into court. Also, see if you can find any other evidence of people being out on the coal island."

"Such as?"

"I don't know; cigarette butts, a Coke can, or something with DNA on it. That would be a lot cheaper anyway and we'd know who was out there last night, if anyone was."

"How much cheaper?"

"More like a couple hundred bucks."

"That sounds like a great idea," Mike replied. "Let's try that."

The more she thought about it, the more Courtney became convinced that someone had been on the island and had put the dogs to sleep. Earl had a boat that he bragged about constantly. But could he really be the unlikely ringleader of the do-gooder faction? And there was Grace Clarkson, that Tim guy, and Jason Erickson. None of them would be likely to risk their law licenses for this case.

It was all probably much ado about nothing. Courtney grabbed a couple of pieces of pita and hummus and got back to work. Later that afternoon, she called Earl, and, to her surprise, he answered.

"Earl, have you decided which side you will work for?"

"Umm, yes, a long time ago," Earl said. "And it's not going to be your team, my friend."

"Score one for the polar bears."

"Look, you can make fun of the polar bears or whatever, but I know you better than you know yourself. You're not that cynical, deep down," Earl said in his confident trial lawyer's tone. He still had his chops. "You're wounded and a little bitter, and you want to get what's yours. I respect that. I always have, Court. But let me tell you, those years in prison helped me to see what it's all about, and there's a lot more out there than just getting what's yours or the thrill of the moment."

"Of course, there is," she replied. He was dead serious and partly right. "There are people. I've got someone in my life now, too. A lawyer my age."

"I'm glad to hear that, and I hope he treats you well."

"He does, Earl."

"Glad to hear it. But I'm also talking about what you do with your time. You're not some true believer in all this corporate nonsense about coal, or whatever."

"I'm just doing my job, Earl."

"Yes, but why is that your chosen job? You know what happened to me, getting sucked in by gambling debts. You told me several times that you were going to be different once you'd paid off your own debts and got yourself a place."

"That's none of your business, Earl."

"You're right; it's not. But I hope at some point that you make it yours."

"Thanks for the advice, big guy."

"You called me, not the other way around."

"You're right, Earl, I hear you. But I called to ask if you had any idea why the coal shipper's dogs were all sleepy this morning?"

"If that's a riddle, I don't get it," he fired back. "What dogs?"

"Never mind, have a nice day buddy."

Earl was a good liar, but he'd seemed genuinely baffled by her question.

Chapter Thirty-Eight

One Split-Second Decision

Earl was exhausted but couldn't get back to sleep after the calls from Grace and Courtney. He got up, drank some more coffee, and looked out at the steel-blue lake. Parts of it were open, which was a first in February. Of course, the climate was changing! It required willful blindness not to recognize it. It was probably too late to stop it entirely already, but it required all-hands-on-deck to at least try to slow it down. You had to be either a highly paid hack or a fool not to see it.

Betty came in and sat down on the leather couch beside him. "So are you going to tell me about yesterday, Earl?"

"Grab a cup of coffee and I'll tell you everything."

He spilled it all, every detail. "Oh my God, Earl," Betty exclaimed when he was done. She immediately took his hand to inspect the dog bite. "This looks a little red and swollen. I think you should get it checked honey."

"It is a little red, but it wasn't all that deep. I'll put some more Neosporin on it this morning and decide this afternoon."

"I probably shouldn't be, but I'm proud of you for trying to do what's right." Betty kissed him and then held his uninjured hand. Then she shook her head and continued. "Even if I think it was crazy to go out on your little boat on Lake Superior! Fighting off dogs! How is Jason's girlfriend, the pastor, doing?"

"No sepsis and she's being released," Earl said, relieved to have told Betty. What he'd done was not egregious. "But she might have some scars on her pretty face."

"That's too bad. She obviously thought it was a good plan, too. I'm surprised that Jason went along."

"He kind of wimped out again and made me decide after Grace and Tim backed out. I should have just called it off." He shook his head. "Your whole life can be changed from one split-second decision."

"Don't beat yourself up. Do you want me to stay home today? I have my book club meeting this afternoon."

"No, I'm fine and Grace is coming up to get those precious coal samples."

Later, Earl was enjoying a delicious, recently caught walleye sandwich out on his deck when he heard a car pull into his driveway. It was Grace. She embraced him, even though he was still not too thrilled with her. "Tell me the whole story," she said.

He told her everything that he could remember. When he'd finished, she looked at his hand. "You better go have this looked at, Earl."

"I probably will, later." He handed her the bag with the samples. "Camille may have paid for these with her face. I sure hope that they prove something."

"Me, too. It was all such a long shot. I should have just rejected the idea more firmly from the start."

"That makes all of us," Earl agreed.

When he heard Grace leave, Earl returned to the couch and pulled the throw blanket over himself. He was so glad to be home; now, all that coal stuff was behind him. He heard the Blue Lake loons wailing as he slowly drifted into a blissful nap.

Chapter Thirty-Nine

Finessing It

Grace had the illicit coal samples. She noticed dark circles around her eyes as she looked in the rearview mirror, backing out from Earl's place. Apparently, Jason and Camille were flying back to California even as Grace had the fruits of their efforts in the back of her Leaf. The bag of coal, a potential trial game-changer, was rattling around in the hatchback's rear.

Her stomach was upset, too. Guilt gurgling. What had the dog done to Camille's face? Earl's hand had looked bad enough. It was unsettling. Tim called her on the drive back.

"Have you decided yet how much you will tell our expert?" he asked.

"Not completely," Grace replied. She was leaning against it. "I'm hoping we can find a way to finesse it."

"Yes. She's sure to want to take the samples back to her lab," Tim said.

"I'm trying to figure out if there's a way that we can exchange bags without her knowing it," Grace admitted. "Frankly, I doubt it."

"Me, too. I think we must tell her, or just not even use those samples."

"We have to use them!" Grace raised her voice. "You should see the wound on Earl's hand! I'm terrified of seeing what Camille will look like. I'm feeling guilty that we waited so long to call it off."

"That was a mistake. Maybe we can get a feel for Tonya Nesbitt and see if we can trust her. We're going to have to insist that she get samples from that quadrant in either case."

"Yes, that was my thought too," Grace said, insomuch as she was thinking straight. "I've worked with her before. She's committed on the environment. A true believer."

"We'll see. I know you're down about it all. Just hang in there, honey."

"Thanks, Tim. I'll let you get back to work. We'll probably both be out of the office all day with the site inspection tomorrow."

"Meet you there tomorrow at nine."

Grace felt a little better after talking to him. She went to bed early, slept surprisingly well, and was out of her door by five a.m. sharp. She probably would have ordinarily gone up the night before if she hadn't had to drive to Blue Lake to see Earl. Now, the plan was to pick up Tim in Eau Claire and then meet with the expert at a coffee shop near the plant an hour before the official Entry Upon Land to get the samples.

"Did you have time to look into the drone idea any further?"

"Just a bit, but it was disappointing." Tim looked out the window, then back at her. "I think Wisconsin's privacy statute has been interpreted to include drone photos. Even the police need a search warrant to use them. So, we'd probably have to get an order from the ALJ to authorize it, or we couldn't get it into evidence."

"So, of course they would do everything right until the case is over. Maybe they already are and there will be no difference in the samples, and all of this will have been for naught."

"It's unfortunate, but it's really not our fault," Tim said firmly. "We've conducted ourselves professionally, and we're doing our best to win this case. I mean, what time did you have to get up this morning?"

"Four-thirty."

"See what I mean?"

She loved the way Tim smiled. It was naturally calming to be around him. He was kind and hot, too. Grace let herself be happy for the rest of the drive up.

Dr. Tonya Nesbitt, a tall brunette in her mid-thirties, was waiting for them in a booth when they pulled into the coffee shop at eight fifty-five. She had an angular face and comfortably messy hair.

Grace had worked with her before, and they greeted each other like old friends. They ordered, and Tonya pulled out her laptop. Grace noticed that she had the photo of the little girl in the breathing apparatus as a screensaver.

"Oh, poor little Lacy," Tim said.

"It's definitely pretty motivating," Tonya said. "So your suspicion is that only a small portion of the pile is actually being protected by the encrusting agents?"

"Yes, we've spent several hours watching and have never seen some areas sprayed."

"That might account for all of the air standard violations." Tonya sipped her coffee. "What are the legal niceties of getting that into evidence?"

"It's tricky because this is a permit renewal, and violations go to enforcement and not permit issues," Grace replied. She was on the verge of mentioning the bag of pilfered coal samples in her trunk but thought better of it.

"We thought of doing a drone film, but that would be hard to get into evidence absent some approval from the judge," Tim said.

"It's not uncommon for permits to get approved with important conditions that are never enforced." Tonya shook her head. "I did a case against a well-known energy company that seems to have a business strategy of just paying fines and doing whatever the hell they wanted."

"I think I know the company that you mean." Tim smiled.

"We better get going; we don't want to be late," Grace said. If she found the right opportunity, she was going to give Tonya the samples at the end of the day.

Chapter Forty

Another Bad Start

"Are you nervous about meeting my parents?" Camile asked Jason as their flight for Santa Barbara by way of Denver took off. A top Twin Cities plastic surgeon had done the stitches on Camille's face and leg and she had confidently predicted minimal scarring. But Camille's face was still a mess now, wet with cream that promoted healing.

"A little. I mean, it would probably be better if you weren't still wearing bandages from a dog attack that I talked you into."

"You didn't talk me into anything." Camille smiled and looked him in the eyes. "I volunteered, remember?" He nodded. "Now you can see why I never made it through vet school."

"I thought it was the weed?" he teased.

"That, too. By the way, I never mention that in front of either Micah or my parents."

"Of course not."

They made it to Denver just in time. The plane to Santa Barbara was surprisingly large and full. The flight went by fast. Jason was dreading meeting her parents under the circumstances. The plane began its descent. It soared out into the blue Pacific and then made the abrupt landing that the pilot had warned them about. There wasn't a lot of room between the mountains and the Pacific.

Just then, Camille leaned over to him. "I keep coming back to the idea that you and Earl saved my life," she said, holding his hand. "Thank you."

"You're welcome," Jason replied. "Thank you for not dying." Camille gripped his hand tighter.

The little airport was a tiny strip between the ocean and mountains. Those mountains in the distance called to Jason. He longed to just be out there or beside the ocean, feeling the mysterious peace that Santa Barbara always evoked in him.

Micah and the Garlands were waiting for them as they got off. There were hugs and handshakes all around. Then they all awkwardly stood waiting for the baggage cart.

"We don't have an automated baggage carousel in SB," Camille observed.

"How are you feeling, dear?" her mother, Simone, inquired.

"Pretty much normal, although some people have started to call me Scarface."

Her father had a hearty and sincere laugh.

"She's joking! She had the best plastic surgeon in Minneapolis do those stitches."

They collected their bags and then drove to Camille's tiny apartment. It was standing room only, but Jason and Miles brought some of the kitchen chairs into the living room.

"We're staying at the Canary downtown through the weekend," Miles said, as he sat down on one of the green kitchen chairs. "Maybe we can take Micah to the zoo tomorrow?"

"I'm not five," Micah scoffed. "Our zoo is pretty lame. How about the skateboard park instead?"

"We'll see," Simone said. "We mainly just want to give your mom a chance to rest. Are you planning on staying here, Jason?"

"Yes, he is," Camille said. "But only if that's all right with you, Micah."

"Of course, Mom," Micah said. "Jason's going to keep teaching me self-defense."

"Oh, I am, am I?" Jason asked.

"These guys get along great," Camille said.

But Jason noticed Simone grimace and shoot a look at Miles. Who could blame them? He was off to a bad start with them.

Chapter Forty-One

Whitefish Dunes

Earl felt relieved that the boat fiasco was behind them and glad to be off the coal case. He was done with both the law and with being a do-gooder. Fuck all that; he just wanted to spend time with Betty.

To that end, he was planning a surprise weekend trip. But where? Since they'd just been to Milwaukee, he was thinking of Madison. But then he remembered Door County, where he and Betty had first consummated their love when he was released from prison.

They'd corresponded and she'd visited him numerous times in that whole last year at Portage. Laurie had offered to pick him up the day of his release, but he told her it made sense for Betty to do it because she lived next door in Blue Lake. But Betty had surprised him with two nights at the Gordon Lodge in Bailey's Harbor. He wanted to book a couple of nights there, where they'd stayed, but it was closed in winter.

So he tried the White Gull Inn, where they'd enjoyed the classic fish boil. Bingo, it was open. He booked them a room with a fireplace in the Cliffhouse cottage. She'd probably like that romantic touch.

"Oh, Earl, that's so sweet," Betty said when he told her. "But what are we going to do in Door County in winter?"

"Our room has a fireplace, and we can bring books and get cozy."

"That sounds romantic," she said, sliding in for a kiss.

"You're right, I didn't mean to be poopy."

The sun was shining, and it was just above freezing as they set off. Earl consciously took back roads through the hills and then got them to Fish Creek just in time for lunch. Betty was literally shining with delight as they were seated at the Cookery.

Earl had been coming to Door County since he was a kid. He'd seen his first play there, a crazy piece about a chain-smoking agnostic priest who accidentally becomes Pope when the cardinals can't agree on a more conventional candidate. Despite its Midwestern wholesomeness, Earl had always associated Door County with the bohemian spirit of that play and the Peninsula Players Theater.

Growing up in a small town outside La Crosse, it had been a yearly tradition for him to spend a week with his free-wheeling Uncle Sal, who lived in Green Bay. Sal was a charming and irrepressible figure who had taught Earl not to be full of the rural fears—including fear of success—that had hamstrung his own farmer and farm-adjacent parents.

Later, Earl had spent a college summer in Egg Harbor, smoking meat all day (and marijuana by night) at a restaurant there. Things were wild in 1975. Young people from all over the Upper Midwest lived in small rooms above their various employers. He'd enjoyed a classic summer romance with a girl named Sarah from Michigan; they wrote old-fashioned US Mail letters all through the fall. Earl met her in Chicago one weekend to say a very sweet farewell. Years later, Sarah had even tracked him down, but he was recently married to Maggie.

Earl and Betty checked into their room and then set off for Cave Point County Park and the nearby sand dunes. It was a sunny day and well above freezing. Earl had no idea what the trail would be like in winter, but the only obstacle to enjoying their hike to Whitefish Dunes were the tree roots that stuck out along the path. They were both wearing hiking boots but could have been in sneakers. There was no snow.

The sun shone off the bits of ice that clung to the rock ledges. The water was mostly open and blue. Standing on the escarpment ledge, they watched the water slap between the sea cave creases. The climate was messed up when both Superior and Michigan had so much open water in late February.

The sound of the water took him back to his Superior misadventure. It had been stupid, but successful. They had the samples and Camille was on the mend and already back in California and being nursed back to health by Jason. The guilt that Grace felt about that and backing out at the last minute would make her even more dogged about winning the case. He knew the type; their righteous displays of ethics were often really a type of personal vanity; she was so much like Maggie.

"Can I take your picture, honey?" Earl asked, to change the direction of his own thoughts as much as anything else. But she was looking fine in her navy-blue puffer and Blue Lake baseball cap. Betty happily obliged and then they took one together. "Let's keep going, we're not far from the dunes."

"By the way, I didn't even know that we had sand dunes in Wisconsin." They passed the remnants of an old shipwreck; there were several out in the lake a mile or two from where they walked. "I can't believe that we have this beautiful place to ourselves," Betty added as they approached the sandy beach below the dunes.

The winter wind was surprisingly calm and warm as they walked the white beach at Whitefish Dunes.

"I love it here," he declared to Betty. "I always come away refreshed."

"Yes, I'm glad that we came. The dunes are a little scrawny, but the water is so clear!"

"Part of that is the zebra mussels. But the water is almost always clear on the Michigan side of the peninsula anyway."

"The waves are mesmerizing. Did you notice the little midsection that is bright blue?"

"Show me, Betty."

A clear wave approached. "There, there." Betty pointed. The water was like an abstract painting of horizontal lines in white, gray, green, and then this half-band of bright blue at its center.

"Oh, yes, that's lovely."

It was just like Betty to notice. She was always in the moment rather than her head. Earl took a deep breath, happy to be alive and with her here.

He got her laughing about his meat-and-marijuana summer in Egg Harbor as they drove up to Baileys Harbor for lunch at a fish place. The place was very busy; people were jockeying for a place at the bar. Earl and Betty nabbed the last two seats. Betty took off her new silk jacket, set it on her seat, and went to the lady's room.

As soon as she'd left, a man aggressively reached over Earl to try to order a drink at the bar. That would have been forgivable, but when he collected the four beers he'd ordered, he spilled some on Betty's new jacket.

"Hey bud, this is not where you're supposed to get drinks," Earl advised him, pointing to the proper area. "You just spilled beer on my girlfriend's jacket."

The man just shrugged. "Okay, boss," he said, stepping away.

Betty was on her way back. "What's up? You look upset?" she asked.

"That man there," Earl began, pointing. "Just reached over me and spilled beer on your beautiful jacket."

"It should come out; don't make a scene."

"It was incredibly rude."

"I know, honey, but you never know who's packing a gun anymore."

"Okay, I guess you're right." But he was still pissed and feeling wronged when their food arrived. Earl was halfway into his grilled tuna wrap when he started to feel woozy. Was it the argument? Whatever it was, his head was spinning a bit. "I'm going to run to the men's room, darling."

Earl did his business and looked at himself in the mirror. A few aging spots on his forehead, but not bad for an ex-con pressing seventy. As he washed his hands, he noticed that the hand that the dog had bitten and licked was puffing up slightly. Shit. Did he bring the Neosporin? Doubtful, though he'd meant to. He washed out his hand as best he could and tried to pull himself together.

"Let's drive back through the park, shall we?" Earl asked.

Betty emphatically agreed, and they entered Peninsula State Park at Ephraim. The park stretched all the way back to Fish Creek, where they were staying. Earl had been coming up here for decades, and now here he was suddenly pushing seventy. He'd even thought of Door County when he was in prison, of the pines, rocky bluffs, and soothing waters of Green Bay and the more boisterous waves on the Lake Michigan side.

"It's lovely even on this gray day," Betty said.

It was true. There was a beech-maple forest and genteel public golf course that looked out over the bluff outcroppings toward the bay. Earl pulled over when he saw this new enormous wooden contraption that led to the Eagle Tower lookout over the bay.

"Let's walk up this thing and have a better look at the bay."

They wound their way up the tower just as the sun opened after being gray all day. The bay and sky were this rich electric blue. It was breathtaking. Earl literally felt a little out of breath, probably just the climb up.

"It's even bluer than Blue Lake, Earl!"

"Well, it's close anyway," he said, quickly adding. "No, damn it, you're right!"

They made their way down and back to their hotel.

"What a romantic day," Betty said as they made their way inside. He knew that look in Betty's eyes. And that was her word. Romantic. Sure enough, she pulled him to her when they got back and checked into their room. "It's so nice that you're just as romantic as me," she said, slipping out of her pants as Earl did the same.

"You know that you drive me crazy, Betty." He held her close. "Let's just give up on do-gooding and have a great time together for the rest of our days."

She took off her sweater and shirt and her matching blue bra. Earl got naked, too. And soon, there she was above him, truly an angel sent to him from the gods. He always felt so close to her when they made love. It was corny, but true, to say it felt like they were one when they cried out together.

"I love you so much, Earl!"

"Oh, Betty, my darling!"

She stared at him a bit as she slid off him and then cried out. "That was lovely, Earl, but my God, look at your hand!"

"Yes, it's been a little red and swollen," Earl replied. "But these purple pimple things are new."

He did feel a little lightheaded when he sat up, and then he realized that he was going to throw up.

Chapter Forty-Two

Something to Say

The monthly partnership meeting was always held in the ornate large Higgins and Clark conference room with the expensive blue leather chairs and a fantastic view of the Chicago skyline. There was the slate-colored Willis Tower, which many still called the Sears Tower, and the cylindrical tan building next to it like a strange, chubby little sibling. The whole crew was arriving, too, and Courtney called the unruly group to order.

Courtney hadn't slept for two nights. She was turning it all around in her mind, a silly dog chasing her tail. But then the night before she finally made her decision, she slept soundly because she knew what she was going to do. Her way was clear.

She didn't want to be Managing Partner anymore.

"I have something to say before we get into the details of things," she said firmly. "I've decided to step down as Managing Partner for personal reasons. I'm just a bit over-whelmed with this expedited coal permit case, and you all deserve someone who can focus more clearly on providing the firm with leadership."

There were a few baffled looks, but then there were some insincere affirmations from two or three of the most likely candidates to replace her. "I think we can vote on your replacement as soon as tomorrow," Arthur Messing, one of them, offered.

"Yes, that's right," said Candice Short, another likely successor candidate.

"That's great," Courtney said. "I will officially withdraw from all personnel matters and other management committees as soon as someone steps forward to take over for me. Now let's move on to other business."

That was all it took. As the meeting dragged on, Courtney felt her spirits rise. The problem that had been plaguing her for months was simply off her plate. Now she had to get ready for her afternoon flight to Duluth for tomorrow's Entry Upon Land in Superior.

Ben drove her to O'Hare that night. "How does it feel, Court?"

"It's a tremendous relief," she said, letting herself feel it. "Change is almost always energizing for me. But this time, I feel sort of settled, I guess."

She didn't add that a lot of the latter was because of how well things were going between them. Courtney had never even wanted to feel settled; it had always seemed so close to settling. But with Ben the palpable feeling of connection was like having another whole self to explore, to discover.

She hugged him close, twice, as he dropped her off.

As she waited for the plane to board, Courtney went over her notes. Then she got an email from Mike Crew. The groundskeeper had found a work glove, an earring, and a piece of gum. Courtney sent all three in for DNA testing. That whole thing with the dogs was fishy.

It was unlikely to be prim Grace's earring or glove; how could they prove it even if it was? Maybe getting some of her DNA from a water bottle or something? But Grace always brought her own Yeti.

Why would they be out on the coal island? It didn't make much sense. They were going to take coal samples on the site inspection. She'd love to talk to Earl Franks about it, but he'd gone over to the other side.

Chapter Forty-Three

Hoopla?

Grace was so wired that she begged off coffee when she met up at the hotel with Tonya and Tim before the coal facility site inspection. Sleep had become an issue since the boat night. Her mind kept creating images of the dogs attacking Camille in the middle of the night. The three of them discussed where they would take samples from and then met up with the others.

Considering the scale of the coal facility, the indoor office was stark and industrial. They met in the break room, which featured dark wood paneling, an enormous Bunn coffeemaker and something akin to a card table and folding chairs that seated ten. The large group going out on the coal lot stood around the table. Grace, Tim, and Tonya were joined by State EPA attorney Dan Martin and his expert Joe Torkelson, Courtney Sharpe, her associate Jake, and Mike Crew, who ran the coal transshipment facility, and their expert Dr. Graham Collins.

Mr. Crew was playing tour guide.

"The privately owned island and the road that we're driving on was man-made from dredge spoils from the 1890s' harbor improvements, like Barker Island, where the marina is located. It's important to remember that this is a transshipment facility. That means that we transfer the coal from railroad cars into the big pile and then load the vessels for delivery through Lake Superior out the Seaway."

"There was a case at one of your competitors in the late

1990s that established that transshipment facilities were not subject to new source performance standards," Graham noted pointedly. "All of the coal comes pre-sized."

"We know, though the two local air permit engineers had thought that they should," Tonya replied a little curtly. Grace liked how scrappy Tonya was. "Let's get on with the tour, and let me collect my coal samples for testing," Tonya said. "I'm also going to be taking some photos."

"Sure," Mike said. "We brought everyone N-95 masks for when we go out to the coal yard. The yard on the island has room for about four million tons of coal and is considerably below that capacity now."

Everyone put the masks on, and then they made their way out to the coal island. The scale of it was terrifying. Three-story mountains of swampy peat pressed over a million years into the familiar, black, soft sedimentary rock that had provided energy for centuries.

"This helps me to understand a statistic that I read the other day," Tonya said. "In 2016, coal still accounted for one-third of all US train freight traffic."

"It's got to go somewhere, and we handle a lot of it here," Mike said. "Despite all the hoopla around alternative energy, we handled millions of tons very efficiently last year."

"Hoopla?" Tonya asked. "They shipped three hundred thousand tons of just wind turbine parts through this same port last year."

"He didn't mean it in a derogatory way," Courtney said. Crew looked taken aback but didn't say a word. Grace thought that Courtney looked good in the mask, which brought out her eyes.

They toured the metal grizzly gate, which separated out unwanted materials before shipping. Lots of dust was raised when the tons of coal crashed down on it before going into the ship container hopper. That was a point of contention in the earlier case.

Grace thought of Earl saving the day with his little boat and felt a wave of guilt run through her as the facility tour continued. Her focus was wandering a bit, but Grace had no doubt that Tonya was taking everything in and would have lots of photos to share as well.

After forty-five minutes, they were done, and Tonya had a large bag of coal samples. How could she get Earl's unofficial samples into Tonya's hands? She'd have to trust her. Grace wrote her a note to meet her in the ladies' room.

"What's up?" Tonya asked.

"We have some more samples, gathered by an anonymous neighbor that we'd also like you to test."

Tonya nodded.

Courtney opened the bathroom door. "Room for one more in here?"

"Of course," Grace replied. "I was just leaving."

"I'm ahead of you in line," Tonya smirked, going into the stall.

Tonya texted Grace from there. ***Meet me outside the coffee shop and I'll grab those flowers.***

Tonya was going to help.

Chapter Forty-Four

Maybe It Was Just the Cherry Pie

Earl was miserable and retching cherries on the passenger's side of his car. They'd already pulled over twice, once in Appleton and now near Beaver Dam, for him to get sick. He'd let her take over the driving after the Appleton episode.

"I'm worried about you," Betty called.

He noticed that her lips were quivering, as he wiped off his mouth with a tissue.

"It's going to be fine," Earl replied. "Maybe me getting sick is just that cherry pie I had for lunch."

"That's possible," Betty said, sounding unconvinced.

Over his protests, Betty had insisted on immediately checking out of the hotel, driving to Madison, and taking him to UW Hospital. Earl washed his mouth out with bottled water and got back in the car.

"It might not be related to my hand at all."

"There's some gum in the glove box," Betty said.

"Thanks." Earl knew that he must have reeked. His hand looked much worse as he reached for the gum. It was swollen, and what looked like purple chicken pox extended up past his wrist.

At last, they made it to Madison. The UW ER docs looked at Earl's swollen hand and started taking blood samples. From what he could glean, the purple dots indicated capillaries were bleeding just under the surface of his hand and lower arm.

He also had a fever of 102F. They gave him an antibiotic drip and admitted him to an intensive care area just for infectious people.

Earl was lying in the ICU like he was at death's door, but he didn't feel all that bad. Even Betty was kept out. What was going on with his hand? Could a little dog bite lead to big problems, even to death?

If this was it, he would be going out in style, making love to Betty like a champ. But poor Betty would be a widow again even though they'd never even married. It would suck to die right when he had finally found happiness with a woman that he loved and respected, who felt the same way. Betty was the real champ.

She'd find another guy. Or at least he hoped she would. Someone with a bit of juice still left in him.

No, Earl thought, that was catastrophizing. It was just a dog bite, for Christ's sake. It had barely broken the skin, and then the dog had licked him for good measure.

But would he ever make it out of this tangle of tubes and misery to marry Betty?

Now, Earl remembered marrying his first wife, Maggie. They were so young and in love, too, but still, they'd struggled. So much of it had been his fault! He'd wasted too much time playing those damn ponies. But part of it was that they were just too different. Earl was a man of appetites, while Maggie loved putting things in order.

Still, marrying Maggie had given him Laurie, the best thing he'd had a hand in. Laurie Little, what a name! Poor thing. Hopefully, she would tell Maggie that he'd tried to do something decent, but this was what he got for it instead.

Now Earl thought of those old cousins he'd seen at the funeral, who he hadn't laid eyes on since that wedding forty years ago. Those losers had hated him until he failed, too. What kind of life was that? Or was that just some usual pattern? Would they show up for his? Probably just to gossip. Earl was glad that he'd recently updated his will.

For some reason, he found himself thinking about the big, sprawling cities that he'd lived in. New York and Chicago. All the traffic and people rushing around from place to place. He could die here right now, and nonetheless, people would still be cutting each other off on the Long Island or the Dan Ryan Expressway.

What did it all add up to? Nothing. Nothing added to nothing, and death.

No, there was so much more than that. There were friends, even if he'd found out how few he really had after he'd gone to prison. Most of all, there was the love of a good woman. He'd been so alone, then, miraculously, Betty had come to visit him in prison.

Out of despair, came joy. Seventy years old, having the most profound love and the best sex of his life, and not being judged as either a hero or a villain but just as a man who loved a woman. A man who wanted to do something positive after fucking up royally for most of his adult life.

Now, here Betty was beside him. He heard Betty saying in a final-sounding way that she loved him, that he'd done far more good than bad on this blue earth that he loved. He tried to answer, but the fever had disabled his mouth and sent his thoughts spinning.

Soon, he was back on the big lake, piloting his little Brother's Keeper. The stormy night waves were rhythmically slapping it on all sides, but he held steady, shepherding his ailing passengers back to safety. All that stress was giving way to release, and now it was a sunny morning on Blue Lake with Betty beside him, smiling. She said something sweet to him that he couldn't make out, but when he turned to her, she was back on the shore, waving at him from their crappy, crumbling pier.

Chapter Forty-Five

By My Brilliant Line of Questioning

Grace met her expert, Tonya Nesbitt, at Fayze's restaurant in downtown La Crosse. They were seated away from everyone else in the back under a large Lebanese flag. Tonya was wearing an outdoorsy green Patagonia parka and some kind of high-tech brown pants.

"Thanks for coming, Dr. Nestbitt," Grace said as they took their seats and ordered coffee.

"Call me Tonya, please!"

"I love this place; it's kind of a local institution. There's lots of Lebanese folks in La Crosse, including one of my favorite teachers in high school."

"Cool," Tonya replied, fidgeting in her chair.

"So what did your analysis find?"

"It was a long drive over," Tonya said, as their waitress approached. She pulled out a document called Preliminary Findings and excused herself to go to the lady's room. "Can you just order me a coffee?"

Grace looked over the preliminary conclusions. Tonya had found that a total of seventy-eight percent of the samples were unsprayed. She had an asterisk and had done another column that still showed more than forty percent unsprayed. When Tonya returned, Grace asked her, "So what does the asterisk mean?"

"For precision and in trying to be scientific, I ran the

numbers with and without the neighbor's samples," Tonya explained. "The ones we've been calling the flower samples. For my final report, I included half samples from those and half that I had gathered onsite."

Grace nodded. "And more than half were still untreated?"

"Yes."

"Is that as significant as I think it is?" Grace asked.

"Yes, it shows that they aren't spraying the whole pile. Period. Full stop." Tonya smiled briefly, but then frowned slightly. "But my question for you is how do you plan to make that a permitting issue?"

"By my brilliant line of questioning?" Grace was stalling; it wasn't going to be easy. She still hadn't fully worked it out. "I guess, first, you redo some of their calculations. And opine that all their calculations, every premise for issuing the permit, are off because of this evidence and, accordingly, that likely explains the air violations and NOVs. That should come in at a minimum. Tim and I are still working on where to go with the implications of that. Probably, then opine that the permit should be reduced by an equivalent fifty to eighty percent."

"That all follows, if this conservative judge allows it in," Tonya replied. Her arms were crossed, and her brows also looked a little skeptical.

"I hear you, believe me," Grace replied.

That was the terrible irony of both Earl and Camille being attacked by the dogs. It wasn't clear how much all their heroic efforts would really help the case. How had they all gone down that rabbit hole together? Groupthink? Whatever it was, Grace had regrets. It had seemed so essential at the time. But was it just an emotional response to the clear injustice of the company's lies? There was such a strong urge to prove that the company wasn't spraying.

They went over the data for fifteen minutes until Grace felt like she understood it. Soon, Tonya excused herself and left for a quick phone conference. Grace felt encouraged and was relieved that Tonya was willing to go along with the rogue samples. And one way or the other, they'd proven that the company wasn't following its permit.

Tonya came back and said, "I can redo the calculations in your office before we meet with Tim. Does that work for you?"

They walked from Fayze's to Grace's office down by the Mississippi. The breeze was alarmingly gentle for February in La Crosse. There were a surprising number of people out on the streets enjoying the beautiful winter day.

"Your city seems to be doing well," Tonya observed.

"Yes, downtown La Crosse is thriving. We have a large Health Logistics company, the university, Kwik Trip, and Gunderson and Mayo Clinics. Tourists, too, in the summer and fall."

"We're just holding our own in Stevens Point. For now, at least. They're talking about major cuts to the university."

Grace set up Tonya to work in an empty office. A few minutes later, she greeted Tim with a kiss. She ran her direct examination of Tonya by him. "What do you think?"

"You nailed it, Grace. I think it would be hard for the Judge to keep out an attack on the logic of their underlying data and calculations." Tim was nodding and smiling. "But do you think Tonya can actually estimate what would meet the standards based on the samples that she took?"

"She's working on it right now in the room next door."

"I think it will work, or it would have worked if your ex was presiding, anyway."

"Yes," Grace replied. She hated it when Tim called Jason her ex. Should she tell him that? "Let's not go there; we have the judge that we have."

"I'm sorry to bring him into it." Tim set his coffee cup down.

"Yeah, Camille is still struggling a bit. Nothing like Earl, mind you."

"So, Earl has that new dog lick illness?"

"Yes, here, I wrote it down." Grace pulled it up on her phone. "The bacteria is called *Capnocytophaga canimorsus*, and it comes from the saliva of perfectly healthy dogs. It can cause sepsis. A guy up north died from it this year, and another guy had to have his legs amputated."

"Weird, so some people are just sensitive to it?"

"They're not sure. One thing I read said that the bacteria may have changed and that the change is likely associated with climate change."

"Poor Earl, but it's one more reason we have to win this case."

They worked all day, and by four, they had Tonya's revised calculations based on her review of the coal sample data. She felt comfortable opining that the existing facility should be reduced by forty percent and that no additional capacity should be permitted.

Grace also gave Tonya a chart Jason had made and a key to his sources, clearly showing the correlation between Lacy's hospital visits, air permit violations, and wind speed.

"This looks promising, too," Tonya said. "There's obviously a strong link in four of her trips to the ER. I hope that the ALJ lets it come into the record. What are our chances?"

"Not great," Grace admitted. "But we can make an Offer of Proof that will at least make it part of the record." Reviewing courts would know that children were likely to be harmed if the permit was issued.

Within a couple of days, Tonya had created an Amended Expert Report Summary that included her revisions and then they talked with her by Zoom and, with a couple of tweaks, sent it on to the other side.

The trial began in three days.

Chapter Forty-Six

Thousand Steps Beach

Micah was at a sleepover at a friend's house, and it was Jason and Camille's first night out in Santa Barbara since their return. Their first night out, period, in a very long time. Camille was recovering well. The face wounds were superficial but still prominent, and they joked that they made another little constellation on her face.

A star, Jason thought. Camille said a tiger. Micah saw a dog. But he was obsessed with getting one and a little biased.

Camille had needed skin grafts from her bum on the deep cut on her thigh. But there was no sign of any infection, and even the gashes on her pretty face and leg were looking better now as they walked below Thousand Steps Beach.

Jason was carrying a cooler bag on his shoulder, which was filled with a healthy light dinner of takeout from Lazy Acres grocery and a thermos full of local Melville Santa Rita Hills Chardonnay. Camille lit a pre-roll that he'd bought for her as they walked along the high cliffs and sagging Monterey pine trees above the Pacific waves.

"This is good for my anxiety." She passed it to Jason. She'd been smoking too much pot since the dog attack, but who could blame her? Not Jason, he was too. "Thanks for picking it up."

Jason drew in a citrus-scented cloud of the Clementine weed and took a picture of Camille with his phone.

"You look beautiful and pretty chill," he said, snapping more photos.

It was true; Camille was looking healthy and relaxed, radiating happiness in her large blue floral hat that set off her high cheekbones and the slightly silly smile that hinted that she might already be a little high.

"This is just what I needed, boyfriend." She drew in a slow draft of smoke.

"Me, too," Jason replied. He still couldn't believe that Camille was going to be all right. After losing Tara, everything terrible seemed highly likely. He had done a video session with his counselor about that. It was a common reaction. "I've had enough. Let's have our picnic on that large rock over there."

Jason poured the wine as Camille assembled their take-out treasures, a nice organic salad and a flavorful chicken-and-peppers dish that they both liked that was too spicy for Micah. After they'd toasted their rare date night, Camille urged Jason to go back to Wisconsin and the coal plant trial.

"I want you to go, honey," she said, emphasizing the second word. "You can help Grace and Tim, and maybe check on Earl if that feels right for you." She paused and then added, "You said that you were feeling a little guilty about it."

"Hah, I thought that you were asleep when I said that!" Jason confessed. "Are you sure that you're ready to be left alone with Micah?"

"Yes! You should go! Check on flights when we get home."

"Okay, I will. I could probably add some value at the trial. This salad is delicious."

"Agreed. How are you? Are you still writing every day? I think it's good for you."

"Yes, mostly about Blue Lake. I love that town. They did such a great job protecting that lake."

"And about Tara, too, I hope?"

"Of course." Had she seen him in tears yesterday? "And Earl, too. I have complex feelings about that guy."

Jason wanted to go visit Earl in the hospital. He'd visited

Earl when he was in prison, but that was mostly just schadenfreude and trying to make sense of things for himself. Now he felt genuine respect and concern for his old adversary, who'd gotten injured trying to save Camille's life.

"Sure, but please join me in a toast to Earl's full recovery," Camille began. "And for him helping you save my life."

"To Earl's health." Jason sipped the delicious wine. "Yes, I'll look into flights after we get home."

"And after we have our underwear dance." Camille smirked, sliding in to give him a kiss.

"Deal," Jason replied. "I've missed our date nights."

Chapter Forty-Seven

At the Top of Her Game

Courtney and Jake flew to Duluth from Chicago on Saturday and then rented a car for the trial. They spent Sunday at their hotel cramming with their expert, Dr. Graham Collins. He was concerned about the coal samples the Objector's expert took and her Amended Report.

"I read Tonya's deposition, and she seems to have laid a foundation for them to at least get this in as Rebuttal," Courtney confessed.

"Her calculations are sound as far as that goes," Graham replied.

"Maybe we should just let it in and then say it's not worth much. More like a back of the envelope than anything that can be relied on," Jake offered.

"That's what I'm thinking, too," Courtney replied. It was uncanny how often Jake was on the same page and line with her. "Can we take that through as far as how you'd under-mine it?"

"Sure, that's not hard at all." Graham smiled. "It really is a back-of-the-envelope calculation. Basically, she's just saying that there will be sixty percent more coal dust because that's equivalent to what her samples said were not sprayed."

"Okay, I'll object, but we could almost just let it in and act like it has no evidentiary value," Courtney concluded. "Now, let's go over your direct again."

They did. The coal sample thing wasn't likely to touch them. This judge wasn't going to do anything with it.

Finally, it was Monday and the trial started. Courtney did the Opening Statement, and it went well. The coal transshipment facility had been in Lake Superior City since the late 1970s, and it had been a good neighbor and provided jobs. It was one of two such large facilities in the area.

This case was on the narrow issuance of an Amended Permit, and because the State had approved it, the Objectors had the burden of proof. The facility's experts had calculated the impacts based upon real-world data drawn from four decades of experience. The Objector's expert was trying to undermine this based upon hypotheticals that were drawn from speculation that parts of the pile were not following permit terms, but that was unproven and irrelevant because it was a matter for enforcement of the permit rather than whether the new permit should have been issued.

The State EPA attorney, Dan Martin, echoed all her points and stressed that the ALJ should not substitute her judgment for that of the agency's air experts, who had issued a preliminary approval. "This is not a case about whether we want to keep using coal at this point in human history. We all have our personal opinions on that, but this is not the place to express them. Rather, this is a simple review of issuance of an air permit by the EPA. There is substantial evidence that it had been issued based on reasonable calculations, and no back-of-the-envelope calculations will overcome that. The permit issuance must stand," he concluded.

Grace gave the Objector's Opening. Her expert's calculations were based upon the ultimate reality, actual pieces of coal from the coal mountain that was such a disruptive presence in the lives of its neighbors. "There was nothing speculative or hypothetical about her calculations, and these calculations, unlike the rose-colored numbers produced by the facility, corresponded with the facts on the ground, namely that the plant that wanted to expand had had twenty-eight Notice of Violations just over the course of the past five years.

Courtney objected to the discussion of the permit violations, and it was sustained.

Expanding the footprint, Grace continued, under those circumstances, would be reckless and would put the lives of children like Lacy at risk. They can't pretend that she hadn't visited the ER more than a dozen times over the course of the past two years, more than one visit every two months. That was not the Wisconsin Grace had grown up in, and the ALJ must see that that is not the future for Lacy and other children in Lake Superior City. "This is a case about two very different Wisconsins. There is the fictional one presented by the company where there were no violations, I'm sorry, Your Honor, no problems, and the real one that Lacy lives in, where she is going to the ER because the coal dust is destroying her lungs."

Grace was good. All of that would have been very effective in front of a jury, where Grace usually practiced. But it seemed lost on the longtime conservative ALJ, who knew how to parcel out state approvals to companies with less than pristine track records.

Courtney was feeling energized. She always relished a hard-fought trial. She took a satisfying sip of coffee as the State expert began testifying. There was still some deep vein of combativeness in her, no doubt related to her personal history. And there was always the pleasure of the moment in a trial, where anything could happen, and it was on her to resist it and control it.

That was the story of her life, and she was just now at the top of her game.

Chapter Forty-Eight

Public Hearing

Jason flew out to Duluth in time for the first day of the coal trial. It was odd to see a case merely as a spectator, as a member of the public at the public hearing, though Grace had listed him as an expert witness on some of the legal issues. He sat in the rear of the courtroom next to a young man who seemed familiar and who greeted him.

Then he remembered, it was Jerry, the guy that had taken Grace and him out on his boat. "How are you doing, Jerry?"

"I signed up to speak, but it's a very long list."

"Yes, I bet."

The first day of the trial, Judge Benson had reserved for opening statements and then public input, as he probably would have done. Dozens of people wanted to speak for and against. Among those who advocated for the facility, a majority were either employees or suppliers. One elderly gentleman, his voice filled with desperation, pleaded, "Lake Superior City is already struggling in 2020. Why would you strip us of these well-paying jobs?" His words were simple yet deeply heartfelt. To him, the need for the permit's renewal was crystal clear.

Another memorable public witness was a soft-spoken young nun, Sister Sabrina, who spoke of the impact of coal dust on children at her school and then cited the Pope's 2015 encyclical on climate change. She had striking brown eyes and short blonde hair.

"The climate is a common good," she began, reading from a document. "A very solid scientific consensus indicates that we are presently witnessing a disturbing warming of the climatic system. The Pope called for lifestyle, production, and consumption changes to combat this warming. Concentrated in the atmosphere, carbon gases from coal do not allow the warmth of the sun's rays reflected by the earth to be dispersed in space. The problem is aggravated by a model of development based on the intensive use of fossil fuels, especially coal, which is at the heart of the worldwide energy system. The Pope concludes, we will witness extraordinary climate change and an unprecedented destruction of ecosystems, with serious consequences for all of us if we don't get off the coal habit."

"I object, your honor," Courtney interjected. "This is interesting theology but not relevant to whether we meet the standards for renewing our permit."

"May I respond, your honor?" the nun asked.

"Yes," the judge replied. "Briefly."

"To say that climate crisis is not relevant to the expansion of a permit which facilitates the distribution of millions of tons of coal across the world and adds an according amount of carbon dioxide and other gases into our common atmosphere would be like the proverbial ostrich sticking its head in the sand. That's exactly what the Pope is saying, we need changes and not just coal and carbon business as usual."

"I understand your point, and I've given you some latitude, but please try to keep your focus on the permit, which is the subject of this hearing, not larger issues for the planet."

"Every journey begins with a small step, your honor," the nun said. Her bright brown eyes looked straight toward Judge Benson. "And this permit renewal represents not one step, but millions of tons of them. I trust you to recognize this in your decision."

"No cross," Courtney said. Dan from the State EPA had none either. Neither wanted to take on that nun.

Ms. Carol Weston, a charming fifty-something teacher at Lake Superior City Elementary, was next. She testified about the number of kids with asthma in her second-grade class and what the days they missed meant for their futures. "We've been observing around thirty-five to forty percent of the kids having asthma-related issues that caused them to miss classes. The average for them is missing three days of school, but they have challenges even on days when they're here."

Courtney stood up and moved toward the witness. "Ms. Weston, you are not trained in medicine, are you?"

"No, I have a master's in education."

"So you're not claiming that the children who have asthma are as a result of my client shipping coal to the Netherlands or any other country are you?"

"No, but I am saying that your client has had many violations of air standards for particulate matter that have made those problems worse."

"Move to strike, Your Honor, she's not competent to testify on that matter and besides you have already ruled that alleged permit violations are a matter for enforcement and not this hearing."

"I'm not going to strike it, but your point is valid, Counsel. Anything else from this witness?"

"Yes, that seems like a bad assumption to me. Maybe I am missing some legal niceties but how can it not be germane that they have violated their old permit as we discuss their right to a new permit?"

"Same objection," Courtney interposed.

"Sustained. That can only be considered if they have had some repeated bad faith actions that have caused actual violations and not just notices of possible violations. Next witness please."

Jerry turned to Jason and opened his palms, as if to say that can't be right, is it? Jason screwed up his face with displeasure and then nodded. It was outside of his job, but Jason had heard that the state would often respond to a Notice of Violation by a new round of testing, which permit holders would see was better before actual violations and penalties were imposed.

Next up were a mother and then two sisters, the Smythe family, one of whom was the little girl Lacy who had been to the ER so many times. Ellen, the mother, explained how there was no question that both daughters had experienced asthma-related symptoms directly from blowing coal dust. She displayed the photos of the white sheets that she'd hung on her clothesline that Grace had shown him at the Driftless Café.

Courtney objected.

"Your honor, all the exact times and the dates of when the photos were taken are clear. I even have those sheets out in my car if you want to see them."

"My objection is as to the cause coming from the coal transshipment facility, your honor."

"I'll allow it. I think that goes to the weight rather than the admissibility of the photos."

Grace said, "This is firsthand direct evidence that is not only admissible, but which should be entitled to great weight because this is the reality of this family's daily life living so close to this facility."

"Thanks for your unnecessary editorial comment, Ms. Clarkson. Go ahead."

She testified how difficult it had been to raise a child with asthma near the coal transport plant. "I was both surprised and unsettled every time she needed to go to the hospital. I was upset that I waited to call or bring her in, thinking I was alarmist and finding out I wasn't. Upset that despite going to the doctor to prevent an attack before the second time, it was not prevented. The number one feeling is always the fear of losing a very precious child." She wiped away some tears. "I heard someone say, 'Why did you buy a place so close to this monstrous coal pile'? And the answer is obvious. The company has it hidden. You can drive around the neighborhood and never know it's there. We didn't even know it was there until we started hanging out our sheets. Now we can't get what we paid for our house if we were to try to list it. That's it from me, but I'd like my two daughters to be sworn in to testify."

No one objected.

The youngest, Lacy, was sworn. She had a head full of blonde curls with a white ribbon tied in them, a striking contrast with the sober adult faces all around her.

"How old are you, Lacy?" her mom asked.

"You know. Four and a half, almost five."

"Do you have problems with breathing sometimes?"

"Lots of times, and then I have to go to the ER."

"Did you have another name for it?"

"When I was little, I called it the Ear. But now I know it means emergency room."

"Do you like going to the ER?"

"No, I hate it. Sometimes I feel like I'm going to choke from coughing." She folded her hands in her lap.

"Does Mommy ever make you come in the house when you're playing outside?"

"Yes, lots."

"Why, do you know?" her mom asked gently.

"The wind blows so much of that black coal dust stuff into our yard. We made a chart that showed that I had to go to the hospital every time the wind blows too much of it for me to breathe."

"Your Honor, you've already ruled that that Chart is not likely to be relevant to this permit case," Courtney said. "I urge you to strike it from the record."

"That's not how I understood your pretrial ruling, Your Honor," Grace said, standing.

"Overruled. The ruling said that on its face it seemed like an enforcement issue, but that I would see if it had some specific nexus to a relevant permitting issue," Judge Benson said.

Jason had a strong suspicion that Audrey Benson was just going to wait to save face and rule that it was irrelevant as part of her written decision. That would be typical of her, of several of his old colleagues.

"Anything else, Lacy?"

"I have a picture book that says the smallest voices can create the most powerful ripples of change. And I hope that it's right!"

"Okay, thanks, sweetheart, let's let your big sister talk now."

"It's your turn, Sylvie!" Lacy called to her sister. But then she added, "I made drawings for the Judge and Grace and Courtney and Dan."

The state EPA attorney, Dan Martin, smiled when she handed him his. "Judge, should we mark these as an exhibit?"

"Sure, we'll mark them as Lacy Smythe Exhibits A-D. And thanks, Lacy, they're very pretty."

"No objection, Your Honor," Courtney said.

Sylvie was twelve, and she read from a prepared statement after being sworn.

"My name is Sylvie Smythe and I live two-tenths of a mile from the coal dump facility. It's been a big part of my life. My parents have many times wished that they hadn't bought this house. They had no idea how bad it would be for us, for Lacy and me." Sylvie smiled at Lacy, who had waved to her. "Now, it would be hard for them to sell it, or I'm sure that we would move. Lacy and I have both had near-fatal asthma attacks. Did you know that last year in 2019, three thousand five hundred people died from asthma?"

"Objection."

"I have footnotes for all of my sources."

"Good job. Overruled," the judge said.

"There have been a couple of close calls for both me and my little sister. Neither of us ever had asthma before we moved here. My friends and I, we loved to play outside," Sylvie continued, her voice breaking up a bit, "but those games have now been replaced by inhalers and doctor visits. The air we breathe, once fresh and clean, has become a toxic reminder of what used to be. I don't claim to know all the legal rules, but how can it not be important that this facility has made us both sick, and destroyed my parents' life savings? That has to be relevant, and worth something."

Next was Walter Messette, a tall Ojibwe man with long black hair who talked about how his people had come to Lake Superior centuries ago, where they found wild rice beds, the food that grows on water from their sacred prophetic traditions.

"You will hear testimony from our expert from GLIFWC later, and you have her report, but I want to speak more about the larger context. European and white culture often separates people from nature, and not knowing it means being distant from our responsibilities for it and for how we've changed it. But how can any of us, Indigenous or European, deny that our climate is changing for the worse? How can we deny that millions of tons of coal are perhaps one of the most significant causes of those changes? The waters of the Big Lake are open in the Wisconsin winter! Wild rice beds were once abundant and now there are just a few areas left. The coal dust from the facility harms us all, especially those in our care, our children, and our elders. Our people prioritize gratitude and finding solutions, helping bring back the human connection with nature and the land. Judge, if you can't deny this permit, cut it down as far as you can," he concluded softly. "Everyone is responsible, especially those who have the power to do something and don't do what they can."

Next up, two workers at the transshipment facility who talked about their good jobs and all their efforts to keep coal dust down. It was their job to keep the dust down, and they were committed to doing it. It was insulting to think that they didn't care about the coal dust, they lived here, too. The second of the workers, a bearded guy dressed in camouflage, was dismissive of all the prior testimony.

"I saw those two girls, and their mom. I have daughters as well, and I would never live so close to any industrial facility. That's why their house was so cheap. Whining about it now and putting those little girls on the stand is just a tawdry play on your emotions, Judge Benson. We need those jobs."

As always, the public comment was tinged with political spin. Jason remembered how exhausting it was to see the country's division so passionately displayed from both sides. Americans had formed themselves into separate factions that simply couldn't understand each other. He was glad not to be practicing law and understood now that this would be his last case.

"Is there anyone else?" the judge called, clearly expecting none.

But a slight older woman of color cautiously raised her hand, and the judge promptly swore her in and asked her name. She carried a manila folder to the stand.

"My name is Reyna Mendoza, and I have lived in Lake Superior City approximately half a mile from the coal facility for the past fourteen years. For thirteen of those years, I lived there with my late husband Bayani Mendoza. But he died from complications of COPD just last March. Bayani did not smoke, and had no other risk factors for lung disease, as this summary of his medical records confirms. His pulmonologist, Dr. Sheri Carlson, confirms that in writing. Bayani's sole risk factor was living near the coal facility."

"I object," Courtney said. "These are not certified medical records."

"Overruled," the judge said, "I will give it the weight I think it deserves."

"Thank you, Your Honor. I will continue with my statement and then offer two new exhibits. Bayani's death should come as no surprise, the preliminary findings of a large new study found that a total of 500,000 Americans have died due to exposure to coal in the past decade alone, that's from 2009 to 2019. Just in America. It's even worse in Asia, where Bayani's and my family live. Coal is not just a killer of the environment and the climate; it's a killer of people, people who are loved."

"I object."

"Noted."

"Here are my two exhibits, first this Certified Copy of my late husband's medical records," she paused to glare at Courtney, "and the copy of the new study on coal deaths."

"I object," Courtney said.

"Overruled, exhibits 651 and 652 are received. I will give them the weight that I think they deserve."

Jason knew that that likely meant none, even though Ms. Mendoza's testimony had the most truth in it of anything he'd heard over the course of the trial. It would be easy for Audrey Benson to discount. Bayani's death is an issue for enforcement, not permitting! Too bad, so sad.

When he'd sat in Audrey's privileged chair, he'd done his best to be fair, to listen and to care. But the system that he'd been so much a part of often made that difficult. The powers that be wrote the laws, and those forces were wealthy and ruthless. Big corporate interests had come after him personally whenever he did something they didn't like.

Meanwhile, the people who suffered environmental injustice were facing so many obstacles just to get through their long days. Their direct experiences were often irrelevant; the whole system seemed designed to ensure that. Jason would do his best to at least have them be heard when he testified on Wednesday.

Sitting in the peanut gallery with Jerry had opened his eyes.

Chapter Forty-Nine

Mansplaining to Her Honor

On the third day of the trial, Grace called Jason as an expert witness. She was in the flow of it, and it didn't seem all that awkward. Courtney objected.

"What's he an expert witness about?"

"He was on our list," Grace replied. "He's clearly an expert on the scope of the ALJ's authority."

Courtney shook her head. "That's a legal issue solely for the judge to decide for herself," Courtney said, emphasizing the "her." "She doesn't need Jason mansplaining her authority to her."

"No, I don't," Judge Benson said with a smile. "But I value my old colleague's opinion, and I'm going to overrule the objection, which could have been made as a pretrial motion."

Grace asked him his name, where he lived and what his old job had been.

"I worked briefly for the current governor, but before that I was a colleague of Her Honor, Judge Benson, as an ALJ."

"Did you have professional experience hearing environmental cases for the State of Wisconsin?"

"Yes, for approximately seventeen years."

"Did I ask you to render an opinion about the ALJ's authority about some of the issues in this case?"

"Yes."

Courtney stood up. "Your Honor, can I have a continuing objection to this whole line of questioning that I think usurps your own authority?"

"Yes," the judge replied. "Go ahead, Counsel."

"Do you have an opinion about whether the issue of spraying is properly an enforcement or a permitting issue?"

"Yes, I do. Even in a permit application or renewal, it's important to evaluate the quality of the data that went into the assumptions that are part of the application. If the assumptions offered by a company are not realistic, then their modeling about the effects of the operation is also not realistic. Garbage in, garbage out."

"Did you review the permit data for those types of inaccurate assumptions and consequences?" Grace queried.

"Yes, and the fact that they're not putting the encrusting agent on the whole coal pile makes many of their assumptions inaccurate."

"I object." Courtney stood up again. "It's not a fact that they're not spraying; that's his own false assumption."

"I'll rephrase, Your Honor. Would you mind sitting down, please, counsel?" Grace asked calmly. Courtney was almost as theatrical as her old colleague Earl Franks. Her Uncle Ray had taught Grace to calmly counter bullying with polite requests. "Thank you. Now let me rephrase the last question. If it is established that the facility is not spraying the whole pile, are their assumptions inaccurate?"

"Yes, that's my point," Jason answered. "And in this case, we have the reality that corroborates that their assumptions were inaccurate, namely the hard evidence of the Notice of Violations and Air Permit Violations."

"I object, Your Honor," Courtney interposed. But she stayed seated. "Those are not hard evidence either, subject to your earlier Ruling."

"Your point is noted, Attorney Sharpe, and Mr. Erickson, as well, and the court will give this opinion testimony the weight that she finds appropriate."

"If that threshold of a lack of spraying is established," Grace began, "do you have an opinion about what remedies would be appropriate, based upon your professional experience to a reasonable degree of probability or certainty?"

"It's my professional opinion to a reasonable degree of certainty that the ALJ could deny the permit outright for more accurate and comprehensive modeling data. Or it would also be appropriate to reduce the size of the permitted activity by sixty percent to conform with the realities that the hard data analyzed by Dr. Tonya has uncovered."

"Thanks, Judge Erickson," Grace said. She took a sip of water. That had gone well.

"I just have a couple of cross questions," Courtney began. "Wouldn't the NOVs and Violations more accurately be described as an enforcement rather than a permitting issue? Yes or no, please."

"Yes, but it's a yes-but answer."

The judge smiled. "Go ahead, Jason."

"Yes, it's obviously also an enforcement issue, but if the assumptions are so far from being accurate and call into question the information provided with the permit application, then it's also clearly a permitting issue."

Courtney seized on that. "So, am I right that what your opinion testimony to this court is that only if she finds the underlying data in the permit application unsound should she find it relevant to this permit renewal?"

"That's generally a fair shorthand summary of my opinion testimony."

"Thank you, no further questions," Courtney said, looking relieved.

"I have just two more redirects, Your Honor," Grace replied. "Is it your professional opinion that the underlying permit data is not sound?"

"Yes, based upon both Dr. Tonya Nesbitt's data, the neighbor's photos of the sheets, and the long pattern of NOVs and the two Violations, yes."

"Finally, is there anything else that you'd like to add to

your testimony?" Grace asked.

"Yes, we must keep some historical perspective on our actions; we're in a solemn moment in our planet's history and need to act in that context. I invite the ALJ to consider the effects of this permit decision on the lives of neighbors and the planet. Sitting in her chair, I remember deciding on a case for a coal-fired power plant. I was very proud that it was the most stringent in US history and became the standard for the lowest achievable emission rate nationwide. So, though I was very proud of that at the time, I now regret not thinking further into the future, and I don't feel proud about approving that coal plant permit at all. The Clean Air Act gives the ALJ considerable discretion in those kinds of circumstances."

"Move to strike," Courtney said.

"I'm not going to strike that, but I'll give it the weight it deserves, which is very little. Cases must be decided solely on the law and the evidence. Anything further?" Judge Benson looked at her watch. Courtney shook her head. "Okay, Mr. Erickson, you're excused. Nice to see you, Jason, and we're adjourned for lunch until one thirty."

Jason had overreached. Grace regretted asking that last question. Her old beau was no longer thinking like a lawyer, much less like a judge.

Chapter Fifty

A One Hundred Percent Match

Courtney was feeling good about how the trial was going. Grace's emotional appeals might play better in the newspaper, or even if there'd been a jury, but they weren't landing with this judge. She'd tried a couple of Wisconsin cases with her before, and Judge Audrey Benson stayed focused on the facts and was very aware of the limits of her authority. Benson wouldn't try to limit the world's coal supply; she would just do her job.

Courtney hit the bathroom during the next break and checked her texts and email. She had an urgent message from the coal sample tester. *The results of our tests found one hit in the state's database: a 100 percent match on the glove with convicted felon Earl Stanley Franks.* That damn Earl had been working with Grace and Tim!

Courtney sat at the trial table, stunned. They had gone on the island to get unsprayed coal pieces, which was no doubt how and why Tonya had reached her alternative calculations. Wow, did that mean that Tonya was in on this, too? Their whole side of self-appointed do-gooders was even more corrupt than Courtney could have imagined.

Courtney was thinking about just when and how to expose Earl, and, especially, when to expose her unethical opposing counsel, Grace and Tim. Should she call a witness or just ask for a sidebar with the judge? Should she involve Jake or keep this all to herself? Maybe file a formal motion with an affidavit from the coal DNA evidence fingering Earl?

But what would that mean for Earl? Courtney also found herself admiring Earl's guts and willingness to put himself out there. She thought of her conversation with him, where he'd urged her to stop being selfish and cynical and to get on the right side of history. Apparently, Earl had taken that all the way to going out onto the coal island to get unsprayed samples.

Despite herself, Courtney was kind of oddly proud of Earl. But another part of her wanted nothing more than to expose the hypocrisy of the do-gooding lawyer crowd. It was an old issue, too.

Courtney had been considered a bad girl in high school, because she'd been edgy and smart and trying to figure out how to reclaim her sexuality after having it stolen. But she knew that the goodie-goodies were no better than her deep down, then or now. She'd love to expose it all in open court.

But what would that mean for Earl Franks? It was probably criminal trespass and enough to send Earl back to prison. She would consider Earl's fate carefully, but first she had to put on her own witness. They could deal with Earl and any sanctions in their rebuttal case.

Besides, Courtney wasn't sure what she was going to do.

Chapter Fifty-One

Some Perspective

The first days of the trial, where the Permit Holder and the Agency presented their case, had gone well enough, but Grace had the creeping sense that the ALJ was just going through the motions. Judge Audrey Benson seemed resistant to emotional appeals about the real-world impacts on the facility's neighbors. Benson took a bureaucratic, by-the-book approach that Grace feared would make her impenetrable to the objector's best arguments.

Like her Uncle Ray, Grace knew how to tug at the heartstrings. But even Ray said that some juries just had no heart. Same with some ALJs.

Grace's expert, Tonya, came on again in rebuttal, and she was an excellent witness. Her calm voice and scientific precision might just be enough to wake Judge Benson from her slumber. Tonya looked into the judge's eyes when she explained how she'd chosen samples based on the observed spraying pattern not reaching the pile's farthest reaches.

Her meticulous testing of the coal samples had been conducted with precision, which led her to conclude that the existing permit was already too large and that this was the likely cause of the twenty-eight documented air permit violations in the past couple of years. She'd even managed a timeline that matched known ER visits and the specific dates of air permit violations. This was met with strong objections from Courtney and Dan.

"Objection, Your Honor," Courtney had said, standing.

"These are irrelevant enforcement and not permitting issues."

"May I lay a better foundation, Your Honor?" Grace asked. She was trying not to look at Jason nodding at her. He was trying to be encouraging but it was a little distracting.

"Go ahead."

"Is it your opinion to a reasonable degree of engineering and air modeling probability that if your calculations are correct, the facility would be likely to frequently be in violation of the existing permit?"

"Yes, to a reasonable degree of probability," Tonya replied.

"And would you hold the same opinion with respect to the proposed Amended Permit?"

"Yes, to a reasonable degree of professional probability."

"My objection stands, Your Honor," Courtney countered.

"I'm going to allow it in, and then give it the weight that I ultimately conclude that it is worth," the judge ruled. "Exhibit 77 is received."

Grace was thrilled. The direct examination had gone as well as she could have hoped, and all her exhibits had made it into the record. There was a brief break and then it was Courtney's turn to cross Tonya.

Courtney almost immediately homed in on the recently revised calculations based on the pilfered coal samples. In her black silk suit, the fiercely intelligent, poised, and attractive Courtney Sharpe was impressive. But, in the more down-to-earth Dr. Tonya Nesbitt, she may have met her match.

"Isn't this just a bunch of back-of-the-envelope numbers that you put together to try to deny this permit issuance?" Courtney asked, her voice rising to an almost accusatory tone.

"Absolutely not," Tonya replied. "Do you want me to explain why it's not?"

"Yes, because that's how both of your fellow air engineers characterized it in their direct testimony."

"My numbers are the only ones that reflect hard science; namely the calculations were based not on some modeling projections but on actual pieces of coal from among that huge pile of coal that is out on that island. There are no assumptions other than that the day that the company allowed me to collect them was a typical day in the life of the facility. If anything, the company could be expected to take every precaution on the day that the Objector's expert arrives to do a site inspection. These are hard numbers that reflect the real-world conditions."

"But all of your opinions are based upon coal samples that only you have tested," Courtney asked. "Isn't that correct?"

"Yes, but those samples have been made available to your expert and to that of the state, and they have had every opportunity to analyze them. Instead of doing that, it's just this drumbeat that my real-world calculations are somehow less reliable than their theoretical model-based ones. They're more, not less, accurate."

"That's all I have," Courtney said. She was smart enough to concede the point and not keep digging the hole deeper.

"Okay, I've hit the wall," Judge Benson said. "It's time for our lunch break. When we come back at one fifteen, we will finish with this witness in no more than ten minutes. So go over your notes, Counsel."

Grace was feeling good about things. So far, so good. But then she remembered. She was supposed to go to lunch with Jason to see if he had anything to add about her direct of Tonya. She was dreading seeing him. She should have never agreed to it. She'd only spoken to Jason once since the coal boat disaster and he'd been unfriendly.

"So, you guys bailed with the Lake Superior-worthy boat because you got a busted taillight warning?" he'd snarled. "That's pretty lame, in my opinion."

"We were on a cop's radar, so there was a record of us on a boat on the same night as the dogs went to sleep."

"I know, but you sent us out on the Big Lake on an eighteen-foot trawler."

"No, we told you to abort for that night," she'd said, trying not to sound defensive.

Now, Jason, dressed for one of their date nights in jeans and a sport coat, came over to her table. "Great job, Grace."

"Thanks, we've got a little over an hour, any ideas for lunch?"

"I wasn't sure how much time we'd have, so I brought a couple of Niçoise salads." Her favorite. "And one for Tim."

"That was thoughtful. Let's find a quiet room to eat them in, and we can go over your notes."

"The clerk said we could use the jury box of an empty courtroom."

They made their way there. Jason pulled the salads out of the Stay Cool insulated bag that they'd used for picnics together. A distant memory.

"The judge was listening to Tonya, and you did a great job to make a record of her calculations even if they didn't come in. I know that I would let them in," Jason said, with his hand covering his mouth full of salad. "Just be sure to get Tonya to express a full-on opinion that the permit should be substantially modified or denied."

"You're right; I have that on my checklist."

They sat eating quietly. Grace was remembering many meals that they'd shared. It was nice to see him again. Life was strange. Jason was looking intensely at his phone.

"Oh no, shit!" Jason suddenly exclaimed.

"What is it?"

"Earl Franks just passed." Jason was tearing up. "From that stupid dog bacteria. What are the odds?"

"Oh, I'm sorry. I know that you had a complicated relationship with him."

"Yes, but I came to respect him." He shook his head. "Look, this just confirms it. You and Tim were right not to come that night. Earl said so, too."

"Thanks for saying that. Speaking of Tim, I better go tell

him. Thanks for lunch and your input." She hugged him.

Tim was waiting inside the courtroom.

"Oh no, Tim!" she called out.

"What is it?" Tim asked.

The courtroom door opened and Courtney entered. The judge was also taking her seat above them.

"I've just been informed that a professional acquaintance, Earl Franks, has passed."

"Fuck," Tim said.

"Did I hear you correctly, Earl Franks has died?" Courtney's face was ashen white. "Who told you that?"

"I just got a text from another colleague. You worked with Earl, didn't you?"

"Yes, he was my supervisor. And a friend for several years. He helped make me a partner." Now Courtney was crying, too. "Your Honor, I'm going to need a minute."

"Of course," the judge said. "I've done a few trials with Earl as well and know what a capable attorney he was. We'll take another ten minutes or as long as you need, Ms. Sharpe."

"Thanks," Courtney replied, sobbing softly.

Grace watched her walk down the hall and take a seat on a bench outside a distant courtroom. That stark bench had no doubt experienced its share of human sadness. Courthouses were right up there with hospitals when it came to sharing sorrow. Now, Courtney was here, alone with her grief. Should Grace approach her?

Something drew her there. "I'm very sorry for your loss, Courtney," Grace offered. Courtney nodded blankly, dabbing her eyes and then blowing her nose into a tissue. "I knew him, but not well."

"Damn straight you knew him." Courtney stood up and moved closer. "Here's what I'll say about that, Ms. Clarkson. You and your self-appointed good guys just used him, the same as the mobster Tommy Calandro!"

"What?" Grace asked, as her heart pounded. What did

Courtney know? "I have no idea what you're talking about."

"You know damn well what I'm talking about," Courtney said. Her eyes sought Grace's and seared hers. "Take off your halo, you stupid fucking hypocrite."

"I'm sorry," Grace replied. "Very sorry for your loss."

Courtney gave her a death stare as Grace headed back down the hall toward Tim. "Let's grab our coats and step out for a walk," she called to him.

It was cold out but clear, but even through her wool coat the sun felt good on her shoulders. Grace was a mess. "Courtney knows that Earl was involved with getting those unsprayed samples," she whispered to Tim. "I have no idea how, but she said that we used him as badly as the mobsters."

"That's not good. But I still can't believe that Earl died getting those," Tim offered, shaking his head. "I feel terrible about that, and Camille's injuries, too." He held her close. "Yes, it's a tragedy, Grace, but we're not to blame. You're not to blame."

"Thanks, Tim."

"Seriously, Gracie." Tim hugged her. "Everyone had their own reasons for going or not going out on that boat. We made the right call in not going. There's no reason for us to feel guilty."

She felt a little better. "But will Courtney turn us in?"

"That's the question of the hour, isn't it?"

They came back on the record fifteen minutes later. The judge had a moment of silence for Earl Franks. But the fight had gone out of both Courtney and Grace, and they limped through the rebuttal case to its end. They would hold their fire until their briefs.

The case had been put into some perspective.

As she packed up her trial binders, Grace remembered the time her Uncle Ray had caught her sleeping on the job when she was a summer law clerk for him many years ago. She'd been working hard, trying to write two briefs and draft a lawsuit complaint, and she'd curled up in a green leather chair in the office conference room. She'd fallen asleep there, just minutes before her weekly meeting with Ray to go over the status of her cases. Instead of getting angry, he'd let her sleep for half an hour before gently waking her. She'd been so embarrassed and felt like she'd been so unprofessional. But Ray had said, "Grace, you've put your whole heart into this job all summer, and you have to remember to keep some of it for yourself, too." Then, they'd had their meeting.

Now, she wanted to wake up from this whole coal facility nightmare.

Grace and Tim wheeled their banker's boxes out to their car. As she was putting the last box in the trunk, a binder fell out and papers flew out of the parking lot and into the street. It was that kind of day. And that was the least of her worries now.

Chapter Fifty-Two

Blue Lake Path

It was a beautiful winter day as Jason drove up Highway 51 to Blue Lake. He'd been surprised to learn of Earl's death and more surprised by how hard it hit him. Now, ten days after Earl's death, Jason still wasn't sure about what to do about Earl's memorial service. But he was driving to Blue Lake anyway.

Courtney had already somehow figured out Earl's involvement in the coal island caper and had threatened to out Grace. True to form, Grace and Tim had sent him an email full of righteous excuses for not attending; they didn't want to further implicate Earl in the coal pile case. Who knew how Courtney might react? All that made sense, but still here he was heading ineluctably back to Blue Lake.

Jason would be reading a novel quietly when he'd remember a scene with Earl and smile. Then there had been Jason's own almost cruel need to see Earl in prison after Tara's murder. And it could also still make Jason angry to remember that Earl had contributed to Tara's death. All of these various memories were baffling, and hard to square with seeing Earl valiantly tie up his little boat to come and rescue Camille.

People were complex, and Earl more than most. He had a roguish charm and brutal intelligence. Jason had spent so much time hating Earl, only to come to respect him in the end. Jason still believed that Tara would not have been murdered if Earl hadn't threatened to bribe him. But, by the same logic, would Earl have died if Jason hadn't got him involved or called him to help him save Camille? No, Jason still felt that the two situations were so different that they couldn't be judged on the same scale. What could be judged squarely, though, was what Camille had said, that Earl had helped Jason save her life.

And Earl had died trying to do something like that for the planet as well, fighting coal.

Grace had mentioned to Jason that she knew that Earl was going to help them after he'd seen the photos of the coal-stained sheets and the picture of little Lacy in her breathing apparatus. Earl had teared up just a bit, though he'd bluffly tried to pretend that it was his seasonal allergies. That was Earl in a nutshell, caring despite himself.

It was hard to grasp that Earl was dead. Apparently not from a dog bite but from a dog lick. That was truly bizarre, and somehow fitting for Earl.

Jason pulled in within a block of the Blue Lake Center, where Earl's memorial was to be held. Now what? He'd driven a couple of hours mostly because he'd been concerned no one would show for Earl, but there were so many cars already parked in the lot that his presence wasn't needed and might be a distraction. He wasn't sure how either Betty or Earl's daughter, Laurie, would feel about him showing up anyway. And Grace was right that Courtney was a wild card.

After seeing the grand turnout, Jason decided to skip the service and do the Blue Lake Path hike instead. First, he dropped off sympathy cards for Betty and Laurie by handing them to an older man in a black suit and tie. Then he drove to the lakeshore path.

The sun was shining bright diamond patterns on the distant frozen parts of the lake. Jason thought of meeting Tara and their walks and secret rendezvous in Blue Lake. So many thoughts and feelings about Tara, Earl, and the whole cycle of life. These things swirled around in his brain and created a kind of pressure, almost like steam that needed to be released.

The hike was helping, and he knew where he was headed.

Now Jason sat meditating on the memorial bench that he'd had put in for Tara. There was a slight breeze that raised feeble little waves in his direction. The sky was mostly gray, but there was a bright orange burst of sun starting to break through to the west above the deep blue water. He closed his eyes, felt the warm winter breeze on his face, and tried to hear the life-giving sound of his own breath.

Chapter Fifty-Three
Wildly, Simply

Courtney's drive from Chicago to Blue Lake was slightly treacherous. It was still early March and there was snow on the ground and icy patches on the roads in northern Wisconsin. Courtney put her Sirius XM on the "old school" rock that Earl would have loved. Bruce was frozen out of Tenth Avenue now, as she made her way up into Wisconsin.

Oh no, *Nights in White Satin!* They'd done it once to that song and he'd said it was one of his favorites. She'd teased him that it was maudlin and melodramatic, like most Boomer music. But it was perfect for her mood now.

Courtney was still debating with herself about what to do with the DNA results that put Earl out on the coal island with the too-sleepy guard dogs. Her antipathy toward Grace and Tim and even their expert Tonya was powerful. All the good that they thought they were accomplishing would be forever diminished by the fact that their efforts seemed to have cost Earl Franks his life.

Sure, maybe her client had been deceiving the regulators about what and how often they were spraying, but that was par for the course. Many of the big energy suppliers, the gas, oil and coal companies, simply preferred paying nominal fines to following costly permit conditions. That wasn't her fault; that was America, like it or not.

Earl had probably led the innocents to this understanding, and they'd tried to catch her client in a lie. Perhaps they even had. Now she was driving to Earl's funeral, weeping to his melancholy music.

But what was the point of calling them out on it now? It might mildly help her case, but why drag Earl through the mud when he had at last done something for someone other than himself? Earl had tried to wear a white hat, but it just didn't sit right on that big fat head of his. She laughed a little.

Courtney had sent Betty both a sympathy card and then a later email and she was surprised to get an immediate response to the latter. *Thank you for your thoughtful card and email. Please come to Earl's Memorial Service in Blue Lake*, with a date and time. *Seriously, please come.* Courtney would have assumed that Betty was just being nice without the *seriously*, and she was still unsure of whether to attend.

Finally, Ben had convinced Courtney to go. "Do you want me to come with you?" he'd asked, putting his arm around her.

"No, but thanks for the offer. I really appreciate it." It was better to suffer both her grief and that undeniable awkwardness on her own. She'd never gone to the funeral of someone that she'd slept with before.

As she approached the outskirts of Blue Lake, she saw a large bird, possibly a green heron, swoop down toward the small part of the lake that was open. Earl had spent several calm years with his contemporary Betty among such bucolic natural pleasures. Good for him.

Despite Betty's background, Earl's memorial service wasn't conducted in a church. It was held in the recently remodeled Blue Lake Center, where the Wisconsin Water Law Conference had been held one year. For a thoroughly disgraced former Supreme Court member and Attorney General, there were a surprising number of cars. She had to walk two blocks to get there.

Courtney made her way in, and there was already a slow-moving receiving line. She recognized his very pregnant daughter, Laurie, from her picture. The poor thing was the very female version of Earl himself. The broad nose that made Earl ruggedly handsome didn't do much for Laurie. She was with her husband and a short older couple, maybe Earl's ex-wife and her new husband. And there was Betty, looking both devastated and beautiful, in a shimmering blue dress.

"Very sorry for your loss, Laurie," she said, patting her shoulder. "My name is Courtney Sharpe, and I was a friend and colleague of your father."

"Thank you for coming; this is my husband and my mom and her husband," Laurie replied. She seemed anxious to be passing Courtney down the line. Did Laurie somehow know about her time with Earl? "Courtney is a former colleague of Dad's."

The ex-wife was far more friendly. "So nice of you to come."

"Earl was a mentor to me; I learned so much law from him."

Betty overheard this exchange and came and gave Courtney a hug. They embraced, saying nothing.

"I'm so sorry, Betty," Courtney finally managed.

"I loved him like crazy," Betty said, tearing up.

Maybe Courtney had loved him a little too? But now she said, "He told me how much he loved you, too. Thank you for making me feel welcome here at this hard time."

Laurie was the only speaker, but she was magnificent. Her father was as complex a person and as hard to make sense of as anyone she'd ever known. Laurie said she loved him fiercely, flaws and all.

"The elephant in this funeral room is that my father did time in prison for trying to bribe a judge at the behest of his client. He lost his job but also the dangerous trap he'd been in at that time stemming from his gambling debts and addiction. His juice, he called it.

"But he had that juice in so many parts of his life. I loved my father, and he loved Betty! Wildly, simply. They had a blast together over the past three years. He'd loved my mom before that. He had so much energy, and he accomplished a lot. My mom used to say 'thank Daddy' every time that I saw a cardinal or a bluebird because he'd helped to ban DDT.

"Later, that put him on the Wisconsin Supreme Court, where he wrote decisions that are still cited on both the rights of gay citizens and the value of preserving wetlands. One of his most famous decisions contained a line about filling wetlands that said it was like destroying public parking for water. If all the public parking is filled, where are we going to park all that floodwater? As the climate changes and flooding becomes more frequent, it's still a question that demands an answer.

"In prison, he gave legal advice that helped free an innocent man. He learned to slow down and think of the implications of his actions. To try to get back to doing good.

"It's possible that he was trying to do good on the journey to Lake Superior, where he got the dog lick that took his life. Sure, he'd tried to bribe a judge, but it hadn't exactly been his own idea. His client had been a scary little creep who'd promptly fled back to Sicily as he let Earl take the fall.

"My father often quoted Robert Frost's epitaph and applied it to himself. Dad, too, had his lover's quarrel with the world. Earl lived his whole life like he loved both people and the world.

"Wildly, simply.

"He will be missed by many here who felt the same way about him."

Courtney felt her throat tighten and the snot and tears on her lip and cheek. She loved that old dude. Earl, who'd been so foolishly full of life, was dead.

Chapter Fifty-Four

Earl Stanley Franks

225

Earl Stanley Franks, age 69, passed away on February 28, 2020, after being licked by an unknown dog carrying a lethal bacterium. Earl was born on September 19, 1951, in Cashton, WI, to James W. and Mary Beth Franks. Earl graduated from Cashton High School in 1969, a three-sport star athlete in basketball, track, and football. Earl won a football scholarship at Michigan University and was the starting middle linebacker for the Wolverines in his junior and senior years, graduating with honors in 1974. He was an All-Big Ten Academic for three of his four seasons.

Earl continued his education at New York Law School, graduating magna cum laude in 1977. Earl returned to Milwaukee and was in private practice for several years before becoming the state's youngest Attorney General in 1982. Earl was instrumental in Wisconsin becoming the first state to ban the bird-killing pollutant DDT. Governor Tony Earl appointed him to the Wisconsin Supreme Court two years later. Justice Franks served as a State Supreme Court Justice for 12 years. During his time on the state's highest court, Earl wrote numerous decisions of national interest that have been cited hundreds of times by other courts. Earl and his first wife, Margaret, founded the Blue Lake Preservation Trust, which now has more than five thousand donor members. After leaving the court, Earl returned to private practice at Higgins and Clark in Chicago, where he was a senior litigation partner. In 2017, his longtime problem with gambling led him to engage in a criminal effort to bribe a state administrative judge, which led to him serving time in prison. While in prison, Earl helped two fellow inmates secure new trials, which led to their later acquittals. Earl deeply regretted his criminal misconduct and spent all his remaining time trying to make amends and make the world better. He loved fishing Blue Lake, reading, playing cards, and sometimes singing in local chorale groups. Earl is survived by his much-loved wife-to-be Betty, his daughter Laurie (Little), and many friends, including his first wife Margaret (Chisolm Ginsberg).

226

Chapter Fifty-Five

Inspiration Point

Jason was back in Santa Barbara, hiking in the mountains near the Botanical Garden. The trail was called Inspiration Point; it was truly an inspiring spot when he at last had made his way up the rocks to the view of Santa Barbara Bay and the islands in the distance. That's when he got a phone call from his brother.

"Justin, how you doing?" he asked.

"Feeling great! Ask me how great." Jason started to, but Justin couldn't contain himself. "Sunny is pregnant! What do you know; we made a baby."

"I'm so happy for you. How does it feel?"

"I'm so excited. I was really starting to think it wasn't going to happen. It's a relief."

"For me, too!" he joked. "That would have been an awkward way to be Uncle Jason."

"Oh, sorry, Sunny and I both agreed about that being a bad idea a while ago. You and I haven't talked. Hey, I've got more calls to make, but you're the first!"

"Thanks, bro. Please give my love to Sunny."

Jason was thrilled. The ocean and mountains below were staggeringly blue and beautiful. Could he be any happier?

Then he saw that he'd gotten a text from Camille while he was on the phone with his brother.

Come home, the decision has arrived in the mail.

Go ahead and open it, he replied.

Are you sure?

Of course, it's your case, too.

It's quite long, but it sure isn't good news.

Disappointing, but I'm not surprised.

Sorry.

I'm going to stay up here and work. Be home for lunch. More importantly, Sunny is pregnant.

Another good news, bad news day.

Chapter Fifty-Six

Everything They Asked For

Grace saw the certified mail that was likely the final decision in the coal plant case. Tim must have gotten his too, because he'd already called her.

"So? How is it?" Grace asked. "I haven't read it yet."

"We lost on everything," Tim confessed. "The ALJ said that the unsprayed coal samples were very concerning, but she refused to require unannounced inspections by the Department."

"Shit," Grace said. "Did she reduce their request at all?"

"No, they got everything they asked for," Tim steamed.

"So, someone died from a completely lost cause?"

"You know the answer, Grace," Tim said.

She was upset and wanted to get off the phone. "Well, we can talk about a possible appeal later."

"Yes," Tim said. "That would be hard because she said we didn't carry our burden. Want to hear my least favorite part? Benson kind of almost scolds us. 'The objectors seem to expect this ALJ to put some kind of brake on the worldwide demand for energy from coal. That would be far above my pay grade or that of any single decision-maker. My job is determining if this permit renewal request meets the legal standards for such issuance. While some of the coal sample evidence is troubling, I find that the objecting parties have not carried their burden and that the permit as proposed must be issued.'"

"Well, screw you, too, Audrey Benson."

Chapter Fifty-Seven

A Pyrrhic Victory

Courtney hadn't really wanted to be done with Sydney, anyway, but the truth was that Earl's death had put her off course and she wanted to talk to her therapist. There were layers of stuff with her feelings for Earl, not all of it grief. Courtney saw the calming artwork and big stuffed chair that had put her at ease with Sydney from the start.

"I've had all kinds of dreams about Earl. And lately, I've been kind of wondering if maybe I loved him when we were hanging out," she admitted about midway through their session.

"Why only kind of?"

"Because that's easier to admit." She looked away. "In my official version, he was just a Senior Partner with benefits."

"And?" Sydney probed. "Are you slut-shaming your own feelings?"

"Maybe." What was it? She'd sometimes been so frantic about her goals that she had stopped to feel things. "I think I figured out that Earl was kind of important to me getting over what my uncle did to me. A safe old guy."

"Yes, that's a fine insight." Sydney took her glasses off and looked straight into Courtney's eyes. "But, of course, it's perfectly fine to have cared for Earl. It was a consensual relationship between adults, and he helped you get to where you are."

"I was just trying to make a new life. A little too focused on that to even be aware of my feelings."

"What do you feel now?"

"I think I'll miss him."

"Of course, you'll miss him."

"Yes, I do already, even though we seldom spoke." Courtney was choking up a bit. "I was half hoping that he would work with me on the coal case. We could have tied up any loose ends."

"Speaking of the coal case, did you do anything with what your investigator had discovered about that?"

"No, I didn't. Why add that to Earl's family's grief?"

"That's another very kind gesture of you. When will you know if you won or lost the coal case?"

"We won. The ALJ noted the unsprayed samples but said that was not a permitting issue but one for enforcement."

"Congratulations, I guess," Sydney said as she gathered up her notes. "I know that you had mixed feelings about it."

"Yes. We won, but it feels very much like a pyrrhic victory."

Sydney stood up and gave Courtney that look that saw right through all of Courtney's artifice. "Here's what I want you to think about before our next session. What do you think Earl might be trying to tell you in these dreams? I doubt if it's anything to do with loving you, perhaps something about how you choose to use your legal talents?"

"Yes! That's exactly what I've been talking about with Ben."

"Great, keep talking. Until next time."

Courtney felt unresolved as she walked out of Sydney's office and got on the elevator. What was going on with her? Something kept tugging at her. Earl's voice. Incorrigible Earl, who was on the wrong side of the law even when he was try-ing to do good.

Years ago, when they were working together, he'd told her, "You don't always have to be an asshole to be a good lawyer." He'd paused and then added, "Though sometimes it helps."

But she was pretty sure that, if he were here now, he'd be saying, "You don't have to be an asshole, Courtney. You can do whatever you want." *You always could*, she told herself. But, no, that was wrong.

It had taken her years and lots of time with Sydney to get to where she was now.

PART THREE:

The Eloquence of the Earth

---

*If I say Gichigami—Lake Superior—a turquoise plain,
stretches infinite, gete-gaming. If I say Wiikonigoyaang,
she invites us to her feast, how many will remember the
eloquence of earth itself?*

\- Kimberly M. Blaeser, *The Eloquence of Earth* -

Chapter Fifty-Eight

He Never Mentioned That

At the height of the pandemic, Jason and Camille had partially moved to a house in Madison. "If we're going to live here part of the time, let's have a proper yard with a garden," Camille had said. Jason sold his condo and found a house on a street that led to Owen Conservation Park, a hundred-acre oak savannah and prairie refuge on the west side.

Camille was doing services by video then, a kind of pastoral digital nomad. That had gotten trickier as the pandemic slowly passed. They'd worked out a living arrangement that seemed to work well for them. They spent the school year at Camille's place in Santa Barbara and the summers mostly in Madison.

Twice a month, Camille would have to fly back to do a Sunday service, but they had plenty of airline miles to cover the costs. They were a family. Micah loved the lakes and going up north to explore Bayfield, Door County, and the North Shore. Their family life was sweet, full of laughter and tenderness.

Jason wasn't a judge anymore, or even much of a lawyer. He was mostly a writer and a reader. He had three rooms in which to write in in the new house in Madison.

Jason would follow the morning sun from his bright lower-level office, then work in the afternoon, bathed in light, from his Norway Spruce-framed desk, and then on to his master bedroom in the evening to sketch out the next day's work. He'd learned that for him, that casual sketching at night when he was loose and relaxed, was the trick to writing longer pieces.

Writing was healing for Jason. Writing well required some healthy habits: listening without rushing to judgment, having empathy for others, learning the craft, and practicing a kind of patient meditation followed by the constant effort to improve. There was the high of either reading or writing a well-made sentence, the thrill of a single line of a poem that had multiple meanings. And writing about nature meant listening to what the earth was trying to tell you, as Indigenous people had done for centuries. A wonderful Anishinaabe poet called it the eloquence of the earth. You could feel her spirit, rooted in the earth, in her poems.

Jason wanted to do that kind of listening, to put himself and his concerns into the context of the natural world. The climate crisis had a thriller-like urgency to it. Would government, corporations, and ordinary people be ready to make the changes necessary to save the world?

Words, feelings, regrets, and ideas poured out of him like water after a late spring snowmelt. He was, in fact, melting something. But now the phone was ringing.

Jason almost didn't take the call. It was from a northern Wisconsin area code. Was it the guy working on the shower remodeling? Had their new light fixtures come in? Probably just a junk or political call, but he'd better take it.

"Is this Jason?" an older female voice asked. "It's Betty Franklin, Earl's partner."

"Hi, Betty," Jason began. "How are you doing? I was very sorry to hear about Earl's death."

"Not sorry enough to show up for Earl's memorial service."

"I didn't want to be a distraction." At least he'd given her a card, if the old guy had remembered to deliver it. "And I'm sure that you know that I had a complicated relationship with Earl."

"Obviously," Betty replied. She coughed a bit. "For some

reason, you thought he had something to do with Tara's death, but that wasn't fair."

"You're probably right about that. But..." He sat at his desk for a second, watching a garden-eating rabbit cross his yard. Then he got up. What did she want from him? "Earl and I had worked through that, or we wouldn't have been out on the boat together."

"Well, all I know is that if Earl hadn't carried that guilt, he probably never would have been out on your hare-brained coal island caper. He'd still be here today."

"It wasn't my idea, Betty. Honestly, if it was anyone's, it was Earl's. But we all made our own choices." He could hear her sniffling. "How are you doing with your grief?"

"It's a bitch, isn't it?"

"I always think of it like weather, with storms that can come up really fast."

"Well, it's still raining a lot, and it's been more than three years since I lost him."

"I'm sorry, Betty."

"It took me sixty years to find the kind of happiness that I had with Earl, and then it was snatched away in two weeks because of you and some goddamn German Shepherd."

Jason wanted to dispute that "because of you" nonsense, but instead he just said, "Yes, grief is the cost we pay for truly loving someone." He thought of Tara and his own voice broke as he said it. "Maybe your anger at me, however misplaced, can help you get through this."

"It's not helping me right now," Betty said. "I just want to strangle you and that Grace Clarkson. At least you picked up my call. She never does."

"Betty, I didn't kill Earl. Grace didn't either. The dog did." How could he get her to understand? "I didn't even want to work with him, for my own reasons."

"Technically, you're right. I know that."

"Would you like to meet up for coffee sometime to talk

"about things?" Jason asked, immediately having second thoughts about the offer.

"Maybe, but it would have to be in Blue Lake. I don't like to drive long distances."

"That works well; my girlfriend and her son and I are renting a cabin on Blue Lake in a couple of weeks."

"Okay, but I'm not letting you off the hook so easily," Betty teased. "By the way, I've got your book, and I'm planning to read it before we meet."

"Thanks for that."

Jason had written a novel, *The Blue Lake Affair*, about losing Tara and all that had led up to it. He'd tried his best to make Earl a sympathetic character. Now that he knew how Earl's story had ended, he wanted to give the man what dignity he could. Jason hoped that might be more lasting than just showing up at his memorial service.

"No need to thank me; I'm just reading it to see if you were fair with Earl or if you made him into some kind of a monster and I have to sue you."

"He wasn't a monster, Betty. He was incredibly brave that night on the boat. And you could tell that he was proud of himself for doing the right thing, however inappropriately." Jason went outside on his deck. "He saved Camille's life that night. Did he tell you?"

"I know he helped you out on the island, but no, he never mentioned that. We should talk."

"We will. Let's leave it there. I promise to call you when I'm in Blue Lake. Thanks for calling, and now I have your number."

"Thanks for picking up. I'll see you then."

Jason tried to get back in the flow of writing, but now he was thinking about both Earl and Tara and feeling too sad. He went out to the garden to see how much damage the rabbits had managed.

Chapter Fifty-Nine

Here's One for You

Grace and Tim each kept their houses even as they'd formed a professional partnership. Clarkson and Gergen had offices in La Crosse and Eau Claire. Their loss in the coal case hadn't harmed their professional reputations but somehow enhanced them. They had plenty of work in both cities. While they had never talked about marriage, they seemed to be establishing the life partnership that Grace had craved since losing Jon.

But then, in May of 2022, just as COVID cases were starting to level off, Tim got COVID-19 and nearly died. He was in the hospital for ten days. Grace was not allowed in his room.

During that depressing time, the US Supreme Court leaked its infamous *Dobbs* decision overturning *Roe v. Wade*. She tried to talk to Tim on the phone about it, but he had a fever and was resting.

Grace was still at work, but everyone else had already left for the day. If the leaked decision was legitimate, younger women would have fewer rights than their mothers. How could that be? She sat in the big leather chair in her office, feeling all alone in a hostile world.

Then her mom called, "Did you hear about the Supreme Court?"

"Yes."

"Do you think it's for real?"

"Yes."

"Those selfish bastards," her mom replied. "A bunch of men who wouldn't know a uterus from a UFO and a woman who wanted to be a Handmaiden!"

"That pretty well sums it up," Grace laughed. "Thanks for calling, Mom, it's good to hear your sensible voice."

People sometimes experienced the world as static, but life and history kept moving on. Sometimes it went in the direction one hoped for, and other times not. That was part of the pain of being human. Things seemed to keep getting worse for Grace.

Tim never fully recovered but instead suffered from Long Covid symptoms that he couldn't shake. Tim's breathing was shallow, his whole body ached, and he would get headaches that put him in bed with the lights off. Long Covid was their relentless companion. Some weeks, he was able to work and seemed to have put it behind him. But then he would have a setback that took him off a scheduled deposition at the last moment.

Grace could fill in sometimes, but not always. It was a strange way to live, never knowing if a plan would come off or not. Their once-active lifestyle had been reduced to doctor visits, medical consultations, and unanswered questions.

Tim found some solace in online support groups of fellow Long Covid patients. Grace sometimes resented the time he devoted to these online activities, as she struggled to keep up with their thriving practice.

In the summer of 2023, they finally decided to hire a young associate, Caitlyn, in the La Crosse office. She was just two years out of law school and had recently moved to La Crosse, where her husband was a physician at the Mayo Clinic Health System. Caitlyn was very bright, and Grace loved her mixture of confidence and willingness to learn.

One Friday night in late June, Grace drove back to Eau Claire to be with Tim after spending a day in court in Black River Falls with Caitlyn. Tim was lying on the couch in his baggy underwear, chatting away with Simone from Chicago on one of his forums. There were dirty dishes in the sink, and his house was a disaster.

"This is how you spend your days now?" she asked. "I mean, really?"

"How did it go in court?"

"It was a long day. It was work." His strategy when she got frustrated was just to try to be super empathetic. But Grace wasn't having it today. "Work, remember that?"

"Of course, I remember that; why are you mad at me?"

"Not mad, just extremely frustrated." She looked at him, frowning. "You couldn't even wear pants when you knew I was coming?"

"You're right, sorry. I'll go do it now."

"I don't want to take you away from Simone in Chicago."

"Don't tell me you're jealous? I've never even met the woman."

"That's only because you're no longer living in the real world. You're just living in cyber chatrooms, like a teenager with acne." Shit, Tim had struggled with acne well into his twenties. He looked wounded as he got up from his sofa, rearranging his light blue boxers. "Okay, not with acne. I apologize. That was mean."

"Yes, it was," he said and went into his bedroom.

He'd left his laptop. Grace thought for a minute and then went over and looked. *Thanks for the pics; here's one for you.* It was what you'd expect—a large-breasted naked woman in her late forties or early fifties—what you'd expect, but maybe with more tattoos.

That was it; she was done.

"I remember now why we didn't make it the first time we dated."

Tim tried his best to deny it initially, but eventually, he relented. "Maybe it's for the best," he said.

It was. Grace was tired of driving to Eau Claire and biting her tongue about Tim's descent. She was tired of being a long-distance nurse and conscience. Tired of the life she'd been leading with Tim.

She got back in her car and headed home to La Crosse, to her own house, feeling profoundly free. It wouldn't be so bad unraveling their practice; at least they hadn't married. She was very glad that she would have Caitlyn with her to keep fighting the good fight.

Chapter Sixty

A Little Less Corporate

"Should we become do-gooders?" Courtney had asked Ben a couple of days after she'd learned the circumstances of Earl's death.

"We'd have to start somewhere. What would you want to do?"

"Honestly, I have no idea." It was true. That had always been true for Courtney. Her childhood struggles had given her drive but not direction. "What about you?"

"We'd probably have the biggest impact just doing what we're doing but coming at it from a little less corporate approach."

Ben was surprisingly excited about the idea. They talked about it for weeks. Then he started showing her some possible firms that had both an environmental and a product liability practice on the plaintiff side.

Eventually, they set up meet-and-greet dates with a couple of them. Finally, things worked out perfectly with Hooper and Cates, where a prominent environmental attorney was planning a retirement, and their product practice was thriving.

It went well. Now Courtney had some municipal clients, progressive and wealthy Chicago suburbs who were serious about the environment and the climate crisis. They went from a firm that had 250 local and 400 national attorneys down to the firm where they were two of sixteen total lawyers. And they were glad that they did.

Ben had gotten involved with big solar projects that were

booming because of the Inflation Reduction Act and the Biden Infrastructure bill. He traveled around the US advising clients on how to navigate both the grant and the real estate solar landscape. Business was thriving.

Ben moved into Courtney's condo in June 2023. They debated getting something bigger, flashier, maybe even out of the city, but there was something appealing, too, about just being satisfied with their simple life together with no rent or mortgage. Mostly, they just enjoyed hanging out a lot. Ben didn't like retreading old ground about past relationships. He was very understanding about her childhood abuse, but he didn't want to hear about her old mistakes.

"Do we ever really make sense of our own pasts?" Ben asked her one day. His father had beaten him severely with a belt many times when he was just a kid. Ben's reaction was to try to make himself strong. He'd done weightlifting, and then, like Earl, played football well enough to win a scholarship to Cal-Berkeley. Yikes, two football players. Who knew that was her type? "At some point one has to either forgive or move on."

Ben had done both, and that was something Courtney admired about him. As for her, she was certainly moving on. Courtney wanted to believe that she made some positive difference, and occasionally she did.

Chapter Sixty-One

Blue Lake Cabin

Camille had given Jason a wonderful fifty-fourth birthday gift. Ten days in Blue Lake at a little cabin with lake access. Micah was going to be doing an Outward-Bound expedition in Colorado. The cabin was at the east end, away from the places he'd shared with Tara.

They'd been looking forward to it all spring, but now, in the early summer drought, the Canadian fires burned uncontrollably and made the sky a scary orange. The climate crisis was now indisputably part of daily life, though some continued to pretend it wasn't. The Air Quality Index in Madison was still a Very Unhealthy 275, and it wasn't supposed to get much better for a couple of days. Chicago and Milwaukee had the worst air quality in the world on back-to-back days. It was 225 at the air station closest to Blue Lake, and that meant wearing N-95 masks when they were outside.

Were those damn masks a constant presence now, in the summer of 2023, too?

Jason had been a little concerned that it would feel strange to be in Blue Lake with Camille. But she was so chill that there was no awkwardness about being in the place where Jason's love for Tara had blossomed. Camille thought that it would be healing for all concerned. They were not morbid about either of their pasts.

This was a refreshing change from how he and Grace had navigated the deaths of her husband and Tara; after an initial burst of crying together, they'd largely avoided talking about either of them for fear of treading on painful ground. Camille spoke openly about what had led to her breakup with her last relationship, Juan, who'd been both a heavy drinker and pathologically jealous.

Blue Lake Cabin was less a rustic cabin than a year-round house, and it had a distinguished history. A regionally famous poet, Nadine Schmeckpeper, had once lived there in the 1940s, and there were photos of her everywhere, as well as excerpts from a nature journal that she had kept while staying there. Two were even framed on the exposed brick living room wall.

September 4, 1945
Out on the sunset gold lake
with still-grinning granny,
looking peaceful, too,
in her shiny silver tin canoe.

Green and Blue Herons
everywhere, a couple
with their wings raised high.
Herons cry as if they knew:
the world finally at peace!
(NS)

September 6, 1945
Foul odor (dead deer?)
emanating from alders—
death still a part of things,
world peace or not!
(NS)

All guests were encouraged to continue the tradition in a black leather notebook. It was a little daunting to write in such a space. All the previous entries had been positive and lyrical, but on the day of their arrival, the sky was hazy and orange from the fires.

Donning his N-95 mask, Jason took his coffee and the Wildlife Journal down to a tree stump above the pier. The morning sun had warmed it just enough as it rose above the red pines. Jason was happy to be back watching the grace of the loons landing and singing their songs to the lake. What did the polluted air mean for them?

He wrote in pencil, not sure whether he would keep it in the journal.

June 28, 2023
Blood orange hazy sky
burning Quebec pine forests
bring lethal climate misery,
even to Blue Lake Cabin.
(JE)

"It feels kind of anti-romantic to be writing about the air quality," he said, handing the journal to Camille.

"Unfortunately, that's part of nature now, too."

By a couple of mornings later, the wildfire air had cleared. Jason and Camille were happy to slip into the pattern that generations had pursued at Blue Lake Cabin. The cabin was the ideal habitat for them. The pier was the perfect place to begin each morning, drinking coffee and vaguely planning their leisurely day. They often took a walk, and then took turns writing in the Nature Journal. This became a kind of ritual, performed after the midmorning walk.

Today, Camille was wearing a T-shirt that encapsulated her philosophy of life. On the front, it said: HARDLY EVER WHINY; on the back: FREQUENTLY OPTIMISTIC. After their walk along the lakeshore path, it was her turn. She wrote quickly and handed the journal to Jason.

July 2, 2023
Native grasses ripple
swaying in the summer breeze,
as the wild rose shrubs sing
with black-capped chickadees.
(CG)

"Sorry, gloomy Gus, some of us are still hopeful," she teased.

"It's not fair," he protested. "You had a day after the fires had cleared."

"I'm going to write an even more hopeful sermon when you go into town."

Camille had encouraged Jason to visit the town center and spend a day mourning Tara. He visited the diner café where he used to meet Tara and the bench where they used to meditate together.

How he'd loved her! Would they have really gone the whole distance, with kids and kindness? He still thought so.

Then he called Earl's partner Betty, and she met him at a nearby state park.

"Don't worry; I'm not as angry as I was," she said in her animated voice.

They walked on a trail beside a beautiful and very mature stand of mostly yellow prairie coneflowers above the lake. The air was once again crisp and fresh, like it should be in summer above a northern Wisconsin Lake. Betty was in short Patagonia shorts and a stylish blue top.

"I just wanted to say that I'm sorry if I blamed you too much for Earl's passing," she said.

"Believe me, I understand." He stopped walking and looked into the eyes behind her sunglasses. "Of course, I did the same thing with Earl about Tara's death. I think he knew that I had gotten over that before he passed."

"I think he did." Betty smiled. Her face looked a little

more worn than he remembered. Losing Earl had taken its toll on her. "At least he stopped calling you 'that smug little Boy Scout prick!' How are you doing with your grief?"

"It comes and goes. And you?"

"Do you know what the worst part was, Jason?"

"The hospital?"

"Yes, for you too?" He nodded. "I'd been in his arms only a couple of hours before I saw him lying there with all the tubes and just struggling to breathe." Her eyes had taken on water. "His breathing was weird, very irregular, and I knew then that he was in big trouble. I had the same experience with Pastor."

"I'm sorry." He put his arm around her, and she moved around for a full hug. He thought of the last time he'd seen Tara. He'd begged them to wheel him in his own hospital bed to see her. It was searing to see her so pale and helpless. He thought of Tara as he hugged Betty and said, "I'm so sorry, Betty."

"I realized just how much I'd loved him."

"Yes, I had a similar experience with Tara. Even the shadow of death brings a person into full view. But I went to my old haunts with Tara today, and I only cried once, so that's progress."

"That is progress. The only other thing that I wanted to tell you was that I thought you were mostly fair to Earl in your novel."

"I'll try to do better in the next one. I'm workshopping part of it on Long Island next week."

Chapter Sixty-Two

Isn't It Ironic?

In early November of 2023, Grace ran into Courtney at a CLE conference on Legal Issues in Solar and Carbon Credit Projects at the Pfister Hotel in Milwaukee. They were sitting no more than a couple of rows from each other, so Grace sought her out at the first break.

"I just wanted to thank you," Grace said. She didn't want to say for what. She was expecting Courtney to ask her that anyway.

But Courtney just looked through her and said, "I didn't do it for you; I did it for Earl."

"Very gracious."

"No, I didn't want one more scandal in Earl's obituary. I mean, Jason had already done enough in that way. Besides, you guys lost anyway."

"We did. You did an excellent job for your client." Courtney had cut her long hair in a way that flattered her face and softened her angles.

"You did a good job, too, other than violating one metric shit-ton of ethical rules." Courtney couldn't contain a smirk. Grace smiled back. Courtney may have mellowed some, but she was still fiercely herself.

"No comment," Grace replied. "I heard that you and Ben are practicing together. That's been a longtime dream of mine, going back to law school."

Courtney's face softened. "What about Tim?"

"Yeah, that didn't work out."

"Life is difficult sometimes, isn't it?"

"Oh, yeah. Nice seeing you, and seriously, I appreciate what you did, whatever your reasons."

"Oh, here's Ben now. You may as well meet him."

He was a super handsome man with a sympathetic, symmetrical face. Lucky Courtney, not poor Grace. Grace repeated that to herself a couple of times.

"Ben, this is Grace Clarkson from the coal case."

How much had she told him? "Nice to meet you, Ben."

"Oh, hello, Grace," Ben said, averting his eyes.

Everything. Courtney had obviously told him everything. Grace's face reddened, and the rash on her chest that had plagued her in college was back. It itched as she made her way back to her conference seat. It was terribly ironic to be lectured about ethics by Courtney Sharpe, an attorney she'd always thought of as a corporate shill.

But Grace knew that she had it coming.

Grace's personal life had always been full of irony, but lately, her professional life was, too. She had made her name with a victory over a large dairy in her signature groundwater case several years ago, but now many other big dairies were coming to her to be her clients. And she was taking them on to represent them in getting carbon credits to sell for installing anaerobic manure digesters that harvested climate-damaging methane. Manure was sometimes as valuable as milk in the California and European carbon markets.

Some of her old clients were aghast and considered her a sellout because those digesters seemed to lock in place the huge dairies that had led to groundwater contamination. However, taking methane out of the atmosphere was an unquestionable good for the climate crisis, so she felt her work was valuable.

The long battle against coal, which Grace still actively followed, also revealed many depressing paradoxes. As early as 2015, the EPA had tried to implement a comprehensive Clean Power Plan that would have led to the orderly abandonment of coal, which market forces were already doing. The conservative courts blocked it and then it was abandoned when Trump was elected. The Biden Administration tried to revive it, but in June of 2022, the US Supreme Court intervened in a highly unusual move to derail it before any other courts had the opportunity to consider it. The EPA had long had authority to regulate power plants, but the Court wouldn't let them do so.

"Capping carbon dioxide emissions at a level that will force a nationwide transition away from the use of coal to generate electricity may be a sensible 'solution to the crisis of the day,'" Chief Justice Roberts wrote but, "a decision of such magnitude and consequence rests with Congress itself, or an agency acting pursuant to a clear delegation from that representative body."

Justice Kagan wrote in her dissent that the court had substituted its own policy judgment for that of Congress. "Whatever else this court may know about, it does not have a clue about how to address climate change," she wrote. "And let's say the obvious: The stakes here are high. Yet the court today prevents congressionally authorized agency action to curb power plants' carbon dioxide emissions. The court appoints itself — instead of Congress or the expert agency — the decision maker on climate policy," she wrote. "I cannot think of many things more frightening."

It was indeed ironic that, after years of railing against 'activist judges,' the newly powerful conservative majority was the most interventionist and disrespectful toward precedent of any during her decades as a lawyer. Their agenda was to dismantle the regulation of industry by government, which they decried as the 'administrative state.' But, of course, those agencies were part of Presidential administrations that, unlike the Court, had been elected by the people.

A couple of weeks after running into Courtney, Grace attended Jason's *Blue Lake Affair* appearance at the Barnes &

Noble in La Crosse. There was a good turnout, and though he'd already sent her a copy, she had him sign books for her mother and a couple of friends. When they were finally free to talk outside in the parking lot, Jason told Grace that she'd been right about the coal island caper.

"I've been meaning to call you to tell you that," he said as he put his things in the trunk of his car. "Of course, I was mad at you at first, but you did an excellent job for your clients and didn't resort to anything illegal to get there."

Grace shook her head. "Yes, of course I did. I used the illegally gained evidence. Knowing how I'd got it. Both Tonya and I have decided that wasn't right. We're lucky that Courtney didn't rat us out."

"Yes, but I was in it even deeper. We should have listened to you and Tim and called the thing off. I'm sorry."

"Thanks, Jason."

"How's Tim?"

"Don't ask. We're done."

"Already?"

"Yes, he was exchanging nude selfies with this heavily tattooed woman in Chicago."

"I'm so sorry to hear that, Grace."

"Are any of you men faithful?"

"Yes. I always had been. I'm sorry that I let you down."

"He's sorry, too, but so what?"

"Try not to let it make you bitter," he said, pausing. "I'm not saying that you are."

"I'm not so much bitter as just done, at least for now." She gave Jason a sympathetic look. "Look, I'm not putting you two in *exactly* the same category."

"Thanks for that. I'm not big on tattoos, for one thing."

She tried to laugh. "You and I had run our course. We weren't married or living together. You never lied to me. What you did wasn't right; it just wasn't as wrong."

"Thanks. That's what I was trying to say about the coal

plant. I think the January Sixth Riot has sharpened my appreciation for the rule of law. People on our side, especially, must stay on the right side of that."

"Yes, we have to, I agree."

Chapter Sixty-Three

Despite Everything

Jason had written much of his first book sitting in the Santa Barbara sand near Thousand Steps Beach. Now, he was workshopping his second novel in the New York area for the second straight summer. It felt like he'd gone full circle, back to where he'd started his adult life after college.

Camille dropped him off and kissed him goodbye at the Madison airport. It had recently been updated and felt more like an actual city airport, with bars and restaurants on a couple of levels and a kind of Frank Lloyd Wright aesthetic with lots of wood and geometric design patterns.

La Guardia had been even more improved. A central fountain played a corny but welcoming city-highlights water light show to the tune of "New York, New York." Some things were improving in the US, too.

He picked up his rental car to drive to the Hamptons. The traffic was miserable. His Google Maps told him it would take him two hours and fifteen minutes to make it to Southampton, but twenty minutes later, he still had two hours and eighteen minutes to go.

Jason turned on public radio and heard an interview with the Swedish author of *How to Blow Up a Pipeline*. He was talking quietly about the need for climate activists to consider going beyond pacifism and even considering targeted violence.

"No!" Jason yelled at his radio. "Don't blow up a pipeline! Stay on the moral high ground!" It was baffling how people responded so differently to the climate crisis.

Some people wanted to blow up pipelines to stop the carbon economy at all costs. Others reacted with defensive disdain to any suggestion on how they could do their small part. They hoarded old lightbulbs and worried about people coming for their burgers and the gas grills they cooked them on. The world of their childhood was the last word. But nostalgia was not a strategy any more than violence. What the planet needed was a plan.

At length, he arrived at the deserted SUNY campus to get his key to a basement dorm with a shared bathroom. He drove into Hampton's Bay to a King Kullen (America's First Supermarket) to get provisions and a bottle of wine. He got so much stuff that he was worried it might break the cheap glass in the shared refrigerator.

His workshop leader was terrific. She was a full professor at a prestigious Southern school with an MFA and a Ph.D., had written two well-received novels, and knew her stuff.

In the evening, she read from one of her books and talked about how to incorporate myth and folktales into your fiction. In her novel, a Black man from Florida had seen his experience falsely retold by a white writer who'd reaped its reward. She'd written it years before Florida had started its thought control efforts to claim that many people held in bondage had benefited from being enslaved. Her novel had been eerily prescient of these efforts to rewrite history.

Poets were the antennae of the species.

One night was a pleasure. One of the writers in his workshop group was very local, and she invited the whole group to her home. Her husband, an attorney, had pizzas, salads, and rosé wines laid out on the kitchen table for them. They sat and ate outside on a patio facing their pool and, beyond that, a pier with their boat and the water. One of the writers said, "I've had this Hampton Water rosé before but never in the Hamptons."

Jason's critique day came, and it was both energizing and

a little disappointing. They spent half of his allotted hour discussing whether there were coal mines in Minnesota and Wisconsin, because one mansplaining fellow had googled it and thought he'd found a fatal flaw. But there were also some good suggestions on how to heighten the fictional tension of his real catastrophes.

Relieved that his critique was over, Jason sat down at a lunch table where a heated discussion was going on. Trish, a self-described middle-aged white liberal woman, had had her piece shot down because she'd tried to tell the story of a Black teenager. Isabelle, a kind but firm Native woman, was encouraging her to rethink her project because it wasn't her story to tell.

"Take some time to process it," Isabelle told her. "Anyone would feel a little defensive right now."

"I've processed it; I just wish that I'd known that before I put so much work into the project. It seems a bit unfair," Trish said.

"Lots of things are unfair," Isabelle replied. "Where we're sitting right now on this campus is my people's land, the Shinnecock Indian Nation."

"The people by the stony shore," Jason said. "Is that right?"

"Roughly. But yes, we're the people who've lived by this stony coast since time immemorial."

"Has there ever been any effort at reparations?"

"Lots of efforts on our part but no successes yet." She shook her head. "The state has not dealt with us fairly, ever, and locally, they're trying to stop us from building a casino."

"I'm sorry."

Isabelle shrugged. "That is the oldest American story. But we're better off than some others because we still have nine hundred acres as a reservation."

On campus, Jason had found nothing of the Shinnecock history, just a plaque on the windmill where Tennessee Williams had written one of his least successful plays. He decided to drive over to Cooper's Beach to lie in the sand to write a new scene by the Atlantic, as he'd so often done by the Pacific.

He saw the tribal shops selling smokes, including legal, pre-rolled joints. That was one way to scratch out a living. He stopped and bought one for the beach.

Getting to Cooper's Beach required driving through the wealthy areas near the beach, with forbidding hedge thickets urging one to keep out at all costs. Gatsby country. Old money. Southampton had been incorporated in 1640, not long after the British had "traded" the land for sixty cloth coats, sixty bushels of corn, and a false promise of military protection.

Now, the beach required a barrier-to-entry fee of $50 to park and enjoy the public waters of the Atlantic. Jason, a fifty-something white man with a brand-new rental car, was waved through without paying. He made his way down to the nearly deserted beach and chased away some seagulls to find a spot to smoke his pre-roll.

The waves rolled in, returning him to his own thoughts. He preferred the open public beaches of Santa Barbara. You could park for free at Shoreline Park and walk for miles. The rich people were less obnoxious about their wealth there, too. But it felt right to be scribbling in his notebook on the Atlantic coast at Coopers Beach, as the waves rolled in and added their timeless and majestic rhythms.

Sure, he was by now a little high, but Jason felt keenly the whole giant breadth of his home country, from this shining Atlantic to the Pacific, where his new California family awaited his return. Sitting at its eastern edge and flying back to the mountains of Santa Barbara tomorrow, he thought of his big, divided country. Many viewed the 'other side' with Manichean disdain. But there was good and evil in everyone. Meanwhile, biology and the life cycle taught us how connected we are.

One of the conference speakers said that Dante had created

so many circles of hell and purgatory because he cared about every kind of sinner. In his charitable moments, Jason could understand why some people didn't want to face the urgency of the climate hours ahead and why others were overwhelmed with anxiety about it. But he was past ready for action!

He sat there thinking and writing. And mostly missing his little family in California. Jason decided to leave the conference early and made a reservation at a hotel two minutes from La Guardia. He packed up and headed back to the city.

On his way in, a car exploded on the Cross Island Expressway. Cars kept surging past the surreally flaming vehicle. The driver was out safely, and a firetruck was on the way within seconds. Jason pulled over to let the firetruck pass and then made his way to his hotel.

The planet was on fire, too. Would its fire trucks arrive in time?

It was now dinnertime, so he went down to the bar to get something to eat and drink. There were lots of brightly dressed Black people; some of the women were wearing sashes and tiaras. "What's going on?" he asked the bartender.

"It's the Ms. Full-Figured Caribbean competition."

As Jason drank his Diatom Chardonnay from Lompoc in Santa Barbara County, he relaxed and felt at home. At home in New York, at home with Camille, at home with the taste of a fine California summer wine.

A beautiful young Black couple sat next to him. She was tall and fit and had her hair elegantly piled above her head with a tan wrap that set off her sleeveless orange dress. He wore a stylish hat and a blue, white, and salmon plaid jacket that went perfectly with his white shirt and salmon slacks.

"You two look very fine tonight," Jason observed, the weed and wine having loosened his tongue.

"Thank you," the man replied. And their conversation was off.

They were there to support a friend from the beauty competition. His name was Miquel and he was originally from

Jamaica, and she was from Guyana. They worked together, trying to build a new model for urban education. They'd just come from Wall Street and had a great meeting to try to scale up their New York efforts nationwide.

"But we've already reached fifty thousand kids," Miquel said.

"Cheers," Jason replied, clinking wine glasses. "This might sound morbid, but you could die tomorrow and know that your life was well-lived." He was thinking of Earl. "You contributed something important."

They embraced when it was time for them to join their friends.

The guy on Jason's other side immediately started talking to him. His name was Pablo, and he was from Laredo, Texas. He had recently married and was extremely happy. How happy? Pablo had gone to a doctor recently because his jaw was hurting from smiling too much.

He and Jason had thriving new relationships in common. They shared pictures. Then, Pablo shared his worry about the climate crisis.

Pablo was leaving for a month of survey work for the installation of large-scale solar projects. It was 117F in Laredo when he'd left, and Pablo's elderly mother lived alone. Yes, he'd worry about her when he was gone. How could he not? Pablo had learned surveying in the US Navy and, at one time, worked for the oil companies.

"I only work for solar now." Pablo shook his head. "I won't work for the oil companies anymore. There's so much going on with both wind and solar now."

Pedro was hopeful. Despite everything, Jason was, too. It was hard not to be when one was in love.

Epilogue

Jason was still hanging out at the Charmant in La Crosse, drinking French wine and eating Spanish olives. Before he lost the thought, he picked up a pen and wrote a little verse about this morning's walk.

> *November Song*
> *The quaking aspen*
> *have taken their shaking*
> *back down to the substrate—*
> *guess it's time for me*
> *to dig deep, too.*

Then the waitress at The Charmant remembered Jason and Tara being there together. "Sorry about your partner," she said softly. Lost in his thoughts, Jason thought at first that she was talking about Camille or even, for a second, Earl. "I read about Tara."

"Oh, yes, Tara was an amazing person and a wonderful writer. I'm Jason, by the way."

"I'm Abby. You guys had something special," she said. "You could just see it."

"Thanks for saying that," Jason replied. "I'm going to have to come back with my new girlfriend, Camille, to see if we pass the Abby eyeball test."

"I hope you do," Abby said, taking away his plate.

Book Club Questions

1. Several characters are haunted by their past. How did each try to move forward after their past experiences?

2. How did each character decide to make the choices that they did in their personal relationships, and in their responses to the legal case? Is it ever okay to do something unethical in pursuit of the greater good?

3. How do people in the real world make choices with respect to concerns about the climate crisis?

4. What parts of the story were surprising or engaging to you?

5. Did the chapter titles work for you? Why or why not? Were there any that stood out to you one way or the other?

6. The author has said that each of the characters are searching for freedom, meaning and personal connection. How is this reflected in the narrative?

Acknowledgments

I am very grateful to my friend Ted Thompson and his Novel Seminar students who read the earliest draft, and to the inspiring group of writers led by Scott Russell Sanders at the *2022 Orion Environmental Writer's Workshop*, as well as the fiction cohort guided by Dr. Ladee Hubbard at the *2023 Southampton Writers Conference* who read and improved later chapters almost as they were being born, and to Kimberly M. Blaeser for trusting me with her beautiful words. She'll always be my Wisconsin Poet Laureate. I'm also thankful for the solitude of my Writer Retreat at *Write On, Door County*, where I finished the second complete draft. Later came responses to my discerning editors Liz Ridley in Milwaukee and Karen in Bellingham, WA, and to picking the brain of my old friend Mary E. for her medical expertise. Finally, thanks to the team at Atmosphere in Austin, notably the insights of my brilliant editor, Asata Radcliffe, who challenged me with my own words, as well as Matthew Fielder and Ronaldo Alves for the gorgeous cover. My late brother Laurence G. Boldt passed before he could read this finished novel, but he was a lifelong supporter of my creative work and an uplifting example of the power of books to change lives. My daughters Allie and Anna have lovingly encouraged and supported my writing from getting my MFA through now two published novels. Finally, I would like to thank my partner, Carol Bingham, for her love and patience during the exhausting creative process of writing a book. I am a fortunate man.

About the Author

JEFFREY D. BOLDT is a graduate of the University of Wisconsin and its School of Law. After a career focusing on environmental law, Boldt received his MFA in Fiction from Augsburg University in Minneapolis in 2019. Boldt's short fiction, poetry, and essays have appeared in literary journals, including *HuffPost* and those affiliated with the University of California, Johns Hopkins, Duke, Rutgers, UNLV, Clarkson, Stephen F. Austin, Minnesota, SUNY, and CUNY. His first novel, *Blue Lake*, published by River Grove Books, was given a Starred Review and named in Kirkus Reviews Best Books of 2022.